Winnie's Quest

Shawn Lamb

Allon Books

Other Books by Shawn Lamb

Young Adult Fantasy Fiction

ALLON – BOOK 1 – STRUGGLE FOR ALLON
ALLON – BOOK 2 – INSURRECTION
ALLON – BOOK 3 – HEIR APPARENT
ALLON – BOOK 4 – A QUESTION OF SOVEREIGNTY
ALLON – BOOK 5 – GAUNTLET
ALLON – BOOK 6 – DILEMMA
ALLON – BOOK 7 – DANGEROUS DECEPTION
ALLON – BOOK 8 – DIVIDED
ALLON – BOOK 9 – IN PLAIN SIGHT
ALLON – BOOK 10 – WAIFS

GUARDIANS OF ALLON – BOOK ONE – THE GREAT BATTLE
GUARDIANS OF ALLON – BOOK TWO – REPRIEVE
GUARDIANS OF ALLON – BOOK THREE – OVERTHROW

PARENT STUDY GUIDE FOR ALLON ~ BOOKS 1-9

ELDAR – BOOK 1 – SON OF ELDAR
ELDAR – BOOK 2 – TRADER OF ELDAR
ELDAR – BOOK 3 – SHIELD MAIDEN OF ELDAR

For Young Readers – ages 8-10
Allon – The King's Children series

NECIE AND THE APPLES
TRISTINE'S DORGIRITH ADVENTURE
NIGEL'S BROKEN PROMISE

THE ACTIVITY BOOK OF ALLON

Historical Fiction

BY LOYALTY TORN
GLENCOE
THE HUGUENOT SWORD

Characters

Highburn Castle, Kingdom of Orrin

Winnie Briggs – age 18
General Conor Briggs – age 45 – Winnie's father
Jayson Clarke – age 22 – son of Simon Clarke
Simon Clarke – age 55 – Lord Chancellor or Orrin
Lord Devon Falco – age 55 – Prime Minister of Orrin
King Pekka of Orrin – age 78
Queen Rona of Orrin – age 45
Lady Eleanor – age 40 – Lady-in-Waiting to the Queen
Captain Tolbert – age 30
Sergeant Cadel
Lieutenant Kincaid – age 50

Morgrath Forest

Rafe – age 40 – Ranger of Morgrath

Piskies

Zoe & Zane – twins – age 18 (human years)
Finn – Zoe & Zane's father
Mora – Finn's wife
Burdock – Priest of the Piskies
Balor

Chapter 1

HIGHBURN CASTLE SAT ON TOP OF A VAST MOUNT surrounded by a deep moat. A massive bridge spanned the moat to the large main gate made of iron and wood. Both ends of the bridge could be closed for defense. The castle rose in two levels. The first level was surrounded by twenty-foot walls with battlements and circular turrets. This level contained the armory, stables, barracks, and servants' quarters. The Great Hall, royal palace, chapel, library, and ministry offices dominated the second level. This offered a commanding view of the countryside. Leaves began turning vibrant fall colors.

The large walled city of Highburn lay before the castle moat. Any enemy foolish enough to attack the castle must first sack the city. This would be no small feat since Highburn boasted a population of five thousand people.

Inside a small apartment in the royal wing, an elderly man of ninety sat wrapped in a robe and blanket near a window. His pale face was deeply lined with age. The dull, almost vacant eyes stared out at the sunset. He wore a cap over his nearly bald head. Wisps of thin, stringy gray hair stuck out from under the cap. He did not move or speak when a strikingly beautiful woman of forty-five sat on the window seat. Flowing long, light blonde hair, held in place by side combs, cascaded down her back. Soft green eyes filled with compassion as she gently touched his arm.

"Ennis. It's Rona."

His eyes blinked but remained focused outside.

"I suppose that means you can hear me."

He blinked again.

"There is so much to tell you, I don't know where to begin." She took a deep breath before she continued. "Word reached Pekka that Conor is dead. His mission failed." Her voice shook with fear. "It may be too late." She lowered her head to regain her composure. She became startled at feeling then seeing his hand on her hand and his eyes looking sideways at her. "Ennis?"

He shook his head. "Not late," came words difficult to speak.

She knelt next to the chair to hear him better. "How with Conor dead?"

"Dresser … hidden." His head slightly moved in a nod.

Rona searched each of the three large drawers. In the lowest one, she found a hidden compartment. Inside lay a small flat box. She returned to kneel beside him. "Is this what you meant?"

His hand made a motion that she interrupted as "open." To her astonishment, the box contained a necklace with a ruby surrounded by silver. Astonished, she could barely speak. "Is this?"

He nodded. "The broken piece."

Her eyes swelled with tears of understanding.

His hand clenched her arm. "My witness … underneath." He nodded at the box.

Rona removed the lining under the necklace to discover a sealed document.

His breathing became labored. He forced urgent words. "Give … now! Read later …" his voice failed. His eyes closed and his breathing grew shallow.

Anxious, she sat on the window seat and seized his hand. "Ennis?"

His eyes partly opened. "Save the crown. Send for Finn when the time comes …" His head lowered with an exhale of death.

Rona covered her mouth to hold in a sob of grief. "Rest in peace with the Almighty, dear Ennis." She kissed his forehead. She took the folded paper and placed it in a pocket of her skirt. She held the boxed necklace next to her chest. "Lord, it is time. Give me the strength." Taking a breath of recovery, she pulled a bell cord beside the hearth.

"You rang, Majesty?" asked the valet.

"Inform the King, his beloved uncle is dead."

The valet felt for a pulse. "*Beloved* is not the word I would use with the King."

Rona glared at him. "It is *my* word you shall relay to the King not your opinion!"

"Aye, Majesty." The chastised valet bowed as Rona passed him to leave.

She quickly made her way from Ennis' small quarters in the rear of the royal wing to her own more lavish apartment. A large sitting room dominated the center of the apartment. The door to the right of the main section accessed the wardrobe with a simple private toilet attached. A door to the left led to the bedchamber. The sitting room was also used for private dining. Upon entrance, two women stood. The first was her lady-in-waiting, Lady Eleanor, a middle-aged woman with streaks of gray in her auburn hair. The second, an eighteen-year-old young woman with brown eyes and long, light blonde hair pulled back in a braid.

Eleanor grew concerned at sight of Rona's upset. "Your Majesty, is something wrong?"

"Prince Ennis is dead. Just now, while I visited him." She blinked back new tears.

Eleanor lowered her head and whispered a short prayer.

Compassion filled the young woman's voice. "Is there anything you need, Majesty?"

Rona softly smiled. "Dear Winnie. No. I have something for you."

"Me?"

"Indeed." She drew Winnie to a far private corner of the room. "Ennis' death reminded me of your birthday last week. Death and birth often go together." She paused to swallow back a lump in her throat.

"Majesty?" Winnie asked, concerned.

Rona's smile did not reach her eyes. "I regret being out of town and unable to help you celebrate."

Winnie shyly smiled. "It is enough you favor me as your maid."

Rona tenderly stroked Winnie's face. "And with Conor's death, it doubly pains me not to have been here with you."

Winnie sniffled back a rise of emotion. "I miss him terribly."

"As do I." Rona regained her composure. "So, as tribute to both Ennis and Conor, indulge me as I give you a present." She pulled the box from her pocket and gave it to Winnie.

Upon opening, Winnie gazed in amazement at the beautiful ruby necklace set in silver.

Eleanor came to view the exchange; she, too, surprised. "Is it—?"

Rona's quick sideways glance and nod for silence stopped Eleanor's question.

"Oh! Majesty. I can't accept this. It's too wonderful for me," Winnie said in awe. She tried to return the box to the Queen.

"I insist."

"But—" Winnie tried to object but Rona placed it around Winnie's neck.

"Ruby is your birthstone. I know Conor would approve."

New tears rose. "He always called me 'his little ruby'." Winnie's voice quivered.

Rona lifted Winnie's chin. "You are a ruby to both of us. Now, since the King is not fond of elaborate gifts, keep it hidden under the neck of your dress. This way it can be close to your heart as a way of remembrance." She tucked the necklace underneath.

"Thank you, Majesty."

Rona's slowly smile. "The sun is down, and soon word will spread and the castle begin mourning."

"Is that what the King will be, in mourning?" Eleanor spoke with sarcasm.

"He may not, but I will. For all his faults, Ennis was kind to me." Rona then spoke to Winnie. "See I have proper mourning attire."

"I doubt it will last a month." Eleanor kept her same tone.

"All the same, I will show respect until Pekka says otherwise." Rona shooed Winnie to the wardrobe.

Eleanor moved close to Rona. "You are taking a risk by giving it to her."

"There has always been a risk. First Arabella and now Conor." Rona's resolute voice turned to a sigh of grief. "The king's declining health prompts action. Time is short. I fear what Falco will do if we can't compensate for Conor's death." She winced in pain and rubbed her temples.

"Rest while Winnie selects your wardrobe." Eleanor gently guided Rona to her bedchamber.

Winnie emerged from the wardrobe with a question on her lips. She found the main room empty and bedroom door closed. No doubt Lady Eleanor took the queen to rest. Questions could wait. She knew her duty but before she returned to finish her task, the door burst open. The King arrived. He appeared his age of seventy-eight with gray strands of hair visible from under the regal skull cap. The gray beard was trimmed but sparse. The rich royal doublet and robe hung on his scrawny frame like a scarecrow. His face drawn and pale from age and illness.

Winnie hastily bowed with her head down. "Sire."

"Where is the Queen?"

She rose but kept her head bent. "She is lying down, Sire. The prince's death upset her."

"Bah! It's about time the old codger died." He swallowed back a coughing fit.

Evidence of the king's ill-health grew each day. As such, Winnie bit back angry words at his disrespect toward the prince and queen.

Pekka scowled as he looked her up and down. "You dressed in black quickly. He isn't even cold."

"I was already in mourning, Sire."

Pekka roughly raised Winnie's head. "Ah. Briggs' daughter. Another failure," he scoffed.

Winnie screwed her eyes shut at his disparaging of her father. She trembled with restraint of not speaking. She often witnessed him mocked or humiliated the queen. Yet now, he included her father, who reportedly died on his latest mission for the King! Of course, no servant enjoyed an encounter with the King. His gruff manner could easily turn into explosive anger over trifles. Declining health intensified those mood swings. Thus, she fought to maintain her temper.

He gave her a shove of release. "Tell the Queen, I expect her at dinner. And no mourning clothes! I intend to celebrate. Now, go about your business."

Winnie gave a quick curtsy and scurried back into the wardrobe. Under the bleak circumstances, she found it especially difficult to deal with the King. She knew her father stressed respect for the King, at least in title. Personally, Pekka even challenged his patience at times. It took all her strength of will to remain silent and respectful as her father would advise. She swallowed back a wave of tears brought on by the thoughts to concentrate on her task. Despite his order, she knew the Queen wanted to honor Prince Ennis while avoiding the King's wrath. Thus, Winnie chose muted colors but not black.

Chapter 2

ONCE THE QUEEN LEFT FOR DINNER, ELEANOR DISMISSED Winnie, as she would tend to the Queen later in the evening. The day brought so many questions for Winnie. Why the gift? Why did the king forbid mourning the passing of his uncle, a royal prince? Most painful of all, why did he disparage her father by calling him a *failure?* He died on a mission for the King. At least that is what was reported. She found it difficult to believe since no body was recovered. As the King's general, he survived so many other missions. Yet, this one was different. She saw it in his eyes before he left.

Over the past month, she sought answers. However, neither Prime Minister Lord Falco nor Captain Tolbert proved forthcoming with details. Even in her prayers for peace and clarity, she felt a strong urging to and learn the truth. Each day, she laid aside the growing urgency to serve the Queen. She loved the Queen. A gentle, kindhearted soul completely opposite the King in personality. She touched the neck of her dress. Perhaps the gift truly was given as gratitude, just like her mother Arabella, who served as the Mistress of the Wardrobe before she died. Winnie even accompanied her when old enough to help. Alas, the compulsion to leave became almost impossible to ignore.

Instead of proceeding to the castle's lower level, Winnie headed to the scholar's office located across the courtyard from the Great Hall. She needed to speak with someone to help her confused feelings of gratitude, fear, and mourning. Her best friend, Jayson, served as assistant to his father, Simon Clarke, Lord Chancellor of Scholars. Good. A light was on in the office. She knocked and entered.

"My Lord Simon."

At one desk sat Simon Clarke, a forty-five-year-old balding man with spectacles. He wore the dark blue scholar's robe over the matching brocade doublet and pants. He grinned upon seeing her. "Ah, Winnie. Come in, child."

"I had hoped Jayson would be here."

"He's in the vault doing research." He noticed her look of disappointment. "Is something troubling you?"

"Another run-in with the King," she complained. "Only this time, he spoke very ill of my father." A lump rose in her throat, and she fought back emotions.

Simon moved to comfort her. "The King speaks ill of everyone. Do not let it trouble you. Conor was a good man."

She nodded and wiped a few tears from her face.

"You can wait for Jayson if you wish. As for me, I have business regarding the prince's estate. Such as it is."

She flashed a forced smile as she watched him take his satchel and leave. For a few moments, she wandered about the office lost in thought. Since Jayson served as his father's assistant, his desk was in the main office. Other lesser clerks worked in the antechamber. She strolled by Jayson's desk. Among the various papers were partial sketches and finished illustrations. A low gasp escaped upon seeing a detailed map with the word *Thorndel* on it. She snatched it up for a closer look, but noise from the hallway startled her. She pocketed the map and hastily left the office.

Winnie hurried to the castle's lower level and her room in the servants' quarters. There she lit a single lamp to examine the map. She sat on the bed to consider what she discovered.

"Oh, father! They won't tell me what happened to you. Will this help to know?" She placed a hand over her mouth to stifle sobs. In doing so, she felt the necklace and withdrew it to regard the ruby. "She said you would approve." She looked at the map again. Since it was among his papers, Jayson might become upset at finding it missing. She had to act quickly.

Winnie went to her small wardrobe to change. Among her clothes was a forest-green dress with a slitted skirt and pants. She wore the outfit when going on practice maneuvers with her father and his men. Also in the wardrobe was a cloak, knapsack, belt with dagger, flask, and sturdy knee-high boots. Once changed into the military outfit, she began gathering items for the knapsack. A knock on the door startled her. She dropped the map on top of the cloak.

"Winnie?"

"Jayson!" she muttered with concern. She turned when the door opened.

He stepped into the light, which revealed a brown-haired young man of twenty-two. His dark blue suit consisted of doublet, pants, hose, and shoes. The quality showed a person of means. "Father said you wanted to see me." He noticed her change in clothes. "Why are you dressed like that?"

Despite his unexpected arrival, she refused to be deterred. "I'm going to learn what happened to my father."

"Winnie, you can't."

Her frustration burst forth. "Stop telling me I can't! I've wanted to do this for weeks. Only you and your father have stopped me. Well, no more!"

"Winnie!" His voice rose in frustration. "What about the Queen? She protected you from Lord Falco."

Pricked, Winnie carefully touched the closed neck of her dress. The necklace still lay safely hidden. "I would not hurt the Queen for anything in the world. Yet I know she would understand." She looked crossly at him. "If you understood, then you would help me instead of trying to stop me."

"I'm trying to keep you from being hurt or worse."

Winnie softly smiled. "Jayson, I appreciate your friendship and advice, but I *must* do this." At his pricked frown, she continued, "Questions have haunted me for weeks. Is my father truly dead? Why no body? And why won't Lord Falco or Captain Tolbert provide answers? Even in my prayers, I sense something is amiss. I feel compelled to discover what it is."

"It's foolish to go alone."

"Then come with me."

Jayson made a scoffing laugh. "That's not possible. My father would hardly approve."

"Your father agrees there is more to this situation than has been said."

"No need to bring my father into this," he chided.

"You brought up the Queen!" She closed the knapsack.

Thwarted, that all his arguments failed, he sat on the bed. His face screwed up in annoyance when he saw a piece of paper lying on her cloak. He recognized the marking and snatched it up. "This is one of my maps! Where did you get it?" When she refused to speak, he stood to confront her. "You took it from my desk!"

"No! Your father gave it to me." She tried to take it back, but he held fast.

"Liar! My father didn't know I drew this."

"Jayson—"

"No! You stole this."

Frustrated at being caught, Winnie lashed out. "I need it to find my way!"

When she reached for it again, he tucked it in his belt. "Maybe not having this will keep you here.

Winnie's lips pressed together in determination. "I'm going whether I have it or not! I remember what I saw." She put on the cloak, then flung the knapsack and flask over opposite shoulders. However, Jayson barred the door. She tried to push him aside, but he wouldn't budge. "So, what will you do? Tell the guards about me? I'll say you helped me."

"Oh! You are infuriating."

This time, when she pushed him, he moved aside. Before leaving, she said, "Pray for me."

"Of course," he willingly agreed.

She quickly kissed his cheek and dashed out into the dark hallway.

Being born at Highburn Castle, Winnie knew every hidden passage and alley. She managed to avoid all the normal guard posts and knew the time of each nightly patrol. The tricky part would be crossing the moat. Even then, she timed her exit through the pedestrian door of the first gate to the guard's steps. She used her cloak to hide from view on the bridge. No guards walked the bridge with such formidable gates at either end.

She flattened herself against the city-side gate. This gate had no pedestrian door, so opening it would be too loud. This meant climbing around the gate on the bridge itself. She glanced over the side. She could not see the water but rather heard the current as the moat was fed by the nearby lake.

Winnie took a deep breath before undertaking the most dangerous part of her escape plan. She carefully climbed onto the bridge rail. Torches lit the front side of the city gate. This provided some light to see, but not enough to clearly find hand and footholds for the way around. Inch-by-inch, she moved each hand and foot. At one point the cloak hood fell back. She didn't dare replace it and risk losing hold of the brick façade.

When she reached the front corner, she paused. By the sound of footsteps, the guard was near her. This move needed to be fast and precise to land on the bridge, but she had to wait until he reached the other side. When the footsteps moved away, she counted off the number of steps. Upon mumbling the final number, she made the jump. Her ankles gave way upon landing, and she fell hard on her knees. She bit her lip to keep silent. A glance showed the guard hadn't heard anything. Quickly, she pushed herself up, but movement proved painful. She willed herself to run into the city. She ducked into a dark street to catch her breath and massage her knees. She peeked around the corner toward the bridge. All appeared quiet. No alarm.

Phase one of the escape plan was successful. Phase two: reach the main gate to the city and wait until dawn to leave with the morning traffic. Then again, she didn't need to escape, since she wasn't a prisoner. She merely wanted to leave unnoticed by Lord Falco or Captain Tolbert. Fortunately, her absence shouldn't be noticed until midday at the earliest.

Once her knees felt better, Winnie silently moved through the streets to the main city gate. She avoided the constables and deputies who patrolled the streets. In a quiet corner near the gate, she settled down in hopes of catching some sleep. Unfortunately, her mind wouldn't rest. There was too much at stake. Thought of her father brought tears to her eyes. His death happened under mysterious circumstances. Compounding unwillingness to answer her questions, Lord Falco wanted her dismissed from service! Why? She hadn't done anything wrong. Only the Queen's intervention stopped that from happening. Winnie clutched the hidden necklace under the top of her dress. Only afterwards did she learn that Master Simon informed the Queen, which prompted her to intercede and thwart Falco.

Being the head royal scholar, the King and Queen highly regarded Master Simon's opinion. As his father's assistant, Jayson was well-studied in law, royal lineage, and Orrin history. He already gained a reputation for his mythological illustrations, heraldry, and maps, which is why Winnie stole the page she needed. *But he took the map! At least I have a general idea of the direction. What about Jayson? No, he wouldn't betray me*, she tried to console herself.

With that thought, she closed her eyes for a short nap. Sound of a nearby rooster woke her. She slept deeper than anticipated, as told by the full light of morning. The gate stood open! She rose, stretched, and brushed off the dust of night. Her stomach growled. She bought two meat tarts and filled her flask with cider at a nearby bakery. She placed one meat tart in her knapsack then began to eat the other. She joined the morning traffic moving through the gate. Blending amongst the crowd lessened the chance of being spotted.

With walking and eating difficult, she hopped onto the rear of a merchant wagon leaving the city. The driver seemed unaware of his passenger. For several miles, she rode before jumping down at a crossroad. From there, she headed east into the unknown. Whatever lies ahead, she has to face it for her father's sake.

"Lord, you placed me on this path. Give me the courage to see it through," she silently prayed.

Chapter 3

BACK IN THE SCHOLAR'S OFFICE, JAYSON STOOD AT A WINDOW to watch the sunrise. He couldn't sleep after trying to stop Winnie from leaving. *"If you understood, then you would help me instead of trying to stop me."*

Her words cut deep. So many questions surrounded General Briggs' death. No answers seemed satisfactory for Winnie. In truth, most of her concerns were dismissed by Lord Falco and Captain Tolbert. This made Jayson wonder how he would feel if it had been his father.

He glanced at the map he held. *Was I right to try to stop her? To take the map?* He sighed with regret and returned to stare out the window. "Lord, please, watch over her," he prayed. He became so lost in thought that he didn't hear the door open.

"You're up early," said Simon. He moved to stand beside Jayson at the window. "Has something captured your attention?"

"Huh? Oh, father."

"That's hardly an answer to my question."

"Sorry. My mind is preoccupied."

"Pre-occupied by what is my question?" Once more, Jayson appeared distracted by something outside. Simon noticed a paper clenched in his son's hand. "Does the pre-occupation deal with the paper you hold?"

"Not the paper. Her."

"Her?" asked Simon, intrigued.

Jayson looked over his shoulder into the room. Cautiously, he asked, "Where is Rodney?"

"Still asleep, I suppose. It's just past sunrise. What is wrong?" he insisted.

Jayson lowered his voice. "Winnie left to find out what happened to her father. She wanted to take this!" He handed the paper to his father.

Simon's eyes widened in recognition. "A map of Thorndel? Where did you get this? There hasn't been a map of the forgotten citadel since—"

"I drew it from descriptions in the ancient texts."

"You? Oh, lad, you've gone too far. This is dangerous!"

"So, Thorndel is a real place, not just a myth."

"Doesn't matter!" Simon waved it aside.

"It does, since that's where Winnie is going. Fortunately, I took it from her."

Simon's startled annoyance returned. "What? She left to go here?" He held up the map. "Why didn't you stop her?"

"Lower your voice!" Jayson warned. Again, he looked back into the room, specifically at the door. "I tried. That's when I discovered she took it from my desk."

Simon hastened to the hearth, struck a match, and lit the map.

"What? No!" Jayson tried to rescue the burning map from his father.

Simon slapped Jayson's hand away. "This must be destroyed. Neither Falco nor Tolbert can learn of your folly."

"What of Winnie?"

Simon allowed the last of the map to slip from this hand into the hearth, where it turned to ashes. "We must pray she never learns the truth."

Jayson fought to contain his temper. "Why?"

Simon's face turned deadly. "Because she will join her father in the grave."

Jayson stared at his father in dreadful comprehension. "You know what happened to General Briggs." When his father began to move away, Jayson grabbed him. "Why haven't you told her? Or me?"

"I just said why I kept silent. Now, you must do the same."

Irate, Jayson said, "Winnie is out there! Alone."

"You can't help her! Now, you must forget about Thorndel."

The door opened and Rodney, their servant, entered, a gray-haired, spry man of sixty. He carried a tray filled with plates and tankards. "Morning, Masters. I brought breakfast."

Simon assumed a pleasant attitude. "Ah, wonderful. Shall we?" He poked Jayson.

Jayson struggled to calm down. "I'm not hungry."

"Of course, you are," the elder Clarke insisted. He handed Jayson a tankard of morning cider. "Drink up and eat. We have a great many assignments today."

As the day progressed, Jayson pushed aside the nagging questions about Thorndel, General Briggs, and his concern for Winnie. He needed to concentrate on work. Several times throughout the day, he caught scolding glares from his father, but no words were spoken. A look was enough to convey disapproval and frustration. Still, he found it difficult to focus on his daily assignments. He felt relief when his father left for his weekly supper with Lord Falco. He knew his father would spend until the wee hours of the next morning going over reports of court activity. The Prime Minister wanted to know every detail.

Once retired to his chambers, the questions Jayson pushed aside came rushing back. He recalled when his father broke the devastating news to Winnie about General Briggs. Since her mother died when Winnie was ten years old, she and her father became close. They shared a deep bond of affection that showed in everything. Not like he and his father. Oh, there was love, but more of respect in an academic manner between the scholar father and son. In fact, his father deferred to him when quick sketches or finished illustrations were necessary. This made the harsh reaction to the map of Thorndel very perplexing. His father never destroyed one of his drawings before! Yet something about Thorndel deeply disturbed his father, and it was somehow connected to General Briggs. Since his father wouldn't elaborate, the best place to find answers was in the undercroft vault.

Jayson slowly opened the door to peek out into the hall. For a moment, he watched and listened. Too much activity. He shut the door just as the clock on the mantel struck eight o'clock. Best to wait another two hours for supper to end and people to retire.

He did his best to occupy himself until the appointed time to leave. Being assistant to the head royal scholar, he didn't need to be too careful in his trek to the undercroft vault. However, he wanted to avoid any place his father, Lord Falco, or Captain Tolbert might appear. Thus, he took the back stairs and servants' passageways. The vault was in the cellar of the royal officers' wing.

Holding the lantern high, Jayson descended the narrow steps. No need for guards down here. There were no valuables to tempt looters and thieves simply papers, books, and parchments related to court and past kings. Again, his position gave him keys to the vault, kept secure for organizational purposes. They didn't want some unlearned individual to wander in and mess up the neatly categorized material.

Jayson used a match to take flame from the lantern to light several candles on the table. A quill pen, ink well, and paper always remained for taking notes during research ventures.

He made his way to the section where he found information on Thorndel for the map. Now, he needed to learn more than the geographic location. Why was it so dangerous? And why keep its location secret?

Once he gathered all the needed material, he sat at the table to piece together pertinent information. He jotted down notes in personal shorthand developed for his own research. Only his father could read it. No need for junior scribes to understand. Any important notes would be deciphered before given to lower-ranking scribes for final presentation.

Confused, he sat back to stare at the notes. "Piskies? Shadowspire?" he thought aloud. "Why would legends pose such danger as to cost a life?" He left the table to gather more information about these new discoveries. Books became piled upon books, and parchments scattered about the table. Jayson furiously wrote shorthand notes. Suddenly, he stopped. His eyes widened in surprise. "The royal jewel!"

Quickly, he gathered his notes, blew out the candles, and snatched the lantern to hurry from the vault. His haste did not cease until he returned to his room, where he locked the door. He shoved the notes into a hidden slot used for personal papers and journals. He locked the slot and put away the key. He tried to bring his labored breath under control. He stared into the empty hearth to consider what he learned.

A knock on the door made him jump in fright. "Master Jayson?" He relaxed at hearing Rodney's voice. Upon opening the door, he noticed Rodney hastily dressed and worried in face. "Is something wrong? My father?"

"No, sir." Rodney quickly entered and shut the door. His voice low and urgent. "Lady Eleanor woke me since she couldn't find you."

Perplexed, Jayson asked, "Why would she want me?"

"Not her. The Queen! Lady Eleanor instructed me to find you and take you immediately to Her Majesty's antechamber by way of the servant stairs."

For a moment, Jayson stood stunned at the turn of events. He rarely received a royal summons. Anything related to the scholar's service was handled by his father.

"We must hurry." Rodney took hold of Jayson's arm.

Swiftly, they reached the servant's stairway leading to the hallway of the royal wing. They skirted the guards to approach the back door of the Queen's chamber. Rodney made a signal knock, to which came a knocking reply. Another rap from Rodney, and the door opened.

"Inside! Quickly!" Eleanor urged Jayson. Rodney remained outside.

Jayson found himself in the Queen's wardrobe surrounded by gowns and all manner of courtly garments and adornments.

"Where have you been? I went looking for you."

"I'm sorry, my lady. I was working."

Lady Eleanor crossly regarded Jayson. "You were not in the scholar's office. Same as you were not in your chamber."

"Research took me to the vault."

Eleanor snorted a huff. "Wait here." She left the candle on a small table before moving to the main chamber. A moment later, she returned with Queen Rona.

"Your Majesty." Jayson bowed. "How may I be of service?"

"Master Jayson. The day has been most distressing. Yet since you are her friend, I summoned you to ask why she left."

Jayson hesitated. A scolding glare from Lady Eleanor prompted him to reply. "I assume you mean Winnie Briggs."

"Indeed. Who else?" said Rona, a bit terse.

"Forgive me, Majesty, it is late, and my mind has been engaged with research." He saw her impatience and discreetly proceeded. "She said it is something she must do—to learn the truth about what happened to *him* and hoped you would understand."

A whimper of anguish escaped when Rona screwed her eyes shut. "It is as I feared!"

Eleanor moved beside the Queen for support. "Majesty, you must take care."

Rona's eyes snapped open. "No! Learning the truth is necessary. Oh, how I wish she had spoken to me first."

"I don't know if even you could have stopped her," said Jayson.

Rona steadily regarded Jayson. "Has Simon told you anything about the general?"

She spoke with an emphasis that he took to mean specific information. "Only that he allegedly died while undertaking a mission for His Majesty and Lord Falco."

"*Allegedly?* Interesting term. Then again, you are a scholar." Rona's steadfast gaze remained fixed on him. "Would your research be in conjunction with what your father told you?"

Jayson fought to contain his astonishment at the question.

Rona flashed a wry smile. "Do not look so surprised. Lady Eleanor told me you conducted research in the vault this evening. No doubt that happened after everyone retired, for that is when I dispatched her to find you."

"Ay, in part," he admitted. "The other part, well, *her* departure troubled me as well."

Rona stepped closer to Jayson. Her voice barely above a breathy whisper. "Continue your research and tell me all you learn. For there is more at stake than you can imagine." She left the wardrobe.

Somewhat dumbfounded by the interview, Jayson didn't move until Eleanor nudged him to the secret door. Dutifully, Rodney escorted Jayson back to his chamber.

The unexpected audience deepened the mystery surrounding Winnie's departure. He recalled she claimed feeling an unrelenting compulsion to discover the truth. Perhaps if he had been more diligent in research before she left, he could have provided her with needed information. Still, she spoke the truth of how he and his father kept dissuading her from leaving. He followed that action by refusing her plea to go with her. This forced him to admit to himself that guilt drove him into deeper research. Now, the Queen also wanted answers. If Winnie could boldly face the unknown, he would muster the courage to face the consequences to aid her and the Queen.

Chapter 4

WINNIE MADE SLOW PROGRESS ON HER JOURNEY. Her boast of memorization was just that—a boast. She didn't study Jayson's map enough to memorize every detail, only enough to recognize the name of several villages and the main road leading from Highburn. After heading east for two days, she came to the first village on the map where the road turned north. For the next two days, she made educated guesses yet kept in a northerly direction. Money ran out at the last village where she purchased food and drink. She stretched the bread, cheese, and sausage until she finished the food on the third morning. Along the way, she refilled her water flask at a farm or village well. She couldn't turn back! Not for fear of hearing Jayson say *I told you so*, but more importantly, Lord Falco would discover her attempt to learn the truth.

Her father repeatedly warned her to avoid Lord Falco. He never went into detail about why. He didn't have to. Just the sight of Lord Falco caused Winnie to shrink back in fear. To a small girl, Falco appeared a dark, imposing figure of a man. The impression of uneasiness continued into adolescence. Now an adult, she saw enough at court to realize Lord Falco's power and understand her father's warning.

The day her father left on his last assignment, he was unusually silent. Normally, he displayed a brave front and encouraged her about his return. Not this time. No amount of coaxing made him reveal his true anxiety. Even when he hugged her before departure, he held on tight. Recalling that day made her eyes swell with tears.

She moved off the path to sit under a tree and regain her composure.

She took a drink from the flask and discovered the water was nearly gone. She needed to find a water source. She glanced up and down the road for signs of a farm. Nothing. This meant venturing into the forest to find a stream or brook. Going too far into the woods could prove dangerous with werebears and splintercats roaming about. Spending a night in the forest would be fatal. Thus, she slept on the side of the road for safety or took shelter in a barn. With the sun at midday, she reckoned enough time to find water before nightfall.

Her father taught her a few skills on how to identify places for water or forage for food. She never put them to any real use before; only during times she went with his men on practice maneuvers. Recalling those lessons, she used her foot to gently nudge aside fallen branches or debris to search the ground for animal tracks. Shortly, she found deer prints in the soft earth. Her father's voice echoed in her mind. *"All animals need to find good fresh water, so follow the tracks, and they will eventually lead you to water."*

After a quarter mile, the tracks led down a short incline into a ravine. Trickling water cut through the ravine, yet not deep enough to fill the flask. She followed the ravine, which grew wider and deeper. Soon, she heard the babbling of a brook where it emptied into a pool before continuing further into the forest. Her appearance startled a doe and fawn drinking from the pool. She splashed some water on her face. The coolness felt refreshing. She cupped one hand to scoop up some water and smell it. She was told to smell for freshness. Anything foul or stale, don't drink. Of course, if deer were drinking from the pool, it was safe for humans. She drank several handfuls before filling the flask. Whereas the water satisfied thirst, her stomach growled with hunger.

Upon standing, she noticed the doe and fawn had not traveled. They stood grazing from a bush with their hind ends toward her. Carefully, she stepped into the water. It reached above her ankle. She moved in such a way as to avoid splashing, yet slipped on the bank and once again startled the doe and fawn. She hastened to the bush to discover …

"Elderberries!" She frowned at the tangy taste. "Not quite ripe, but it's food." She ate a handful of them. When she stepped away from the bush something crushed beneath her foot. She bent down. "Chestnuts." She hadn't noticed the chestnut tree nearby. Whereas berries weren't easily stored, she gathered chestnuts to roast beside an evening fire.

Suddenly, she heard a scream!

Frightened, Winnie flattened against the tree to determine what screamed and where it came from. Hearing another scream, she shoved some chestnuts into the sack and reached for her dagger. Through the trees, she saw a small figure running, followed by a larger shape.

"Help!" a high-pitched child-like voice called.

Foolish it might be, but Winnie hurried in the direction of the cry for help. She couldn't see clearly, but only heard a child whimpering. She dashed around another tree to discover a splintercat cornering a child against two boulders. The huge, black feline with large hunches, a white chest, and yellow eyes made ready to pounce.

Winnie snatched up a rock to throw at the beast and shouted, "Hey!"

Angry at being stuck, the splintercat turned toward Winnie and let out a roar. She instinctively stepped back. When the splintercat leapt at her, she moved aside and slashed out with the dagger. She felt the feline's claws rip into her right shoulder. The force knocked her to the ground where she lost the dagger. Searing pain burned her right shoulder. Hearing the splintercat roar, she grabbed the dagger with her left hand. This time, she thrust forward with all her strength to meet the attack. The blade sank deep into the splintercat's chest just as the feline fell upon her. The impact rendered her unconscious.

"Zoe! Zoe!" called a frantic male voice.

"Here!" replied the female. Frightened, yet curious, she pushed herself off the rocks. She stood around four and a half feet tall. By her body shape, she was not a child, but rather a teenager. Her woodland clothes were dusty and dirty from her attempted escape. Long red hair once pulled back, now partially undone. She brushed her hair strands behind her pointy ears. Large, bright green eyes stared at the unmoving splintercat lying on top of what appeared to be a human female, who also lay not moving.

The male arrived. He looked almost identical in appearance with shoulder-length red hair. "Are you hurt?"

"No," she answered, still distracted by the sight of the motionless cat and human.

"We must go!" He snatched her hand.

"We can't leave her."

"Of course, we can. She's human." He tugged on her arm.

"No, Zane!" She pulled away from him.

"It's bad enough you wandered off. Now, you want to help a human?"

"She saved my life!"

Zane became perplexed by the statement. "What do you mean?"

"Exactly what I said. The splintercat cornered me, but before it could attack, she arrived and distracted it." Zoe became distressed. "It may have killed her instead." She picked up a branch and slowly approached Winnie. Ever so careful, she poked the splintercat. It didn't move or make a sound. A faint groan came from underneath the feline. "Zane! She's alive. Help me move the splintercat."

Together, they pushed and rocked until the beast rolled off Winnie. Zoe knelt and inspected Winnie's shoulder. "The wound is very deep. It will fester if left untreated."

"There's nothing we can do about that."

Winnie stirred. Her eyes blinked open. She gasped at seeing two small, pointy-eared individuals staring at her with large green eyes. "Who are you?"

"Easy. You're badly hurt," said Zoe.

Winnie groaned and felt her shoulder. "It burns."

"Splintercat claws are dangerous," said Zane.

"Can you stand?" asked Zoe.

"I don't know. But who are you?"

"I'm Zoe, and this is my twin brother Zane. I'm the one you saved from the splintercat. What is your name?"

Winnie became confused. "Winnie Briggs. But I thought you were a child."

Zane scoffed. "We might appear that way to humans."

Stunned, Winnie exclaimed, "Piskies!" She sat up but doubled over in pain to clench her rib cage.

"You need help to heal your wounds." Zoe encouraged Winnie to stand. However, once on her feet, Winnie fainted. Zoe immediately knelt to touch Winnie's forehead. "She's already feverish! We must get her to Mother."

"Zoe—!" Zane began to protest.

"No! I won't let her die after she saved me. Now, let's make a litter for her."

Chapter 5

Zoe and Zane pulled the litter of branches and fern leaves over the uneven forest floor. Winnie lay on the litter not moving.

"Humans are heavy," complained Zane.

"Oh, shut up! We're almost home."

"Father won't like this."

"He will once I tell him what happened."

Zane stopped on the overlook to take a breath. Below lies the Piskie village. On either side of a large brook stood small, thatched homes. A few more elaborate homes were carved into the trunks of enormous oak trees that grew along the banks. Lights came from the homes as twilight grew darker. Boulders served as walkways between the banks. To Zane's right were wooden steps leading down the brook.

"We're going need help to carry her down. I'll fetch my friends. You wait with her."

Zoe knelt. Winnie's face was pale and sweaty. "We're here. You'll get the help you need. Just stay strong." Her words made Winnie groan.

"It's a human!" said one of Zane's friends.

"Why did you bring her here?" demanded another.

Zoe stood to confront them. "Because she was wounded by a splintercat to save me! Now, grab the litter and take her to my mother."

Despite some grumbling, Zane and his friends each took a corner of the litter to carry Winnie down the steps to the village.

The sight brought curious onlookers, and soon a crowd gathered. Gasps and murmuring about Winnie could be heard.

"Stop!" an older male Piskie commanded Zane. "Put it down."

"Elder Burdock, we can explain—," began Zoe.

"Who gave you permission to bring this *human* to our village?" demanded Burdock.

"No one, but—"

"Silence!"

"Elder Burdock," said Zane.

"Silence, I said!"

"Mama!" Zoe shouted upon seeing her parents' approach.

"Lady Mora. My Lord Finn, do you know of this?" inquired Burdock.

"No," replied Finn.

"Mama!" Zoe began with anxiety. "This human female became seriously wounded by a splintercat when she saved *me* from the beast. We must help her before she dies from claw poison."

Unmoved by the reason, Burdock scoffed, "You need not bring her here for that."

"It would have been too late to leave her and fetch my mother." Zoe pointed down to Winnie. "Even now, she is fading."

Mora knelt to examine Winnie. "Aye. The poison has spread quickly. I must act fast, or she will not last another hour."

Burdock made an angry grunt to the contrary. Finn gripped Burdock's shoulder and firmly said, "She saved my daughter. I will not let that debt go unpaid."

Burdock's jowls tightened in disagreement, but when Finn's expression hardened, he reluctantly yielded. "As you say, my lord."

Finn told Zane, "Take her to our house."

Zane and his friends bore the litter as instructed. His parents and Zoe followed.

This home was the largest in the village. The massive oak tree trunk of twenty feet in diameter served as the main entrance. From either side of the trunk, a thatched-roof house extended twelve feet long by twelve feet deep, ending in the high bank. The house had two stories with all the windows facing the river. A chimney cleverly hidden beside the trunk allowed smoke to rise. Inside,

Zane and Finn gently laid Winnie on the sofa in the main room. Her feet hung off the edge, so Zoe moved a chair to support Winnie's feet.

"Zoe, help me with the preparations," Mora said.

"Father, I'm sorry about Elder Burdock," Zane said.

Finn waved it off. "Burdock is always angry about something."

Zane glanced to where Zoe aided their mother. He quietly spoke to his father. "I tried to stop Zoe from bringing her here."

"Why? Because of Burdock?"

Zane shrugged. "Partly. But it is dangerous."

"More dangerous for her than us," he said of Winnie. Seeing Zane frown, Finn moved his son to a corner of the room. "Would you rather it be Zoe lying there?"

"No, of course not!"

"Then why are you reluctant to show mercy to the one who saved your twin sister?"

Zane sighed with regret. "I'm not."

At Zane's despondency, Finn asked, "Then what is it?"

Zane hesitated. When poked by his father, replied. "My preoccupation with finding some black truffles caused Zoe to wander off and straight into trouble. I raced to find her, but I was almost too late."

"Black truffles are a delicacy, but not worth your sister's life."

Zane nodded. "All I wanted to do was get Zoe home safely. The human—"

"Did what you failed to do," Finn finished the statement. "Leaving her wounded would not have satisfied a guilty conscience." For a moment, he and Zane watched Mora and Zoe tend to Winnie. Finn said, "We must pray for the Almighty to spare her so you can make amends to both her and your sister."

"Winnie Briggs is her name."

"Briggs?" Finn repeated in surprise. "Are you sure you heard that name?"

"Ay. Could she be related to ...?" Zane stopped when Finn raised a stiff hand.

"Finn!" Mora waved him over to the bed. Her face was anxious. "Look." She gently lifted a chain found under the neck of

Winnie's dress. Attached to the chain was a small ruby surrounded by silver with tiny etchings. "Where could she have gotten this?"

"By the heavens," Finn murmured, astonished. He then whispered in Mora's ear, "Zane said her name is Winnie Briggs."

Mora's eyes widened in surprise as her gaze shifted between Winnie and the necklace.

He gripped her shoulder and spoke a warning, "Burdock cannot learn of this. Not yet."

Mora regained her composure to nod agreement. Both jerked at a knock on the door.

"Quick! Put it under her collar!" Finn turned to see who arrived and shielded Mona from view.

He ducked under the threshold to enter the home. Upon standing, this was a human male of around forty years old in leather forester ranger clothing, complete with a cloak and knee-high boots. From his belt hung a dagger with a bow and quiver slung over his shoulders. His dark, shoulder-length hair and short beard.

"Rafe?" Finn moved to meet the new arrival.

"I heard you had a human female here."

"Word travels fast," Finn scoffed, laughing.

"I was passing through when Burdock told me." Rafe crossed to the foot of the bed. His brows knitted in surprise recognition. His eyes darted to Finn.

To cover Rafe's reaction, Finn asked, "Did Burdock tell you what happened?"

"Something about a splintercat and Zoe." Rafe caught Zoe's eye.

"She saved me and killed the splintercat."

Rafe's concerned gaze passed to Mora. "Will she live?"

"I've done what I can. It's up to the Almighty."

"We will pray for her," said Finn to Mora. "You and Zoe fetch supper." He stepped closer to Rafe and tugged on the man's arm. When Rafe leaned down, Finn whispered, "I'm told her name is Winnie Briggs. Is that true?"

Rafe regarded Winnie with a mix of sympathy and worry, as he whispered, "Aye."

"You two quit conspiring and come to the table," Mora said to Finn and Rafe.

"We weren't *conspiring*," Finn spoke in light-hearted dispute. He sat at the head of the table while Rafe sat on the floor. Being human, he was too large for Piskie chairs.

"You can't fool me. I know you both," Mora countered.

When all were seated at the table, Finn spoke a blessing over the food and added a prayer for Winnie's recovery. Mora dished out the food, giving Rafe a larger portion of supper, which consisted of vegetables and bread.

Finn grinned and poured dark brown liquid into Rafe's cup. "First draft of black mead."

Rafe eagerly drank. He smacked his lips with a contented sigh. "Nectar of the forest."

"Admit it. This is the real reason you're here this time of year," Finn teased as he poured more mead into Rafe's cup.

"And Mora's cooking." Rafe chuckled. "I also brought grain for your winter storehouse."

"Oh, I hope you didn't get it from Farmer Denis. Many complained of the poor quality," said Mora.

"We are fortunate Rafe takes the risk to bring us grain," Finn told her.

Abashed by the rebuke, Mora quickly apologized to Rafe. "I meant no offense."

Rafe washed down food with mead before he replied. "None taken. I noticed the same about Denis' crop from what little bread I made myself. I bought double my normal winter ration from Kenzie. I told him all the signs point to a very harsh winter."

With supper finished and dishes done, Finn, Zane, and Rafe sat beside the evening fire while Mora and Zoe watched over Winnie.

"She wakes!" Zoe said.

Winnie's eyes blinked then opened. She balked at the sight of Mora. "Who?"

"Don't be frightened," Zoe said softly. "You're safe in our home. This is my mother. She knows the healing arts and has tended to your shoulder."

"Thank you," said Winnie weakly.

"It is we who should be thanking you for saving our daughter," said Finn. He, Zane, and Rafe crossed from the hearth to the bed.

Winnie looked curiously at Rafe. "You're large for a Piskie."

He chuckled. "No. I'm human. Like you."

"Enough talk for now. She needs nourishment," said Mora, then to Winnie, "I'll fetch you some broth then you can sleep some more. Any questions can wait until morning."

Chapter 6

THE FOLLOWING DAY, WINNIE SAT UP ON THE SOFA EATING a vegetable porridge. She used her left hand to raise the spoon to her mouth since her right shoulder still hurt. Zoe sat on a stool beside the bed while Zane, Finn, and Rafe ate breakfast at the table.

"Thank you. That was good." Winnie gave the bowl to Zoe.

Mora brought over a cup. "This elixir will help with pain and healing."

Winnie took the cup and smelled the contents.

"It's not poison, if that is what you fear," said Mora with a hint of insult in her voice.

"Oh, no!" insisted Winnie. "You have been so kind. I just wanted to learn what was in it. I smell garlic, ginger, and a bit of apple, but not sure of the others."

"You know herbs?" asked Mora, curious.

"Some, from what my father taught me."

Mora sent a quick, sly glance to Finn before probing Winnie with more questions. "Your father was a healer?"

Winnie shook her head as she drank.

"But he taught you about herbs?" Mora sat on the foot of the sofa.

"Only what to look for in the forest, if needed."

"Healers forage for herbs. We found chestnuts in your pouch." Mora stared directly at Winnie, who shied from the intense gaze. "You said he wasn't a healer. Then maybe a ranger like Rafe?" She motioned to the table where Rafe and Finn closely watched the exchange.

"Rafe?" questioned Winnie.

"Me," said Rafe.

Winnie again shook her head and drank to avoid answering further.

Rafe moved to stand beside Mora. "He is a soldier."

Surprised, Winnie looked at Rafe. He continued when he had her attention. "You told Zoe your name is Winnie Briggs. You are the daughter of General Conor Briggs."

Winnie became upset. "How do you know that?"

"Easy!" soothed Mora. "Rafe means no harm."

"Indeed." Rafe wore a friendly smile. "I've known your father since before you were born."

Now curious, Winnie asked, "Did you know my mother also? Before she died, that is."

Rafe sighed with melancholy. "Aye. We all knew each other. Now, let me ask you a question: what are you doing in Morgrath Forest?"

"I needed to refill my flask when I heard a cry for help."

"That's part of an answer. However, it's a long way from Highburn Castle. Especially for one traveling alone."

Winnie flinched and tried to stifle a yawn.

"Enough questions for now. She still needs rest," Mora told Rafe. She took the cup from Winnie to give Zoe. "Lay down." She pulled the covers over Winnie. "Sleep." Mora kindly smiled.

Winnie closed her eyes. Mora stopped Rafe's inquiry, but questions stirred Winnie's mind. Who was Rafe? And how did he know her parents? Despite the fatigue, she couldn't sleep. Instead, she lay listening to her hosts. Mora spoke to Zoe about fetching grain for baking. Zane announced he would go foraging. The door opened and closed twice. Just as she started to drift off to sleep, she heard Finn speak, his voice low but understandable.

"Conor must have told her about us. Why else would she be in Morgrath?"

"No, I don't believe so. He took an oath."

"There is no other explanation than he betrayed us!" Finn's voice rose and quickly *shushed* by Rafe.

Angry, Winnie sat up. "My father didn't betray anyone! When he gave his word, he kept it!"

"Then how did you know to come to Morgrath?" demanded Finn. The elder Piskie's features fixed with suspicion.

"I said before that I needed to find water to refill my flask, so I searched for a stream. I didn't know the forest was called Morgrath. Nor that Piskies lived here. Or about Rafe!" She grew agitated. "You both seem to know more about my father than me!"

"Well, I'm sure Conor will tell you—" began Rafe.

"He's dead!" she declared in a quivering voice.

For a moment, Rafe and Finn stood in stunned silence. "Dead?" repeated Rafe. "When?"

Winnie wiped the tears from her eyes. "Last month."

"How?"

She shook her head. "I don't know. Lord Falco wouldn't tell me anything about the circumstances. He wasn't even brought back for burial …" her voice cracked. Their questioning gaze forced her to continue. "I left to learn if Lord Falco told me the truth and my father is truly dead. And if he is, what happened to his body?" Overcome, she wept.

Mora and Zoe returned. Seeing Winnie upset, Mora immediately moved to comfort her. "Here now. Why are you crying?"

"I'm afraid we upset her," said Rafe with regret.

Irate, Mora pointed to the door. "Out! Both of you!" They knew better than to argue.

Finn and Rafe walked a short distance from the oak home.

"Hard to believe Conor is dead," said Rafe, low and mournful.

"Indeed," muttered Finn in half-hearted agreement.

Rafe's expression changed to anger. "You don't sound regretful."

Finn shook his head. "I don't mean to be unsympathetic. He is … *was* human."

Angered by Finn's continued disregard, Rafe lashed out. "Conor would no more break an oath and betray you than I would!"

Finn stared up at Rafe. The ranger's staunch expression told him that he pushed too far. "I'm sorry. I'm merely concerned for my tribe."

"*His* daughter saved your daughter's life and nearly died in the process."

Struck by the reminder, Finn sat on a large oak root that protruded from the ground. "I owe her a life."

Rafe sat beside Finn. His tone softened. "Our goals are the same: survival of the Piskies and restoration of the crown. It is that to which Conor agreed and swore the oath."

"You think that is what got him killed?" Finn followed Rafe's thoughtful glance back toward his home. "Oh!" he said with sudden thought. He seized Rafe's arm to tug the human closer. When Rafe's ear to near his face, Finn spoke. "She wears it!"

"It?"

"Part of *Scrutern!* Mora found she wore it while tending her wounds."

Struck by the report, Rafe declared, "Conor's death prompted her to act. This means time is short."

Finn blinked in astonishment. "You mean the girl is—?"

"Hush!" Rafe snapped yet made a curt nod of affirmation.

Finn muttered in Piskie and finished in the common tongue. "May the Lord guide us."

"Amen," agreed Rafe.

Finn leaned close to Rafe to ask, "Do you think she told the girl?"

"I doubt it. Her behavior shows ignorance. However, I won't know for certain until I speak with Winnie *privately*. That means, you must find a way to get Mora from the house."

Finn shook his head. "She won't leave until the girl is recovered. Even then, you know how stubborn Mora is."

"Ay, she has to be, she's married to you."

Finn sent a hard jab into Rafe's side. The ranger made an ooff! sound before he laughed.

"Still," began Finn, "best wait a few days before trying anything. She's already suspicious of us."

Curious, Rafe looked sideways at Finn. "So, she wasn't teasing us about *conspiring*. She knows."

"Not completely. I've given her vague answers about our recent activities. It's dangerous enough they knew Connor. Now his daughter comes with Scrutern!"

"After what happened with Winnie and Zoe, your family is now *fully* involved."

"Ay," Finn woefully agreed. "Zane questioned me about the possible connection between Winnie and Conor. Yet now you tell me there is more."

Rafe clapped Finn on the shoulder. "My friend, it is time to tell your family everything."

"Mora, but not the twins."

"Why? They are adult members of the tribe."

"Not yet the rank of *elder*."

"Does that really matter? Winnie is thrust into the middle of this. And there is more danger to her now that she has Scrutern." Rafe's grip on Finn's shoulder tightened. His tone firm. "The time has come to act. I'll give you three days before I return. If you haven't told them by then, get them all out of the house so I can slip in an speak with Winnie." Rafe departed.

Chapter 7

LORD DEVIN FALCO SAT AT THE ELABORATE DESK IN HIS office and shifted through a large stack of papers. Early morning light filtered through the windows. The deep crimson Prime Minister's robe hung over the back of the chair. The red, feathered cap lay on the desk. He loosened the collar of his black and red doublet. Salt-and-pepper beard and hair betrayed his age of fifty-five. Long gaunt features made any look from his steel-gray eyes more intense. The hollow cheeks gave evidence of the gastric illness which plagued him most of his adult life. Any food brought him was bland and unseasoned. In fact, an untouched tray of breakfast sat on the edge of the desk. The only item consumed was a tankard of honey ginger mead.

Falco glanced up at a knock on the door followed by an entrance. A sturdy man dressed in the uniform of a royal officer entered. He was thirty years old and in peak physical health. His appearance greatly contrasted Falco.

"Captain Tolbert. What news?"

"Not much, I'm afraid."

"You've learned nothing of the girl's whereabouts?"

"No, my lord."

Disgusted, Falco tossed a quill pen onto the desk and sat back. "Briggs must have told her something! Why else would she suddenly disappear?"

"If he did, she spoke to no one about it."

Falco learned forward on the desk; his eyes focused on Tolbert. "Did I not command you to have her watched?"

Tolbert stiffened under the intense gaze. "You did, my lord. And I followed your orders in assigning men to the task."

"Then how did she leave unnoticed?" Falco demanded.

Tolbert stood at a momentary loss of what to say, but knew he had to respond. "She grew up in the castle. As Briggs' daughter, she could explore at will."

"Or, maybe those loyal to Briggs looked the other way," said Falco in a tone of angry suspicion.

"I thought of that, my lord. I put several of them in the dungeon for interrogation, including Briggs' aide, Lieutenant Kincaid. He stubbornly insists he knows nothing."

"Perhaps, a permanent example should be made of Kincaid."

Tolbert's manner told of hesitation. "My lord, Kincaid's absence from duty caused concern. So much so, that Master Clarke senior came to the dungeon upon learning of the interrogation. He told the jailer that without proof of a crime, he would summon the Council and inform the King. The jailer released Kincaid …"

Falco's abrupt rising from his seat made Tolbert stop speaking. The Prime Minister's cold steely gaze forced Tolbert to take a step back in fear. The captain gathered himself to stand ramrod straight and looked over Falco's head to avoid the piercing eyes.

"Clarke will rue the day he interfered!" Falco flinched in pain and rubbed his abdomen. He took a long drink of the mead. "Send out four patrols. One in each direction. Find the girl!"

Tolbert slapped his sword in acknowledgement and left.

Falco refilled the tankard. He crossed to a window to consider the situation when the door opened again. To his surprise, King Pekka entered.

Falco hurried to put down the tankard and greet Pekka. "Sire! Why do you trouble yourself to grace my chambers when I could have come to you?"

Pekka waved aside the comment with impatience. "I may be old, but I'm not completely infirmed. Can you not see, I am dressed for our weekly hunt?"

"Sire, is that wise? What will the physicians say?"

"Curse the physicians! If I am dying, I shall go on my own terms." Pekka scrutinized Falco. "Why are not dressed properly?"

"Forgive me, Sire. My mind has been preoccupied."

"The Briggs situation," Pekka scowled.

"Ay. Since the general's demise, there has been no progress."

"Not Conor. The girl! Rona is distressed by her disappearance. Apparently, she's fond of the waif. A replacement child, I suppose. Though it is her fault I have no heir!" Pekka spoke with disdain.

Considering Pekka's foul mood, Falco needed to be diplomatic. Lack of an heir touched on a sore spot with the aging King. Thus, he replied, "The Queen does seek to please you, Sire."

"Three stillborn births and two miscarriages. Bah! I need a living son before I die."

"Is that possible considering the Piskie curse?"

Irate at such brashness, he glared at Falco. "Beware your words!"

Falco did not recoil from the warning. "It is a well-known fact, Sire. Everyone has whispered it after each failed attempt."

Pekka spat on the floor. "That is what I think of Piskies! But you have not answered my question about Briggs' daughter."

"According to Captain Tolbert, there is no word of her whereabouts. Yet," Falco hastily added to stem Pekka's annoyance. "Assure Her Majesty, all diligence is being given to find her."

"I don't give a fig about *assuring Her Majesty*!" Pekka's eyes narrowed in suspicion. "Answer me truly. Did Conor confide in her? Is that what made her leave?

Falco stroked his chin in a delay of how to answer. However, he noticed Pekka's rising irritation. "I have found no evidence that General Briggs disclosed the nature of his task to anyone. She, however, deeply grieved her father's passing. She could have simply left in a state of despondency."

Pekka's scowl caused deep wrinkles in his aged forehead. "*If* you're wrong, and he did, her absence could jeopardize everything! So, find her! Learn what went wrong with Conor's mission! And get dressed for the hunt. We leave within the hour!"

Falco made a short bow when Pekka passed him to depart. Again, he picked up the tankard, took a drink, then crossed to the window. Indeed, answers were needed. Too much was at stake. Pekka's illness added urgency. However, the whole situation could unravel if the jewel is not found! A task entrusted to Briggs. He recalled the reluctance of the renowned general to accept the mission. It took much convincing from him and Pekka before Briggs finally agreed. Despite not finding evidence to the contrary, could he have told the girl? What could she do that her father could not?

"Too many questions!" Falco paused in drinking when he spied Jayson crossing the courtyard to the ministry offices. Unaware of being observed, Jayson continued his course.

Falco moved from the window. He put on his robe and cap. In quick strides, he left, intent on making his way to the scholar's office. Servants, nobles, and soldiers acknowledged the Prime Minister. On his part, Falco only gave a passing reply to nobles while ignoring servants and soldiers. All except Lady Eleanor. She remained in a low courtesy.

Falco stared down at her. "Tell me, my lady. How fares the Queen this day?"

Eleanor slowly rose. "She is well, my lord."

"Really? I've heard reports of how the absence of the Briggs girl upsets her."

Eleanor assumed a neutral posture under his scrutinizing gaze. "Naturally. Like Mistress Briggs, the girl serves Her Majesty well."

"I beg to differ. Her abrupt departure could be considered a sign of betrayal."

Eleanor keenly regarded Falco. "By whom? It is rumored she left to find her father. Whom we know is as fiercely loyal to the King as Arabella was to the Queen."

Falco straightened with hauteur. "Mind your tongue when speaking to me!"

Eleanor bowed in submission to the rebuff. "Your pardon, my lord. My loyalty to Her Majesty got the better of me."

"Beware, such loyalty. It can be costly when viewed in light of recent events."

Eleanor swallowed back anxiety at the threat. "Aye, my lord."

"Return to duty. Yet remember what I said and keep your tongue." Without waiting for a reply, Falco continued to the scholar's offices.

Falco's unexpected arrival surprised Simon and Jayson.

"My lord!" said Simon, concerned. "Did I miss an appointment?"

"No, Lord Chancellor," said Falco, politely. "I came to inquire about young Master Jayson's latest drawings." He casually strolled over to Jayson's desk. Papers, maps, illustrations, and such were easily visible. "His Majesty asked about them yesterday. He is fascinated by your discovery of the ancient artifacts and eager to see them illustrated."

Jayson rose when Falco approached. "The descriptions vary from detailed to vague references. Those more precise are finished. Others are sketches of possibilities." He handed Falco three completed color illustrations.

"Impressive." Falco placed them on the desk. "What of the ancient crown and jewel?"

"Surprisingly, there is less detail about those. Most passages tell of their splendor without specifics." Jayson picked up three sheets of drawing paper. "These are some sketches from what information I could glean."

Falco studied the drawings. "I don't see much difference."

"I started with the basic drawing of royal crowns throughout history. Most are similar."

"Where would the royal jewel be located?"

"Center prominence." Jayson pointed to the drawings.

Falco again studied them. "How long for finished color illustrations?"

"Two days for each and a day to dry, so one week."

"Do so." Falco gave the sketches back to Jayson. "The King is most anxious to see them when complete. He might even call upon you this evening when we return for the hunt."

Jayson bowed when Falco turned to leave. However, the Prime Minister paused at the door. "Oh, the Queen is most distressed learning the Briggs girl—I forget her name—has been reported missing. Is she not a friend of yours, Master Jayson?"

Jayson appeared flustered by the question. "I … I know her."

"Perhaps, you know where she can be found? For the Queen's sake. After all, Her Majesty spoke up for the girl at your father's request when it was obvious she needed to be dismissed." Falco's eyes narrowed on Jayson.

Simon intervened. "I'm afraid we have no knowledge of her whereabouts, my lord."

"No, indeed we do not!" Jayson agreed.

"And if my involvement has caused the Queen distress, I shall immediately offer my humblest apologies to Her Majesty," continued Simon with sincerity.

Falco flashed a tentative smile at Simon. "We both know your intervention was well-intentioned. Although, perhaps, misguided."

Intimidated, Simon made a low bow at the waist.

When the door closed on Falco's departure, Simon urgently whispered to Jayson. "Now do you see why I destroyed it! Falco suspects something. He even made observation of your desk in search of it."

"All the more reason to be concerned for Winnie!" Jayson countered.

"You can't help her. You don't even know where she is."

"I know where she is heading."

Simon snarled. "Take care, boy! You will be the death of us all if you don't." He pushed his son back toward his desk. "Start on the illustrations."

The unnerving interaction with Lord Falco made it difficult for Jayson to concentrate on drawing. Falco's mention of Winnie totally caught him off guard and deepened his concern for her. Although grateful for his father's intervention, it proved his father correct about Falco's suspicion. Also, mentioning the Queen heightened his concern about passing along further information. Although he found nothing of any serious consequences to explain the general's mission.

As he completed the final line art for the first illustration, Jayson paused to stare at the center of the crown. A sudden realization struck him. "The royal jewel is not in the current crown," he spoke under his breath.

"What did you say?" Simon asked. He was passing Jayson's desk when he heard speech.

Jayson momentarily regarded his father as he debated whether to repeat himself. "Eh, nothing. Merely self-critiquing the drawing."

The answer didn't satisfy Simon. "Are you sure?"

"Ay. Just considering the configuration for the royal jewel. I assume the center. But could it be located elsewhere?" He pointed to the drawing. "On the top perhaps?"

Simon studied the finished line-art. "It is all speculation."

"Sir." Jayson rose when his father moved from this desk. When Simon paused, Jayson drew his father to the other side of the room, away from the door. Still, Jayson kept his voice to a whisper. "Do you believe the royal jewel exists?"

"What kind of question is that?"

"You scolded me about the map. If that is real, could the jewel be real as well?"

"Both are legends and best left that way."

"But the King and Lord Falco insisted I include it in the illustrations. Why, if only legend?"

Frustrated, Simon rebuffed, "You ask too many questions."

"Isn't that what being a scholar is about? To ask questions and explore the possibilities?"

Simon nodded at the retort. "Aye. Only some possibilities are best left alone. Finish the illustrations like you told Lord Falco." He went to nudge Jayson back to the desk, but thought better and held fast. "Speak no more of these *possibilities* in public."

"Aye, sir."

Despite many unanswered questions, Jayson returned to his desk. The jewel and Thorndel remained mysteries he hoped to solve with more research.

Chapter 8

ELEANOR FINISHED HER TASKS BEFORE RETURNING TO THE Queen's apartment. The encounter with Falco unnerved her, not for herself, but rather for the Queen. Naturally, Winnie's departure troubled Rona. Eleanor anticipated the reaction when word reached them. However, the rumors and speculations proved more distressing for Rona. In her position as lady-in-waiting, Eleanor tried to bolster the Queen's spirit. To some extent, she succeeded.

When Eleanor entered, Rona sat at her personal dining table in the main room of her apartment. She ate a light luncheon.

Rona smiled, pleased. "I see you were successful." She spoke about the cloth and ribbon Eleanor carried.

"Ay, Majesty." Eleanor appeared distracted in her reply. Her expression seemed worried.

"Is something amiss?"

Eleanor placed down the items to sit at the table beside Rona. Her voice low. "Lord Falco accosted me. He is suspicious and considers Winnie's departure a sign of betrayal."

Disturbed by the news, the fork slipped from Rona's hand. "We must allay his suspicion."

"It is difficult considering the commotion her absence has caused. First the general, and now her. He grows bolder since learning of the King's declining health."

Rona looked pointedly at Eleanor. Determination reflected in her eyes. "That is the reason I gave it to her. Neither Pekka nor Falco must know of its existence, or all is lost." For several moments, she sat in deep contemplation. Eleanor patiently waited. Finally, Rona spoke again. "Fetch Master Jayson."

Stunned by the request, Eleanor asked, "In broad daylight?"

"The King has left on his weekly hunt. Falco usually accompanies him." Rona made a *shooing* motion. "Quickly."

Eleanor left as ordered. Upon arrival in the scholar's office, she found Simon sitting at his desk consulting with Rodney. Jayson stood at a bookcase across the room.

"Lady Eleanor," said Simon, a bit surprised.

"Forgive the intrusion, Lord Chancellor. Her Majesty dispatched me to inquire after Master Jayson."

"He is at the Queen's disposal." Simon motioned toward Jayson.

She flashed a humorless smile. "Master Jayson, Her Majesty is curious about some historical mythology she came across while reading this morning. She believes you can answer those questions."

Jayson's surprise mirrored his father's. However, Eleanor carefully turned her back to Simon and sent Jayson a prompting glare. He immediately changed his attitude. "I will do my best to provide any information Her Majesty requires." He returned the book to the shelf. He nodded to Simon. "Excuse me, sir."

No words were spoken as Eleanor escorted Jayson directly to the Queen's apartment via the main door.

"Master Jayson Clarke, Your Majesty," Eleanor announced.

Rona sat on the sofa to receive her guest. "Master Jayson. Good of you to come."

He bowed. "I'm at your service, Majesty."

"Come." She patted the sofa.

Jayson sat beside the Queen. "You have questions, Majesty?" he asked in a tentative tone.

She smiled with reassurance. "We can speak with some freedom. The King and Lord Falco left for the weekly hunt."

Jayson slightly relaxed. "Still, summoning me to your apartment is unusual."

"I'm certain Eleanor gave a reasonable excuse."

"About Your Majesty reading historical mythology and wanting answers," he confirmed.

She lightly chuckled. "Exactly. So, you have nothing to fear in telling me what you have learned."

Jayson tilted his head, hesitant. "I haven't learned too much, as time for private research has been limited to avoid conflict."

"Let me be the judge." Her gaze fixed on him. "Tell me."

Her resolute tone prompted him to comply. "What I found surrounds the legend of the royal jewel. In fact, the King and Lord Falco commissioned me to make illustrations of a new crown that incorporated the jewel. But it doesn't exist. At least, as far as I can tell."

The startling news made Rona look to Eleanor. "A new crown!"

"Steady, Majesty," Eleanor warned.

Curious, Jayson watched the cryptic exchange. "I, too, believe there is significance in the request, but uncertain as to what or why? My father tells me to ask no questions, rather concentrate on the illustrations."

Rona regained her composure. "Master Simon is wise. What else can you tell me?"

"While most consider the jewel and Thorndel to be legends, it seems unlikely with the King and Lord Falco so interested in my drawings. Why want the jewel placed within a new crown? Then, he inquired if I knew anything about Winnie's departure and where she might be heading—"

Alarmed, Rona interrupted him, "Who questioned you?"

Her anxiety surprised him. "Lord Falco, when he came earlier to view the illustrations."

"Then he didn't leave with the King!" Rona said, fearful.

"No, Majesty," Jayson quickly spoke. "He mentioned going on the hunt."

She sighed in relief.

With polite curiosity, Jayson asked, "Majesty, why such interest in Winnie?"

The question aroused Eleanor's wrath. "That is an impertinent question, Master Scholar!"

Rona put up a hand to still Eleanor's objection. "Master Jayson has been very accommodating. He deserves an answer." Her face hardened when Eleanor began to object, which caused Eleanor to back down. Rona's attitude softened toward Jayson. "As the general faithfully served His Majesty, Arabella served me as Mistress of the Wardrobe. Winnie assumed those duties. I'm naturally concerned for her welfare. Yet, you know Winnie's position. So, that answer should suffice."

"To her position, aye. But why your interest in history and mythology? What has that to do with Winnie?"

"Master Scholar!" Eleanor chided.

To this, Rona became irate. "That is impertinence."

Jayson flinched at the rebuke. "Forgive me, Majesty. I don't mean to be rude. I'm only trying to understand why this sudden interest from various parties."

"Master Scholar! A good servant obeys without explanation," Eleanor scolded him.

Jayson flushed with embarrassment at the continued rebuke. He stood and bowed to Rona. "Again, my apologies, Your Majesty. Will there be anything else?"

Rona sat stiff in royal dignity. "That will be all for now, Master Scholar. If I have further need, I will send Lady Eleanor to fetch you."

"I am at your service, Majesty." Jayson bowed and slowly backed away. He didn't turn from Rona until Eleanor opened the door for him to depart.

Eleanor joined Rona on the sofa. "Will you tell him?"

Rona shook her head. Thoughtful eyes remained on the door. "No. And it is obvious Simon has kept his son ignorant."

"But you are risking his life if he is discovered providing the answers you seek."

Rona looked sharply at Eleanor. "More than his life is at risk if everything fails!"

Preoccupied with thoughts about the interview, Jayson didn't hear his father's inquiry when he returned to the scholar's office.

"Jayson!"

At the commanding tone, Jayson realized he was being addressed. "Oh, sir!"

Simon's frown told of immense displeasure. "Return to work. We shall speak later about the matter that interrupted you."

Jayson stared at the illustrations scattered upon his desk. He abruptly rose and approached his father. "Can we speak now, sir? In private."

Simon closed the book he held. "Rodney!" He waved for the servant to leave. Once alone, Simon drew Jayson to a far corner of the room, away from any doors or windows. "Well?"

Indecision made Jayson hesitate. "I'm uncertain where to begin. My research has caught attention."

"From the Queen."

"Aye."

"And?"

"What should I do about it?"

Simon placed a hand on Jayson's shoulder. "You do what all good scholars do. Answer discreetly. Give only what information is requested, nothing more."

"Couldn't that be considered lying?"

"No!" Simon snapped. He then eased his tone to calm when Jayson pulled back at his harsh response. "Often, those making inquiries are not ready to hear all the details. Nor should we divulge everything we know. It may prove hazardous for everyone concerned. Do you understand?"

Jayson cocked a wry grin. "About not divulging everything, aye. It is this sudden interest in a new crown that perplexes me."

"Ah!" said Simon with comprehension. "So, that is what she wanted to know about." His brows knitted in consideration.

Jayson observed his father's reaction. "Her inquiry doesn't surprise you like it does me."

"Why should it? After all, the King requested the drawings."

Jayson's demeanor changed to brooding consideration. "Somehow, it is connected to Winnie's departure. That is what puzzles me." He noticed his father stare at him, a spark of deliberation in his eyes. "Sir? Is there something I should know?"

Simon waved it off. "Not at present."

Jayson grew annoyed. "You have been dismissive of my inquiries and research since Winnie left. Why?"

Simon stiffened at the coarse tone. "Take care, boy. There is much scheming at court. It is best to steer clear. Answer the Queen with discretion and avoid Falco whenever possible."

Irate, Jayson would not be put off. "Why do you treat me like a child by refusing to answer? I'm a grown man, who will someday assume your office."

Simon's ire matched his son's. "Then on both those terms, you should understand that a grown man sees his duty for what it is and abides by it. Your duty is to finish those illustrations." He flinched in sudden pain, which caused Jayson to immediately regret his anger.

"Sir? Is it your head?"

Simon grunted and nodded.

"I'll take you to your room and have Rodney fetch a remedy."

Chapter 9

ROM A HIDDEN SPOT ACROSS THE BROOK, RAFE WATCHED Finn, Mora, Zane, and Zoe leave the Piskie village. The fact that the entire family left told him that Finn had not yet spoken to them about the situation. Going to Finn's house would not be considered abnormal under any circumstances. However, Rafe didn't want Mora to see him. He waited until they disappeared into the forest before venturing across the brook to the house. He paused at the door when the thought occurred to him that Winnie, too, had left. He pushed the thought aside and entered.

"Oh!" exclaimed a startled Winnie. She sat at the table eating. She wore makeshift Piskie clothes since hers were torn and soiled. Not being as tall as Rafe, she could sit in a chair, although the table was quite low.

"I didn't mean to scare you." Rafe smiled.

"I wasn't expecting anyone since the family just left."

"I asked them to leave. Rather, I asked Finn, so you and I could speak alone."

Winnie became guarded. "Why would you do that?"

"Easy," soothed Rafe. He flashed another smile. "There is nothing to fear. I hope you're feeling better."

"I am. Thanks to Mora. I should be ready to continue my journey tomorrow."

"*That* is what I want to speak with you about." Rafe moved a chair from the table to sit on the floor opposite Winnie. "Remember, I said I knew your parents."

"How? You're a ranger."

"I wasn't always a ranger. I used to be a soldier under your father's command. Conor was a good man. A good commander. And a good friend." Melancholy crept into Rafe's voice.

Keen to his change in demeanor, she asked, "Did something happen?"

"Let's just say, circumstances arose that changed things."

"And you became a ranger because of that *change?*"

He nodded. "Aye."

Winnie grew confused. "If you left service so long ago, why speak with me alone? What can I tell you?"

"Do you know any history about the Piskies and Thorndel?"

She glared suspiciously at him upon hearing *Thorndel.* "Why do you ask?"

Rafe nodded and cocked a grin. "I see you have heard of Thorndel."

"What if I had?" she demanded.

"Did Conor tell you?"

Winnie grew angry and pressed her lips together in determined silence.

Rafe's face and tone turned harsh. "Did Conor tell you?" When she remained silent, he seized her arm. "Did he?"

"No!" She winced in pain. "You're hurting me."

Rafe released her. "How did you learn about Thorndel?"

Winnie heaved a half-hearted shrug to assume a casual posture. "I've heard tales since childhood."

"Really?" began Rafe in sarcastic disbelief. "Is that what made you leave Highburn, tales from childhood?"

Again, she didn't answer.

Rafe scowled with frustration. "Winnie, I don't mean to be harsh, but truthful answers are more important than you realize. The future of Orrin is at stake."

Winnie stared at him from under knitted brows. "My father said the same about Orrin before he left. It was the only thing he said." She swallowed a lump in her throat.

This time, when Rafe took hold of her arm, he did so with sympathy. "Tell me about the day he left."

Winnie blinked back tears. "He was unusually quiet and grim. Not himself at all."

"Did he say anything to give a clue of why his behavior was altered?"

Winnie struggled to answer. "No … maybe. He mentioned Lord Falco. A slip of the tongue really. He warned me to stay away from him while he was gone."

"Do you know how many men went with Conor?"

She shook her head, raw emotions making words difficult. "None. I watched him leave alone." Eyes filled with distress as she leaned across the table. Her anxious voice was barely above a whisper. "But I know he was afraid! For the first time, I saw fear in his eyes."

"Conor was no coward." He patted her arm. His encouraging smile was short-lived as he changed the subject. "How did you come by the jewel you wear?"

Winnie's hand protectively gripped the neck of her dress. The jewel is still hidden.

"Well?" he insisted.

Winnie removed her hand. "What's it to you?"

"If it is what I think, then it is part of a jewel that is precious to the Piskies."

She shrugged ignorance. "I don't know about that. It was a birthday gift."

"Who gave it to you?" Despite her reluctance, Rafe again spoke with impatient emphasis. "Winnie, remember what I said about the importance of truthful answers. I'm trying to uncover the truth about what happened to Conor. The jewel may be a clue."

"Honestly, I don't know since the queen …" she stopped at realizing what she said.

"So, the Queen did give it to you," he said with confirmation.

Frustrated with herself, she said, "She told me to keep it a secret."

"Did she tell you anything about the jewel and why you?"

"No," said Winnie, perplexed. "I did wonder since it's such a beautiful jewel set in silver. I'm just a servant."

Rafe coughed back a catch in his voice. When she looked curiously at him, he changed the subject. "Can you tell me anything else about the day Conor left?"

She sat back to recall. "I saw a hastily drawn map near his saddlebag. Half-folded but open enough to see a word," she looked at him and said, "*Thorndel*." Tears again swelled. "I don't know if he ever made it or died along the way. I don't know what happened to him!"

The door opened, and the family returned.

"You upset her again?" Mora accused Rafe. She comforted Winnie.

"I'm afraid it was necessary," replied Rafe.

"Finn told us *everything* about General Briggs."

Finn lifted Winnie's cheek. "Your father was a brave and honorable man. He became a good friend to this family. We mourn his loss with you."

"Rafe said you met him when he stumbled upon your village," said Winnie.

"Ay. General Briggs swore to protect my tribe and restore order to Orrin. I apologize for my earlier behavior. What happened with Zoe was a shock, but no excuse for being rude."

Zoe gave Winnie a cup of honey mead.

"Lord Falco sent Conor alone to find Thorndel. Most likely in search of the jewel. Alas, something went awry," Rafe told Finn.

"Why would Lord Falco want the jewel?" asked Zane.

"To be crowned king," replied Rafe. "Pekka has no acknowledged heir and is unlikely too given his advanced age."

"But the Queen is younger," said Winnie.

Rafe flashed a wry grin at her. "It takes two to make a baby."

Winnie blushed. "I know that!"

Rafe bit back a laugh at her naivety. "Did you ever wonder about the decades age gap?"

"Maybe," she sheepishly admitted.

"Pekka's first queen died giving birth to a stillborn son. She was fifty-five at the time. Many believed a younger woman could achieve Pekka's desire for an heir. Rona was twenty when she married a fifty-three-year-old king. Now, Pekka is nearing eighty and possibly dying."

"Why is the jewel so important?"

"The jewel is special to the Piskies, who are considered *king makers*. Using the jewel, they helped the realm of men rule Orrin. However, it was captured by men two hundred years ago during the Great Struggle between men and Piskies. It ended in victory for men, while beginning the demise of Piskies, who went into hiding. Pekka's family used the jewel to ascend the throne."

Finn took up the explanation. "However, Pekka made a horrible bargain with Balor, a treacherous Piskie who promised him unnatural long life if he returned the jewel to him. Unknown to Pekka, his Uncle Ennis wanted to stop the bargain and secretly broke off a piece. When Pekka discovered the damage, he flew into a rage and imprisoned Ennis. Since he couldn't fulfill the bargain, Balor pronounced a curse that no male heirs would be born to Pekka."

Winnie appeared confused. "If the king still has the jewel, why did Lord Falco send my father to Thorndel to find it?"

Rafe's shoulders sagged. "Sadly, the jewel inadvertently came into Balor's possession. It is now somewhere hidden in Thorndel."

"Whoever possesses the jewel can claim the throne," said Finn.

For Winnie, the answer drove home the ramifications. "My father is Falco's pawn to become king!"

"You were given the broken part Falco doesn't know exists." Rafe pointed to her neck.

Her hand instinctively went to the collar while her eyes darted anxiously to the Piskies.

"They know. Mora discovered the necklace while treating your wounds," Rafe explained.

Winnie considered what was said. "Prince Ennis died shortly before the Queen gave this to me. She said it was a birthday gift since my birthstone is ruby. But from what has been said just now, this goes beyond a simple gift.

"With rumors of Pekka dying, Rona knows time is short. You are now its keeper because Falco cannot find it and restore the jewel," Rafe said.

Winnie nodded. "The King has been ill of late. The royal physicians are constantly coming and going from his chamber." She touched the collar of her dress. "I left Highburn to finish what my father started, although ignorant of what or why."

"Do you know where to find Thorndel?" asked Rafe, curious.

"No. Jayson took the map," she grumbled in annoyance.

"From your father? The map you mentioned?"

"No, another one. More detailed."

Rafe sent a glance of inquiry to Finn. The elder Piskie replied to the look. "I know of none that exist. When Thorndel fell, the way became obscured, and we went into hiding."

"Who is Jayson?" asked Mora.

"Assistant Scholar to his father—" Winnie began.

"Simon Clarke," finished Rafe. A fond smile crossed his lips.

"Ay," agreed Winnie. "Do you know him also?"

"Oh, I know Simon very well. He's my older brother."

Winnie grew wide-eyed. "You're Jayson's uncle. The one he believed died years ago."

Rafe winced and sighed. "Sorry to hear that."

Mora gave Rafe a cup of mead. She softly smiled with sympathy.

"Papa, how did Thorndel fall?" asked Zoe.

Finn's face grew harsh. "Driven by lust for power, Balor made a pact with men. During the battle, he seized control of Thorndel and unleashed the werebears and splintercats from the depths of Shadowspire. This action aided men to victory and drove us into hiding to avoid total annihilation."

"The Almighty allowed it?" asked Zane with astonishment.

"Good and evil exist in the world. While we Piskies aren't invincible."

"But *why?*" insisted Zane.

"The wisdom of the Almighty is not always available to us." Finn put up a hand to stop his son from further inquiry. "We must trust there is a reason."

Winnie's quizzical gaze shifted between the Piskies. "The battle happened two hundred years ago, while the deal with Pekka was fifty years ago. How is Balor still alive?"

Finn grinned at her befuddlement. "Piskies live five hundred years. I was eleven years old when my father died in the battle, so I remember it well. Balor was once his friend," Finn's tone turned somber. "He was two hundred and eighty years old when he betrayed us. Balor is still alive."

"If you are two hundred and eleven years old, then how old are they?" Winnie motioned to Zoe and Zane.

"We are ninety years old. Which is equivalent to your teenage years," said Zane.

"In ten years, we will be considered adults and given the title *Elder*, like Burdock and others. Yet not permitted to marry until we turn a hundred and twenty-five," added Zoe.

Finn touched Winnie's shoulder to get her attention. "My family owes you a life debt. Because of that, and in memory of your father, we will help you find Thorndel so the whole jewel can be safely returned to Morgrath and into our keeping."

The offer stunned Winnie. "You would do that?"

Rafe finished the mead before he countered Finn. "You can't leave. Not without arousing Burdock's suspicion as to why," he spoke with emphasis. He tossed a quick glance to Winnie before he continued in a neutral tone. "Me, I can easily accompany another human."

Finn frowned in reluctance. "True. Burdock would not take kindly to me escorting humans."

"I'll go," Zane volunteered. He turned to Winnie. "I must make amends for my unwillingness to help after you saved Zoe."

"Me too!" added Zoe. "It was me she saved."

"Not with us," began Rafe. "We'll leave separately in the morning and meet at the river fork in the afternoon. From there, we can take the lowland pass north. Agreed?" he asked Finn.

"Agreed," said the Piskie patriarch.

"She's not leaving for two more days!" Mora firmly interjected. "She needs more herbal baths to completely heal the wound, food to regain her strength, and time for her clothes to be repaired." She then said to Winnie. "These flimsy garments won't survive the weather up north. Our tailors will fit you with proper clothes more suitable for the journey."

Zoe placed a hand on Winnie's shoulder to stop an objection. "Don't argue with Mama. You've seen how she handles Papa and Rafe."

"True." Winnie tried to hide a grin as she took a drink.

Chapter 10

THE GRAY LIGHT OF DAWN PIERCED THE TREE CANOPY. Winnie and Rafe left the oak home. No one else in the village was awake. Mora supplied them with root vegetables, bread, and mead for the journey. Rafe's quiver was filled with new arrows. He led Winnie in the northerly direction to the outskirts of the village.

"How far is the river fork?" Winnie asked.

"Half-a-day's journey."

"That's why you told Zoe—"

"No names!" Rafe warned. "We aren't far enough from the village to speak freely."

She flushed with embarrassment. Despite agreeing to help her and being Jayson's uncle, she found Rafe to be a bit abrupt in manner. In thoughtful silence, she followed him. For two hours, her mind dwelled on the events since leaving Highburn. Most of her journey was based on educated guesses from what she remembered on the map. However, nothing prepared her for discovering that the legends of Piskies were true!

She was grateful for Mora's healing expertise after her near-deadly encounter with a splintercat. She heard soldiers tell stories of the beasts. Of course, soldiers tended to exaggerate when swapping stories. Reality became far different from the images created while listening to those campfire stories. Zoe would not have survived the attack. Despite the Piskie's age of ninety, Zoe and Zane still appeared as children to her eyes.

During her time in the Piskie village, she remained inside the oak home. The family kind and generous. The most surprising part was their faith in the Almighty. Burdock visited twice. Despite his grumpiness, he behaved with civility towards her. Rather, Mora made certain Burdock kept to his manners while providing spiritual guidance. She learned he served as high priest among the Piskies. Finn and Rafe told her more history of the Piskies and about the conflict with men. Apparently, it came about due to jealousy among men of how Piskies guarded Thorndel and limited access to the Almighty. Of course, that wasn't true, from the Piskie perspective. They freely shared knowledge and never forbade those among men who willingly sought the Almighty. However, they did test the individual's sincerity. It was their duty to protect the sanctity of Thorndel.

Winnie also learned herbal remedies while helping Mora during preparation. Like a shadow, Zoe remained by her side. Zane came and went. Not that he acted standoffish, merely tending to chores or foraging with friends. Still, the attitude difference between the twins noticeable: Zoe sweet and Zane serious. She still found it hard to believe they were ninety years old since they acted more her age. What the other Piskies thought of her remained unknown. At least the family made no mention of it.

On the day of departure, she and Rafe left just before dawn. She noticed mostly thatched homes along the creek bank. A few others also carved into the trunks of large oak trees. If not for needing water, she would never have learned about the Piskies. She considered it providential. Each day, she prayed for the Almighty to guide her steps. She not only learned the existence of Piskies but also that Finn and Rafe knew her father! They even made a secret pact with him. She glanced ahead to Rafe. He proved to be more than Jayson's uncle. He confessed to being a former soldier under her father's command.

"How long did you serve with my father?" Her question broke the long silence.

"Six years."

"I still find it strange I don't remember you since I recall most of the men who served with him." When Rafe didn't answer, she said, "My father wasn't the only one with whom you had a falling out, was he?" Again, Rafe didn't reply. She grew frustrated. "I need answers if I am to trust you."

Rafe stopped to confront her. "You ask too many questions."

"*You* started by questioning me."

"And *you* were reluctant to answer. But I am to trust you about Thorndel."

Thwarted, Winnie crossly regarded Rafe.

"It's obvious you're not accustomed to secret activities," he commented.

"I'm not totally ignorant," she spoke in wounded defense.

"You are unskilled in such matters. Don't deny it. I know Conor wanted to protect you."

"He taught me some survival skills."

"Surviving in the wilderness is different than navigating the dangers at court."

"I managed to leave unseen."

"I'm sure your absence has been noticed by now."

"I *knew* that would happen. Only, I hoped to be further along in my journey."

Rafe suddenly became alert and signaled Winnie for silence.

With wary curiosity, she glanced about in search of what captured his interest. A hulking shape moved through a distant thicket. She let out a surprised gasp when he snatched her arm and drew her behind a large mound.

"Quiet!" he said in a scolding whisper. "Let's hope it didn't hear us."

Winnie made silent inquiry by shrugging her shoulders.

"Werebear," he spoke in her ear.

Winnie shrunk back in fear. Rafe carefully removed an arrow to notch his bow. She followed his example to unsheathe her dagger. Her hand shook. Tension rose as they listened to snorting and sniffing grow closer.

With a growl, the werebear stood on its hindlegs and reached ten feet tall. The head resembled a wolf with large yellow eyes and elongated fangs that dripped with saliva. The body was that of a massive grizzly bear covered in grey fur that ended with a wolf's tail. Six-inch claws appeared capable of slicing a man in half.

Rafe rose to fire the arrow and struck the werebear in the left shoulder. Wounded, the beast roared in anger. It swiped at Rafe. The claws barely missed as he dove aside. Winnie bolted in the opposite direction from the mound.

"Don't run!" Rafe shouted.

Too late! The werebear leapt over the mound to pursue Winnie. Rafe shot another arrow that lodged in the beast's back. It stopped to roar at Rafe. When it again stood on its hindlegs, the ranger fired a third shot. The arrow struck the werebear in the other shoulder.

Abruptly, two vines sprang up from the ground to wrap around the beast's hindlegs up to the hips. It slashed at the vines. Tree branches lowered like fingers to grab the front legs of the beast to prevent further damage to the leg vines. Zoe and Zane appeared on opposite sides of the werebear. Their faces showed intense concentration with arms outstretched toward the beast. In unison, they spoke the language of the Piskies.

Rafe launched two more arrows that landed in the werebear's chest. The beast fell to all fours. In wild rage at the numerous wounds, it let out a deafening roar that brought Rafe to his knees. Zoe and Zane struggled to remain standing as the roaring continued. Zoe collapsed to the ground, which allowed one vine to disappear back into the ground. Zane's knees gave way, yet he maintained control of the other vine. Winnie returned and jumped onto the back of the beast. She plunged the dagger into the base of the werebear's neck. It reached back, grabbed her, and tossed her aside. She landed hard on the ground, where she lay stunned.

Rafe regained his footing and took careful aim at the beast's head. When it rose up to roar again, he let the arrow fly straight into its mouth. The ground shook when the werebear fell dead. For several moments, no one moved, as each took time to recover.

Rafe made his way to Winnie. "Are you badly hurt?"

She shook her head. "You?"

"My head rings from that roar, but I'm fine." He looked for the Piskie twins. "Zoe? Zane?"

Zane helped Zoe to sit. She simply nodded. "We are well," Zane replied to Rafe.

"Glad you arrived earlier than expected," said the ranger.

When Zoe fell, she lost the small pot attached to her knapsack. Zane helped her readjust the knapsack with the pot.

"We followed you and Winnie. Father thought it best to leave before anyone woke."

Winnie stared at the beast. "I've never seen a werebear before. Far scarier than a splintercat."

"And harder to defeat," said Rafe.

Winnie's curious attention turned to the twins. "Nor have I seen Piskies' power."

"I would be surprised if you had," said Zane.

"What else can you do?"

"Being creatures of the forest, our powers deal with nature."

"Then what do you use the pot for?" Winnie indicated Zoe's knapsack.

"To cook the vegetables," Zoe said matter-of-factly.

Rafe chuckled when Winnie blushed. "You obviously don't travel much in the woods."

"I've managed well-enough," she huffed in reply.

Rafe's grin quickly faded at hearing a distant sound. "I suggest we leave immediately. If the werebear has a mate, it will come searching for its other half." He helped Winnie to her feet. He yanked the dagger from the beast, wiped it clean on the fur, and returned it to her.

"What about the arrows?" she asked.

"Too deep to remove. Now, come."

Despite lingering soreness from the werebear, Rafe encouraged his companions to move quickly. He led them to the river. They paused for a drink.

"Into the water. We'll walk in the shallows along the bank," said Rafe.

"Why?" asked Winnie.

"To hide our tracks and scent." Rafe held out his hand for Winnie to step into the water.

"It's cold!" she complained.

"Better cold than facing another werebear." Rafe then helped Zoe and Zane to step off the bank before he took the lead.

For three miles, they continued in the shallows. The current became faster and rougher. Winnie and Zoe slipped a few times on the slick river bottom. At a bend, Zoe fell underwater.

"Zoe!" Zane grabbed for his sister.

Winnie, too, reached for Zoe and fell face-first into the turbulent water. Winnie managed to grab Zoe, but the swift current tore them apart. Winnie fought to keep her head above water as the current pulled the straps of the knapsack and flask tight around her throat. Dragged underwater by the suffocating straps, Winnie removed the sack and flask. She quickly broke through the surface and gasped for air. A nearby cry made her look for Zoe. The young Piskie bobbed up and down in the water, the current too powerful for someone so small. Winnie used the current to reach Zoe.

"Head for shore!" Winnie shouted. Together they struggled to swim sideways against the growing whitecaps. The roar of rushing water grew louder as they neared the waterfall.

"Zoe! Winnie!" Zane waved to get their attention. He and Rafe ran along the bank. "Swim for the rock!" He pointed to a large boulder ten feet offshore in a shallow part of the river.

Together, Winnie and Zoe aided each other in the effort to reach the boulder. Exhausted, they desperately clung to the boulder. Water splashed when Zane and Rafe entered the shallows.

"Zoe! Give me your hand!" Zane pulled her onto shore.

Rafe aided Winnie onto the bank. Both girls collapsed, exhausted and breathing heavy. They shivered, and their lips were blue from the cold water.

"Watch them while I find a place to build a fire," Rafe instructed Zane.

Zane rubbed Zoe's hands to warm them, then did the same for Winnie. He spoke encouraging words, while they waited for Rafe to return. As time passed, Zane anxiously looked in the direction Rafe left. Zoe's eyes began to close.

"No! Stay awake," he urged his sister. Zoe blinked to remain alert. "Winnie, wake up!" Zane shook her. With a start, Winnie's eyes snapped open. "Rafe! Hurry up!" Zane shouted. He continued to stimulate Zoe and Winnie to stop them from falling asleep.

Finally, Rafe returned. "Carry Zoe. I'll take Winnie."

Rafe lifting her made Winnie wake up. "What's happening?" she weakly asked.

"I'm taking you someplace warm."

Rafe led the way to a small cave further down the river near the waterfall. It provided enough room for adequate shelter from the elements. A good-sized fire was underway. Rafe gently placed Winnie on the ground to sit against the rear of the cave and close to the fire. Zane did the same with Zoe.

"We need to remove their shoes and cloaks. The fire will warm their feet and dry out the garments," Rafe told Zane. While Zane saw to Zoe, Rafe asked Winnie, "What happened to your sack and flask?"

"I had to take them off or be choked to death."

Rafe quickly felt Winnie's neck. "Where's the necklace?" he asked with great concern.

Startled by the question, Winnie felt her neck and collar of her dress and bodice. She relaxed at feeling something in the bodice. She discreetly turned and brought the necklace out from where it had slipped down. "The clasp is broken, but the rest is intact."

"Let me see it." He took a moment to examine it. "It's simply bent. Easy to fix." When he noticed Winnie shiver, he put the necklace in his pouch. He carefully warmed his flask of mead over the fire. "Drink." He offered it first to Winnie then to Zoe.

"That's the second time you saved me," Zoe said to Winnie.

"I think it was mutual." Winnie shivered.

Rafe gave her the flask to drink more mead. "We'll remain until morning so you both can rest and recover. And I'll fix the clasp."

"What about food since I lost my sack?"

Rafe kindly smiled. "Don't worry. I have enough flatbread, apples, and carrots for a couple of days. Now, sleep."

"I can find some kig yar for a soup tonight. It will help to warm them," said Zane.

"Very well. I'll stay with the girls," said Rafe. "Only be back before dark—with or without mushrooms!" he called after Zane. The Piskie waved an acknowledgement.

Winnie and Zoe woke to the smell of soup. Winnie rubbed her arms, as the chill of twilight added to the remaining dampness of her clothes. "How do we eat the soup?"

Zane pulled four Piskie-sized bowls from his knapsack. "Mama thought of everything." He used it to scoop out some soup from the pot and give it to Winnie. He did the same for Zoe and Rafe before helping himself.

"Oh!" said Winnie in surprise. "I thought this was mushroom soup. It tastes like the chicken in the porridge Mora gave me."

Rafe explained, "The Piskies don't eat animals. They do indulge in fish on occasion, but not meat. Kig yar is a mushroom favored for the rich heartiness it gives to soups, stews, and porridge. For us, it has the same consistency as chicken."

"Yet they make cheese, so they have cows."

"For milk, butter, and cheese," said Zane. "We let the cows die of old age, not slaughtered for meat."

Winnie tried to tuck her bare feet under her skirt.

Rafe put the dried sock and boots on her feet. "Should be nice and warm from the fire. As should your cloak. And I fixed the necklace clasp." He fitted the chain around her neck.

"How?" She tucked the jewel under the dress collar.

"I use my knife to straighten it enough for the hook to close."

Zane gave Zoe her dried cloak. Zoe pulled her knees up and wrapped her cloak around her entire body.

Once they finished the soup, Rafe told the girls, "Now, sleep some more," then to Zane, "I'll take the first watch."

Chapter 11

BY MORNING THE GIRLS FELT WELL RESTED. AFTER A QUICK breakfast, they continued. Winnie and Zoe followed Rafe while Zane continued as rear guard. Rafe kept them moving at a hurried pace, only stopping for a brief rest and a quick drink of water. By midday, Winnie insisted on pausing to eat. Finding a stream, the group refilled flasks and ate stale bread and cheese. They softened the bread by pouring a little water on it.

"Maybe more mushrooms for dinner?" asked Winnie.

"Depends on where we stop," said Zane

"I know a cave where we can spend the night. It's near a lake, so we can catch fish," said Rafe. "Now come, we must make it before dark."

By mid-afternoon, the pace slowed as the forest grew thicker with dense foliage. Fallen leaves crunched underneath their feet. The humans pushed vines and branches from their faces. The Piskies simply ducked under to avoid the brush.

"Couldn't you have found a less mangled way than through a thicket?" Winnie chided.

"It would take too much time to go around," replied Rafe.

"I didn't realize we were on a time schedule."

Rafe used his knife to hack a vine. "The more time we take, the more vulnerable we are to werebears and splintercats. Especially in fall, as prey grows scarce in the cooler months. The direct way gives us a chance to pass undetected."

The thicket ended at a small meadow. Winnie stopped Rafe. "How do you know the way to Thorndel? Have you been there before?"

"No." Rafe sheathed his knife. "I know the general direction is north. Same as you."

"There is Shadowspire," said Zane.

"What is Shadowspire?" asked Winnie.

"A large shadowy peak that guards the valley pass to Thorndel."

"Some say it's haunted," added Zoe, nervously.

Winnie appeared skeptical. "I don't believe in ghosts."

Zane shrugged. "Whether ghosts or not, it's the only way to Thorndel."

Still skeptical, Winnie asked Rafe, "How far north must we travel?"

"Ten days. Once at Norwood, we can inquire about Shadowspire."

"I assume Norwood is a town," said Winnie.

Rafe nodded. "The most northern city of Orrin. It is said Shadowspire lies beyond."

"But none dare venture past Norwood into the Unknown Region!" said Zoe with dread.

"More ghosts?" asked Winnie, sarcastic.

Zoe blushed and shrugged ignorance. "It's just what I've heard."

"Our supplies won't last ten days," Zane told Rafe.

"There is a farm a half-day's journey from the cave. We can replenish there. Now, we've talked enough. Let's keep moving." Rafe led them in a run across the meadow to the woods on the opposite side.

The following day, the group ventured near the farm. Rafe halted just inside the trees. Being mid-day, the farm workers were busy with last-minute harvest prep for winter.

"Is that the Farmer Denis homestead?" asked Zane.

"Aye," replied Rafe. "You and Zoe wait here out of sight. Winnie and I will barter for supplies. Unless you have money?" he asked Winnie.

"No, I used all I had after five days."

"Denis knows me, so just stay quiet and let me do the talking."

Winnie walked beside Rafe to approach the farm. Rafe hailed the field workers. They recognized him and returned the greeting.

A short balding man with a scruffy beard arrived. "Well, well. What brings you back so soon?" Denis asked Rafe. He spied Winnie. "And not alone." He flashed a rakish smile.

"This is the daughter of an old friend I'm training to help with my duties."

"A female ranger?" Denis made a scoffing laugh. "That would be a first." Again, he stared at Winnie, who grew uncomfortable under his leering gaze.

Rafe stepped into Denis' line of sight. "Since she's under my guidance *and protection* I came to barter for some more supplies."

Denis' crafty glance shifted between Rafe and Winnie. "What do you have to trade?"

"Same as usual during the winter months. Keeping watch of your livestock at night for werebears and splintercats. Only this time, there will be two pairs of eyes."

Thoughtful, Denis stroked his shaggy beard. "I can give you a sack of potatoes, a peck of carrots, and onions."

"Flour?"

Denis shook his head. "Stock is low."

"A small bag then." Rafe leaned close to Denis and wryly spoke. "It would be nice to have someone bake fresh bread for a change."

Denis grinned. "Very well. A small bag. Wait here while I fetch them." He waved for two of his men to accompany him. They disappeared into the barn.

Winnie whispered to Rafe, "He makes me nervous."

"He's harmless enough."

"To men perhaps."

The comment concerned Rafe, who spoke with assurance. "I won't let anyone hurt you."

Her attempted smile faded. "Let's hope he doesn't take too long." Although only ten minutes, the wait felt longer to Winnie.

"Here you are," Denis announced. "Ten pounds of potatoes." He waved a fieldhand to give Rafe the sack. Then to Winnie, "These are the carrots and onions. The bag of flour is on top of them in this sack. I assume you can carry it."

"Of course!" She reached to take the smaller sack from him. However, Denis didn't immediately let go, as he once more stared at Winnie.

Rafe's harsh clearing of his throat made Denis release his hold. "Thank you. We'll put up the supplies and return before the first snowfall to keep watch." He motioned for Winnie to leave. She was eager to do so and led the way from the farm.

Behind them, on the opposite side of the barn, a group of soldiers waited in the partial shadow of the building.

Not until they reached the road did Rafe hear hooves. "Quickly! To the woods." He shoved Winnie forward, which made her stumble and drop the sack. "Never mind it!" He grabbed her arm to urge haste.

Zoe and Zane emerged from hiding just as Rafe and Winnie reached the trees. Together, they ran into the woods with soldiers in pursuit. Unfortunately, they didn't get far before being surrounded by ten mounted men.

"Winnie Briggs," scoffed one of the soldiers.

She smirked, her voice scoffing in return. "Sergeant Cadel."

"Lord Falco has been looking for you."

She tried to mask her nervousness at the news. "What could he want with me?"

"I don't ask questions. I just follow orders to find you and take you back to Highburn."

Her nervousness became anxiety. "Let the Piskies and Rafe go!"

"So, these are Piskies," Cadel said about Zoe and Zane. With haunter he looked down at them. "It is believed your kind was wiped out for being such troublesome creatures."

"What do we do? Kill them?" asked a soldier.

"No—" Winnie began to object when Rafe's hand on his shoulder stopped further speech.

"Aye! They could cast a spell on us!" added another with disgust.

"We don't cast spells!" Zane hotly disputed.

Cadel reached down to grab Zane by the hair. The Piskie winced in anger but made no attempt to fight back. "Keep your mouth shut, wretched devil!"

The rough action horrified Zoe. But when Rafe moved to defend Zane, Winnie physically stopped him. She urgently spoke to Cadel. "Sergeant, please! Let them go. They are innocent."

"Can't do that. They are aiding you … a known criminal."

"Criminal?" echoed Winnie, shocked. "What have I done?" she asked in a shaky voice.

"That's for Lord Falco to explain." Cadel regarded Zane. "I could kill you. However, Lord Falco will find your involvement very interesting." He motioned to the soldiers who spoke. "Use your sashes to wrap their heads and hide those devilish ears. No need to upset the populace." He released Zane. He saw Rafe's jowls flex with anger. "Why do you look familiar?"

Rafe didn't reply. His narrow glare was enough to speak his disdain for Cadel.

Despite the shock of being branded a criminal, Winnie confronted Cadel. "You served with my father. Do you truly believe me a criminal?"

Cadel's frown showed a hint of indecision. "As I said, I don't ask questions. I just follow orders. The same as your father did. May the Almighty rest his soul. Now, get moving." He took the lead with three soldiers, while others flanked the group, and two were in the rear.

Winnie held Zoe's hand as they walked. "I'm sorry," she somberly said.

Zoe couldn't respond. Distress kept her fearfully silent.

"It's not your fault. The Almighty will help us," Zane spoke with encouragement.

"It's been my prayer since I left. But I never thought this would happen." Winnie sniffled.

"Quiet!" Cadel scolded Zane. "Speak again, devil, and you won't reach Highburn alive! And leave those sashes on until I say otherwise, or that too will be your death!"

Zoe screwed her eyes shut in fear at the threat. Winnie placed a comforting arm about the Piskie's shoulder to hold her close.

Cadel glanced skyward. Shadows grew longer in the late afternoon sun. "We must move faster to reach the inn before nightfall."

"Then I suggest you let us ride," Rafe chided.

"You'd be wise to heed my warning, ranger. Insolence won't be tolerated!"

"Sargent," began one of the men. "I'm afraid he's right. The sun will be down in a couple of hours. We won't make it with them walking."

Cadel again glanced skyward. Abruptly, he spoke. "You! With me." He indicated Winnie. Rafe helped Winnie mount behind Cadel. "You two take the Piskies," he instructed two soldiers. "Your hands will be tied to prevent any tricks," he said to Rafe. He waved another soldier to deal with Rafe. The ranger gave no resistance to the binding then mounting.

Chapter 12

FOR FIVE DAYS, THE CAPTIVE GROUP SWITCHED BETWEEN walking and riding. Speech was limited, even during the night. Winnie's regret increased with each passing day. Regret for involving the Piskies and Rafe, but most of all, regret for failing her father. At times, intense anger swelled at Jayson for taking back the map. If she had it for the journey, she never would have met the Piskies or Rafe. *Was that really a bad thing?* Her mind argued. Mora saved her life while Rafe, Zoe, and Zane took great risks to help her. Because of them, she learned more about her father than she knew upon departure.

What good does that do me now? Her mind warred between regret, gratitude, and reason. Frustration hindered any attempt to pray and find some clarity to the situation. Her father always told her the Almighty heard and answered prayer according to faith. Since leaving Highburn she began to question the strength of her faith.

The few times speech became possible, words were few and barely above a whisper. Rafe told her to carefully remove the necklace and hide it. She placed it in the pants pocket under the skirt. Yet by his continued interest in the necklace, she knew some secret lay behind the Queen's gift. In truth, it puzzled her upon receiving such an exquisite jewel. Her befuddlement grew when instructed by the Queen to keep it on her person but hidden from view. Just like Rafe, the Queen said answers would come in time. Now, being a prisoner, what time did she have? Would any of the mystery surrounding her father's death be unraveled before something happened to her?

As if reading her mind, Zane spoke with reassurance of the Almighty. Zoe held Winnie's hand when they walked. Rafe made comments about her father and how he would be proud of her attempt. Again, what good would that do since she failed to finish what he started? Still, Winnie kept the darker thoughts to herself so as not to upset her companions. They tried to encourage her.

Near twilight of the sixth day, Cadel allowed them to ride into Highburn. They managed to reach the city before the gates closed for the night. Throughout the journey, Zoe and Zane wore the red sashes around their heads to cover their ears. A few humans commented on the inclusion of *children* in the group while others remarked about their uncommon visible strands of red hair. Neither Cadel nor his men replied to anyone regarding Zoe and Zane. They remained stoic in duty while maintaining a soldier's disinterest toward the populace.

The castle bridge gates normally closed two hours after sunset. The exception happened when the royal couple hosted a special event, then it remained open until midnight after guests departed. Activity in the castle courtyard told of just such an event.

Winnie kept her head down, although her eyes shifted to view the goings on. Returning like this isn't what she wanted. To her dismay, she spied Jayson crossing the courtyard. He halted when their eyes met. She looked away as anger at him returned. Her head jerked up when Cadel stopped his horse and the sergeant spoke.

"Take them to the dungeon while I speak with Lord Falco." Cadel nudged her to dismount.

Once more, she caught Jayson's gaze. He watched the scene from a safe distance. Anger towards him faded at seeing his distress. She noticed Jayson's expression change to wariness upon sight of Rafe. Did he recognize his uncle or just curiosity about the man captured with her? The visual exchange didn't last long as soldiers escorted her, Rafe, and the Piskies from the courtyard.

On his part, Jayson struggled to maintain a calm demeanor at seeing Winnie with Sergeant Cadel. He knew about the patrols ordered to find her. Scuttlebutt around the castle told of Falco's intent to have Winnie arrested, although the charge remained vague. Since she left, he buried himself in work to avoid Lord Falco or Captain Tolbert. It was enough that Lord Falco inquired about his relationship to Winnie. He didn't want to become connected to any trouble. Then again, he couldn't help but continue his secret research about Thorndel, Shadowspire, and the missing royal jewel. Somehow, everything was connected to General Briggs' disappearance. Now, Winnie returned as a prisoner. Only she wasn't alone! Surprised curiosity at seeing Rafe caused both trepidation and excitement. Could it really be him?

Jayson hastened to his father's chamber. Simon retired early due to a headache that kept him from the royal party. Upon arrival, he found him in bed. "Father! They captured her."

Simon blinked back pain, which caused some confusion. "What?"

Jayson sat on the bed. "Winnie! But she isn't alone. I believe *he* is with her. At least I think it's *him*," he spoke with emphasis.

The intonation in Jayson's voice made Simon suspicious. "Who?"

Jayson looked directly at his father to say, "Uncle Rafe."

Startled, Simon momentarily stared at Jayson. "Are you sure?"

"I believe so. He has a beard and older. But when our eyes met, I swear it was him." Jayson grew despondent. "From what you told me; I never thought I'd see him again in this life."

"He didn't abandon you. Abandoned us."

"You told me he died! You lied." Jayson spoke with angry hurt.

Simon grew remorseful. "You were only ten. I had to tell you that to keep us safe. To keep Rafe safe."

The answer didn't satisfy Jayson. "Why?"

"I wasn't privy to all the details, since Rafe is good at keeping secrets. When I pressed him, he declined to involve us since it posed great danger. However, he said it dealt with Conor."

The answer confused Jayson. "I thought you and Uncle had a terrible falling out. The shouting frightened me. Not long afterwards, you told me of receiving word he died."

"The argument was a show to keep us above suspicion. He would not willingly hurt his favorite nephew."

"I'm his only nephew," Jayson chided.

Simon ignored the comment. "Although he knew that would eventually happen due to our hasty plan." He sighed with regret and some pain. The conversation was threatening to revive his headache.

"So, you both argued, he left, then you lied to me about his death to protect us?"

"Aye. Only now that he is back, it could bring up a dangerous past. Especially since he is with Winnie. I wonder how they met?"

Jayson contemplated the revelation about his uncle. "This situation is filled with twists, complications, and unknowns." His shoulders sagged as he sighed. "Rafe aside, if I hadn't taken the map from her, neither of them would be locked in the dungeon."

Simon grabbed Jayson's arm. "No! You were right to do so. Thorndel is a perilous place where only the most courageous dare venture. Not an inexperienced girl."

"She doesn't agree."

"You spoke to her?"

"No. I saw her anger when she spotted me. My foolish action allowed her to be captured! And now Lord Falco will punish her! And uncle." Emotions propelled him to pace in anger. "Why? She's done nothing wrong!"

Simon rose to stop Jayson. "Steady, son. You can't blame yourself. Winnie undertook the venture of her own accord. You tried to stop her."

"I should have gone with her like she asked."

"You too would be in the dungeon, and Falco in possession of the map," Simon rebuffed.

Frustrated, Jayson lashed out. "This goes beyond the map! I could have told her the history of Thorndel, Shadowspire, and the jewel. She didn't know what to look for if she got there. But I do!"

Simon's gaze narrowed with suspicion. "You did more research in the vault."

"You taught me to search for truth. My information, joined with the map, could have helped her avoid capture and complete what General Briggs could not."

Simon flinched in sorrow and backed away from Jayson.

Uncertain of the reason for withdrawal, Jayson asked, "Father? Is it your headache again?"

Simon shook his head, yet still grimaced.

Jayson studied his father's posture. This appeared to be remorse and not pain. He feared the meaning. "Did you hide some truth from Winnie about General Briggs' death?"

Simon's shoulders sagged, and his voice was weary in reply. "No, I told her the truth. Or what Lord Falco told me to tell her."

Baffled, Jayson asked, "Then what?"

Simon rubbed the temples on both sides of his head. This time, his headache returned with a vengeance. He sat on the bed and motioned for Jayson to join him. "Like you, I wanted to protect her from the *truth* of his mission."

Jayson regarded his father with understanding. "You knew he was going to Thorndel."

Simon blinked back pain before he spoke. "I provided the information needed, which included a quickly sketched map."

Stunned, Jayson found words difficult. At least at first, then he became angry. "But you burned the map I drew!"

In hushed words of caution, Simon said, "I told Falco the only copy in existence was the one I made for Conor. If he found yours, he would accuse me of lying and throw us both into the dungeon."

Jayson's anger returned. "She is in the dungeon due to the lack of information you gave her father, but wouldn't let me give her."

Simon's shaky voice of regret barely audible. "Aye."

For several moments, a deep, profound silence passed between father and son. Jayson's pained voice broke the silence. "She will be punished without knowing why."

"No!" Simon spoke in his strongest voice yet. "I will do all I can to stop that once I know the charge. For now, all we can do is pray."

Chapter 13

MEANWHILE, THE GREAT HALL BUZZED WITH FESTIVAL activities. All four massive chandeliers were lit. Also lighting the hall were large wall sconces attached to each of the sixteen pillars holding up the magnificent arched ceiling. The pillars were divided with eight on each side of the Hall. Guest tables lined up in two rows in front of the pillars. High Table for the King and Queen sat on a raised platform facing the guests.

Fitted with royal robes and his regal crown, Pekka appeared jovial despite his pale and haggard appearance. He smiled and laughed at the honored guest seated to his right. He ignored Rona. Despite the growing tension between the royal couple at failure to produce offspring, Rona dutifully attended Pekka. Banquets and special events served as a distraction for them both.

Falco sat at the end of the table nearest the platform. He appeared to be enjoying himself in conversation with another guest. Captain Tolbert arrived. He leaned down to whisper in Falco's ear. Despite the interruption, Falco maintained a favorable attitude.

"Excuse me," Falco said to the guest. He followed Tolbert to an exterior door at the farthest end of the Hall. There he met Sergeant Cadel. "So, you found her."

"Aye, my lord. Only she was not alone."

Curious, Falco asked, "She has accomplices? From Highburn?

"No, my lord. A ranger and two …" Cadel carefully glanced around before leaning toward Falco to say, "Piskies."

"What nonsense is this, Cadel?" Tolbert chided.

"Honest, captain. My lord. I wouldn't believe it if I hadn't seen it with my own eyes."

Aware of his surroundings, Falco drew Cadel outside. His eyes narrowed dubiously at the sergeant. "You saw them?"

"Aye. They are in the dungeon with the Briggs girl and ranger."

Cadel's answer infuriated Falco. "You brought them here? How many others saw them?"

"Only my men. I ordered them into silence upon pain of execution. As for anyone else, I had their heads wrapped with a sash to hide the ears. In truth, they appear as children in size and face, only with uncommon red hair." Cadel motioned with his hand to show height. "No fear or alarm has been raised." After a moment of silence, he asked, "What are your orders, my lord?"

Falco made an abrupt wave of dismissal. "That will be all, sergeant."

Cadel slapped his sword in salute and left.

"Do you want me to interrogate them now or in the morning?" asked Tolbert.

Falco thoughtfully stroked his beard. "The morning will be soon enough. I must gather information about our unexpected guests. Make my excuses to the King about court business."

The best place for such information came from the scholars. However, he noticed Simon absent from the banquet. He directed his steps to Master Clarke's personal quarters. The door opened just as he arrived. Jayson appeared at the threshold for departure and was startled at coming face-to-face with him.

"My lord!"

"Ah, Master Jayson. I'm glad to find you here also."

"My father retired due to a terrible headache."

"I thought as much when I noticed his absence from the banquet. However, a serious matter has come to my attention that requires immediate answers." Falco motioned for Jayson to accompany him inside the chamber.

Simon rose and donned a dressing gown. "My lord. I thought I recognized your voice."

"I'm sorry to disturb you, Lord Chancellor, but I need information that cannot wait."

Simon waved to Jayson, who in turn offered a chair to Falco. Once the Prime Minister sat, Simon also took a seat on the bed. "What type of information, my lord?"

"History and mythology."

"Jayson is the expert in those areas, my lord."

"Of that I am aware. Although there may be legal ramifications that will require your services." Falco directed his attention to Jayson. "Tell me about Piskies."

"Piskies?" repeated Jayson, a bit caught off guard. At Falco's nod, Jayson took a moment to think. "They are woodland creatures who were tasked with caring for Morgrath Forest and the hills surrounding the valley of Thorndel. It is said their deep connection with nature gives them special powers."

"To cast spells?" asked Falco.

Jayson's brows knitted in consideration. "Not that I have discovered in any of the ancient writings. Then again, it is believed Piskies were destroyed over two hundred years ago during the Great Struggle between Piskies and men for supremacy in Orrin."

"Would it surprise you to learn that Piskies still exist?"

"It would indeed. There have been no reported sightings in centuries."

Falco rose and sternly said to Jayson. "Prepare a report about Piskies and have it ready by first light." That said, he abruptly left.

Simon reached for Jayson to again join him on the bed. "You must proceed cautiously. Falco doesn't ask for anything obscure without a reason."

"I found mentions of Piskies in my research but didn't consider them important enough to investigate further."

"Obviously, he does."

Jayson thought out loud, "Maybe it deals with the two individuals with Winnie and uncle?" He immediately answered his own question. "No, they appeared to be children. Maybe they are uncle's children."

Simon groaned in pain. Seeing his father's headache had intensified, Jayson nudged him under the covers. He then fetched his father a cup of poppy wine. "Drink this."

Simon complied, but wouldn't release the empty cup when Jayson went to take it. "Whoever they are, you must tread carefully."

"I will. Now, rest." He kissed his father's forehead and left.

Jayson proceeded directly to the undercroft vault. Lord Falco's unusual request only added to the mystery of Rafe's involvement with Winnie. What connection could there be between Winnie, Rafe, and Piskies? According to his father, Rafe's departure twelve years ago dealt with General Briggs. The disclosure that the fake argument helped to facilitate Rafe's departure still annoyed him. His father's lies about Rafe's death made it worse. *But to protect us,* he argued with himself. His current position required keeping state secrets, which sometimes meant not telling the whole truth. *What happened in the past that is so dangerous now?* Answers may lie in what he uncovers about Piskies.

Falco went to his office after meeting with the Clarkes rather than returning to the banquet. The news of the girl's capture and the possible discovery of Piskies upset his stomach. Until then, he enjoyed specially prepared food and the company of fellow nobles. His servant kept a supply of white wine steeped with cumin and anise, stocked in both the bedchamber and office.

After warming a cup of remedy over a candle, Falco sat at his desk to contemplate the latest development. Most of his thoughts turned to speculation based upon myths and legends handed down for generations. He hoped Jayson could provide more enlightening details about Piskies than childhood stories.

His consideration turned to Conor and his daughter. The only logical conclusion was Conor *did* tell her about his mission. However, Tolbert reported that soldiers loyal to the esteemed general knew nothing. *Why tell a girl and not his most trusted compatriots?*

A knock at the door startled him. "Come."

A royal page entered and bowed. "My lord. The King requests your presence in his private chambers."

Mildly surprised, Falco asked, "Is the banquet concluded?"

"No, my lord. The King retired early."

Falco adjusted his minister attire for a formal interview before he accompanied the page to Pekka's chamber.

The King shed his robe and crown for a dressing gown. He appeared tired and unusually pale. However, when the page announced the Prime Minister, Pekka's countenance turned furious. Pekka's rough dismissal of the servant alerted Falco to a royal scolding. He assumed a submissive posture in a low bow.

"Sire—" Falco began, only to be cut off in mid-sentence.

"Why did you not tell me about the Briggs girl and her companions in the dungeon?"

Briefly surprised by the question, Falco knew the moment called for diplomacy. "I did not wish to disturb the evening until I ascertained all the facts."

"Facts?" thundered Pekka. The show of emotion made him cough. Despite the coughing fit, he snarled with annoyance. "She disappeared, which distressed the Queen, and then is apprehended by soldiers along with three questionable companions. Are those the *facts* you want to ascertain?"

Falco fought to contain his irritation at Pekka's continued anger. Unfortunately, this type of interview proved commonplace, but irksome for those subject to royal wrath. "No, Sire. It is the identity of the three companions that I am in the process of determining. Along with any connection to the Briggs girl."

"And have you done so?"

"I will when the report is complete."

Pekka's face showed intense displeasure. "The throne room at nine o'clock tomorrow morning! I want those answers." He motioned for Falco to leave.

Chapter 14

URING HIS PRIOR RESEARCH, JAYSON READ SOME FACTS about Piskies along with Thorndel and the jewel. However, he felt the jewel provided the main clue to General's Briggs' death, so that is where he focused his attention. Consulting his notes on which books he previously used, he dove deeper into the lives and lore regarding Piskies. Some of the oldest manuscripts contained facts about them. Jayson sat back in the chair to consider what he just discovered.

"Red hair?" He mused under his breath. "Winnie, did you stumble upon Piskies?"

He hurried to gather his notes and left the undercroft. He hadn't realized the lateness of the hour until he reached the courtyard. Horses and carriages of guests were gone, and only soldiers patrolled the grounds. Regardless, he headed to the dungeon. The jailer accosted him and refused admittance.

"This is of vital importance!" Jayson stressed. "The Prime Minister wants my report by first light! Now, let me see the prisoners or I will tell Lord Falco how you hindered me in the performance of my duty."

Grumbling curses, the jailer grabbed a torch from a wall sconce and escorted Jayson to the cell. It was a large room where multiple prisoners could be housed. Leg and arm irons were attached to the wall to restrain the more violent criminals. However, Winnie and the others remained free to roam the cell. Ten feet up the wall, a small, grated window admitted moonlight and torchlight from the courtyard. Their arrival allowed more light into the cell.

"Five minutes!" the jailer angrily told Jayson.

"Leave the torch." Jayson waited until the jailer left. "Winnie."

"What do you want?" Her voice tight and face set.

Jayson approached her to speak in a low urgent voice. "I understand your anger, but I haven't much time. I need answers so I can help you."

"Like with the map?"

"Winnie, please! Your life is at stake. And so are theirs!"

Rafe moved to stand beside Winnie. "Hardly the place to have a family reunion."

"Indeed, Uncle," agreed Jayson with sobriety. He moved the torch to better view Zoe and Zane. "By the Almighty, it is true," he murmured with astonishment.

"You know who we are?" asked Zane, mistrustful.

"An educated guess from what I've discovered in the ancient manuscripts." He pointed. "Your hair color. While I assume the sashes are to cover your ears as a disguise."

Winnie explained to Zane and Zoe, "Jayson is a scholar of mythology and Orrin history. He often knows more than he says." She then asked Jayson, "Is that why you are here? To recite Orrin's history?"

Her continuing sarcasm pained him. Still, he ignored the feelings to wave everyone closer and speak confidentially. "Falco charged me with preparing a report on *their kind* by first light."

"Why?" asked Zane, still mistrustful.

"I don't know exactly, other than suspecting your identity. My coming here confirmed his suspicion. What he intends to do with my report is unknown."

"So, you will tell him about us!"

"*Shhh!*" Jayson tried to quiet Zane. "No. I needed the confirmation so I can be prepared for whatever he plans. With knowledge comes wisdom, and with wisdom—"

"Comes resolve," Rafe finished the quote.

Jayson flashed a smile. "Aye, Uncle. I still remember." The smile quickly faded at hearing the jiggling of keys to announce the jailer's return. With great remorse and purpose, he regarded Winnie. "Please know, I sorely regret my earlier misjudgment. I wish I could undo it. Yet I swear by the Almighty, father and I will do all we can now to help. I won't leave you in here! Any of you."

The door opened. "Time's up!" the jailer said.

Jayson looked at Rafe. Despite the years apart, a strong connection remained between uncle and nephew. Questions raised by this discovery about the past must wait. The present required immediate attention. He flashed a smile of encouragement at Winnie before he left with the jailer.

When the door closed, the cell again grew dark save for the shafts of moonlight and torches coming through the small window. Winnie stared at the door. Her mind was a whirlwind of emotions about Jayson and news of the current situation.

"Do you trust him?" Zane asked Winnie.

Her response came measured and deliberate. "I've known Jayson since childhood."

"That's not an answer. You are very angry with him."

Indeed, she had been angry with Jayson. And now? When speaking of regret, his eyes held a depth of tenderness and resolve she never seen before.

"Jayson will keep his word," Rafe spoke when Winnie delayed in response.

Zane directed his harsh questioning to Rafe. "You are confident in a nephew you haven't seen in over a decade?"

Rafe stared down at the Piskie with unflinching conviction. "I helped to raise him after his mother died. I taught him that quote about wisdom and resolve. Swearing by the Almighty is not a statement to be taken lightly."

Zoe took Winnie's hand to get attention. Innocent green eyes looked up to the human. "You do trust him, don't you?"

Despite the perilous circumstance, Winnie knew in her heart the answer. "I do."

In the scholar's office, Jayson began to assemble his report. Several times, he stopped due to the uncertainty of wording or how much information to include. Something about the situation with the new crown and royal jewel gnawed at him. According to Orrin tradition, dating back centuries, whoever possessed the crown and jewel could become king. He received a royal commission to design a new coronet capable of incorporating the jewel. Why? Pekka was already king, only without an heir. Falco sent General Briggs on a secret mission to Thorndel, the formidable citadel that housed the precious—yet now missing—jewel. Did Falco want it to become king himself? Or some plan with Pekka? The commission would suggest that the king and Falco work together.

"Too many questions!" he murmured in frustration. He jerked around in fright at hearing a knock at the door. He took a deep breath to calm down before he opened the door.

"A message from the Prime Minister." A page held out a piece of paper for Jayson.

"Does it require an answer?"

"No, sir."

"Very good. Thank you." Jayson shut the door and returned to his desk to read the note. "Nine o'clock?" He glanced at the mantle clock. Three-thirty in the morning. He closed his eyes and bowed his head. "Lord, you must help me with this. Lives are at stake." With a deep breath of resolve, he took up the pen to resume work.

Once more, the door opened. Simon held a lantern as he approached the desk.

Jayson noticed his father looked pale. "You shouldn't be here. I can see by your face that you're not recovered."

"That doesn't matter. I couldn't sleep if I wanted to."

Jayson fetched a chair for his father to sit across from him at the desk. Simon placed the lantern on the desk and seized Jayson's hand.

"Forgive me for not confiding in you sooner."

Jayson tenderly smiled. "There is nothing to forgive. You helped the general, as I want to help Winnie." He resumed his seat.

Simon leaned forward to speak in a hushed, hurried tone. "Falco's visit troubled me deeply. Along with my conscience." He squeezed Jayson's hand in emphasis of his words. "You are right about the jewel. It is real, just like Thorndel. And the jewel was the objective of Conor's mission. It is said whoever possesses it will be king of Orrin."

Probing, Jayson said, "Pekka is already king."

"*Not* Pekka," Simon spoke with a deadly intonation and steady gaze at his son.

The meaning was clear to Jayson, who spoke with certainty, "Falco."

Simon nodded. "Conor was fiercely loyal to Pekka. How Falco convinced him to undertake the task is unknown. Whatever he said unnerved Conor to a degree I've never seen before. He woke me in the middle of the night with an urgent plea to watch over Winnie in the event he did not return." He grew despondent in reflection. "It's as if he knew his fate."

"Is that when you drew the map?"

Simon blinked back pain of a headache. "Aye. Conor needed as much information as possible. Perhaps now you understand why I destroyed your map. If Falco could intimidate Conor, he would surely overwhelm you and devastate Winnie." He again became remorseful. "I tried to prevent that because of my promise to Conor. Alas, she faces Falco's wrath. I won't let that happen!"

Jayson curbed a smile. "I visited the dungeon after leaving you, and assured Winnie we would do all within our power to help." He picked up the letter from Falco. "Unfortunately, I only have a few hours to complete the report. The King summoned a council meeting in the Great Hall at nine o'clock."

"Tell me what you've discovered in your research. I'll add what I know, and together we will finish the report."

Chapter 15

WINNIE COULDN'T SLEEP. THE SENSE OF FAILURE AND regret overwhelmed her. Tears rolled down her cheeks as she stared at the stars outside the dungeon window.

At times her lips moved in silent prayer for strength to face whatever fate awaited. She also asked forgiveness for failing her father and pleaded to spare the Piskies and Rafe. She became startled when Rafe moved beside her. He placed a finger to his lips for quiet, as he motioned to where Zoe and Zane slept.

"You are not facing this alone," he spoke in a whisper.

"I should be."

"Providence works in mysterious ways to aid us when we need it most."

Curious, Winnie looked along her shoulder at Rafe. "My father often said that."

"I know. He used it frequently when bolstering us for a mission." Rafe then quoted, *"To your duty be true. Honor the king. Trust the Almighty with your souls. Do not fear the outcome or your fidelity. Providence works in mysterious ways to aid us when we need it most."*

Winnie wiped the tears from her face. "I've been trying to remember that. But it's so hard. At least he was here to help me when mother died."

"He loved Arabella dearly."

"He still speaks … spoke of her." She corrected herself from the present tense to the past. "Even before he left on that fateful day, he mentioned her."

Rafe placed a comforting hand on Winnie's shoulder. "Know this: when the general charged us with a mission, we saw it through to completion."

The moonlight only showed part of Rafe's face, but that was all Winnie needed to see the depth of his determination. "There is more you have not told me about you and my father."

"The time is not right for such disclosure." When she drew back in suspicion he added, "By the Almighty, I promise when the time comes, we shall speak. For his sake, I will not let his sacrifice be in vain. So, trust me, as he did."

Again, she observed his resolute tenacity. She slowly nodded in agreement.

"Now, try to get some sleep. It will be dawn soon." He coaxed her to lie down.

Jingling keys alerted them to the jailer's approach. Winnie sat up. Rafe held her shoulder in support. Zoe and Zane awoke when the door opened. Two soldiers entered with the jailer.

"You! Come with us," one commanded Winnie.

"Why? Where are we going?" she asked, fearful.

He ignored the questions to grab her. Rafe sprang into action to defend Winnie. The second soldier clouted Rafe on the back of the head and sent him sprawling to the floor.

"Rafe!" Winnie shouted as they dragged her from the cell. She found it useless to struggle against the soldier's hold. "Do you know my father?"

Neither soldier answered.

"General Briggs!" she declared.

Again, the soldiers remained silent. Once up from the dungeon, they escorted Winnie through back passageways. At one point, the second soldier removed a torch from its place on the wall. He took the lead down a narrow corridor. She became concerned, as this was not a normal route.

"Where are you taking me?"

This time, the soldier holding her covered her mouth. "Quiet! We must be careful."

Although curious, she complied and spoke nothing more. When they stopped in a dimly lit back hall, she recognized …

"Lieutenant Kincaid."

"*Shh!*" Kincaid placed a finger to his lips. He took a torch from the soldier and told them, "Wait here." He smiled at Winnie. "Fear not, but be quiet."

They entered a small closet that turned into a narrow stairway, which forced them to proceed single file. She carefully followed the stairway to where it ended at a door.

"Mind your words," Kincaid warned. He made several knocks on the door. An answering knock came. He slowly opened the door.

Winnie shielded her eyes against the new source of light. He drew her inside a room she immediately recognized as the Queen's wardrobe. Inside was "Lady Eleanor," she murmured in surprise.

"Keep your wits, girl," Eleanor said before she left.

Although Winnie knew the room well, being there in a clandestine manner late at night concerned her.

A moment later, Rona arrived with Eleanor. She wore a dressing gown, her hair down. "Winnie," Rona kindly spoke.

"Your Majesty." Winnie made a deep curtsy.

With a tender smile, Rona touched Winnie to stand. "Child, your absence worried me."

"I'm sorry. That was not my intent, Majesty."

Rona lifted Winnie's chin. "What was your intent?"

"To learn what happened to my father."

"I see you share Conor's determination. However, with that comes a danger you do not fully understand."

"Perhaps not. Yet the mystery surrounding his death deepens with what I have learned."

Rona studiously regarded Winnie. "And for that knowledge, you will face consequences from which I cannot shield you. Although I wish to the Almighty I could."

"You are the second person to speak such regret to me this evening."

Intrigued, Rona asked, "Who was the first?"

"The ranger captured with me."

"His name?" Rona asked with hurried apprehension.

Hesitant, yet knowing she needed to answer, Winnie carefully replied. "Rafe."

Eleanor quickly covered a murmur of surprise. "Majesty."

"Easy." Rona took gentle hold of Eleanor's hand.

Their reaction surprised Winnie. "Do you both know him?"

"What we know is not important. Your knowledge is the issue," said Rona.

"But, Majesty, Rafe is innocent. Along with the … others captured with me," she said with discretion. "I beg you to protect them."

"I fear my protection is of little use against Lord Falco and the King."

"Then why have soldiers bring me to your chambers?"

Rona's fearful gaze fixed on Winnie. "Where is the gift I gave you?"

"When we were captured, Rafe told me to hide it." Winnie pushed aside her skirt to reach for the pants pocket, but Rona's sudden grip stopped her from withdrawing the necklace.

"Continue to keep it safe."

Winnie released the pocket. "Majesty, why did you give it to me?"

Tears swelled in Rona's eyes. "It is best I do not answer at present …" her voice trailed off in upset. She abruptly withdrew, which prompted Lady Eleanor to step in.

"Enough, girl."

Winnie set her chin in defiance. Although, she noticed Eleanor's eyes showed upset beyond the warning. "My lady?"

Eleanor resisted speaking. Instead, she motioned for Kincaid to take charge of Winnie. Eleanor left the antechamber.

Winnie understood the dismissal. She went quietly with Kincaid back to where the other soldier waited. They parted ways with Kincaid for the return trip to the dungeon.

Zoe and Zane eagerly greeted her. "What happened?" asked Zoe, anxious.

"What did they want?" asked Zane, simultaneously with his twin.

Winnie ignored them to inquire of Rafe, who sat where she left him. "Are you hurt?"

He flashed a rakish smile. "I've been hit in the head before. But, no, I'm not hurt. Where did they take you?"

Winnie sat beside him and replied in a whisper. "To the Queen. Although, I don't know why. She would not answer me. A lot like you in ambiguity! Speaking of," her tone changed to annoyed. "The Queen and Eleanor know you. How?"

Rafe lowered his head to hide the beginning of a smile.

"Well?" Winnie demanded.

Rafe's demeanor changed to firm. "Trust me."

Frustrated, she sat back against the wall with her arms folded.

"Don't be angry," began Zoe. "Rafe can be trusted. Just like you said, you trusted Jayson, despite being angry with him."

Winnie's expression gave way to a wry smile at Zoe's encouragement.

"You look tired. Have you slept?" Zane asked Winnie.

"No."

"Lie down. Zoe and I will remain awake and pray for the Almighty to give you rest and Rafe to recover."

Despite the activity, Winnie felt the weight of fatigue. This time, when she lay down, she drifted into a dreamless sleep.

Chapter 16

SHORTLY BEFORE NINE O'CLOCK IN THE MORNING, JAYSON and Simon arrived in the throne room. Despite wearing the full courtly dress of high-ranking scholars, both appeared tired from a sleepless night of preparation. Simon sent to the royal physician for a stronger pain remedy to soothe his headache. Jayson's youth helped him look better than his father.

Other ministers and officials began arriving. Captain Tolbert posted guards in the customary places around the Great Hall for a Royal Council meeting. All the tables from the banquet had been cleared, and the long red and gold rug had been replaced down the center of the Hall. The elevated platform now contained a single ornate throne of mahogany and gold with embroidered cushions. A lesser throne for the Queen was placed near the bottom step of the platform. Another way Pekka showed disdain for Rona was by lowering her royal position to equal that of officials and nobles.

Falco stood on the floor on the opposite side of the Queen's throne. He spied Jayson and Simon upon approach. "Have you completed the report?" he asked Jayson.

"Ay, my lord." Jayson held out the paper to Falco.

"I can't read them here!" chided Falco with impatience. "Be ready when called upon to answer any questions put forth by the King." He waved for Jayson and Simon to take position a few paces behind him.

The sound of a trumpet alerted all to the King's arrival. Pekka walked with halted steps as if the robes hung too heavy for his thin frame. One step at a time, he mounted the platform. He nearly fell when sitting, exhausted by the energy needed to move.

Queen Rona dutifully followed Pekka while Eleanor accompanied her. Rona waited for Pekka to be seated before assuming her seat. Eleanor stood behind the Queen's throne. Rona's eyes scanned those assembled and stopped upon spying Jayson. In that brief exchange, she conveyed her worry. He made a careful nod, joined with a small smile of encouragement. She averted her gaze when the herald pounded the staff for attention.

"This Royal Council meeting is called to order. All give heed to His Majesty King Pekka!" The herald bowed to Pekka and stepped aside.

"Lord Falco, where are the prisoners?"

"In the dungeon awaiting your summons, Sire."

Pekka scowled with intense displeasure. "You know what I wanted to interrogate them. They should have been here already."

"Reasons for the delay will become apparent when they arrive."

Pekka's frown deepened. "Captain Tolbert! Bring them at once."

Tolbert clapped his sword in salute and withdrew.

Winnie slept better than anticipated, and a bit surprised to find herself still in the dungeon. "My dream was more pleasant than reality," she grumbled.

"Thank the Almighty for small blessings," said Zane. He sat with his back against the pillar beside which Zoe slept.

Hearing noise from outside the cell, Rafe went to the door. "Someone's coming," he warned the others. He stepped back at the jingling of keys. The sound woke Zoe.

The jailer arrived with Tolbert and six soldiers. "All of you are to come with me. Bind his hands. And hers as well." Tolbert indicated Rafe and Winnie to the jailer.

He placed shackles on them. "What about the children?"

"The rope should suit them well enough."

The jailer fitted the rope around the waist of Zoe and Zane to keep them together with enough slack to be led.

"Where are we going?" asked Winnie, fearful.

"You'll find out soon enough. I advise you to remain silent unless spoken to," Tolbert said. "You two, bring the children."

A soldier took the rope from the jailer for him and his companion to secure Zoe and Zane.

The remaining four soldiers took up position of escort around Rafe and Winnie. This trek was done in the open instead of back alleyways and hidden corridors. They traveled through the rear courtyard to enter the main building. From there, they moved down the rear hallway to a side door of the Great Hall.

Winnie's heart raced at the sight of so many people. She knew enough of court activity to realize this was an official assembly. As general, her father attended many such gatherings. A few times, he allowed her to secretly watch from a hidden closet. Now, she became the center of unwanted attention. All eyes watched them move to stand before the King! She caught Jayson's gaze. *Will he keep his promise?* she wondered. The pounding of the herald's staff startled her, and she jerked forward. She noticed the Queen appeared anxious. Eleanor's brow wrinkled with somber joy as she appeared to stare at them. Or was it Rafe she looked at? Winnie flinched at feeling a touch came on her elbow. Rafe. She saw a surprising calm reassurance on his face.

"Give heed to the King!" shouted the herald.

Pekka sternly glared at her. "Winnie Briggs. This is hardly what I expected from the daughter of our most renowned general."

"Sire. I don't even know why I'm here in chains. What did I do?"

Pekka cocked a curious brow. "You are unaware of the charges against you?"

"Aye, Sire. All I did was leave to learn the truth of what happened to my father. Is he dead? If so, what became of his body?"

Pekka sneered in disgust. "General Briggs betrayed us!"

The declaration stunned Winnie as well as those assembled. She fought to find her voice among the disbelieving murmurs.

"No! That can't be true! It's a lie!" she shouted. Passion made her step forward.

Despite the shackles, Rafe grabbed Winnie to stop her.

"Are you calling me a liar?" Pekka demanded.

"No, Sire. Whoever brought this false charge."

Falco stepped forward. "I brought the charge against General Briggs. Same as I do now against you."

Jayson nudged his father at the announcement, but Simon focused sharply on Falco.

Winnie's jowls tighten with rage. "You told me he died. Now, you accuse him of betrayal. How can the dead betray the living?" Rafe's tightened grip stopped her from speaking further.

"Sire!" Simon moved to stand beside Falco. "I received no formal charges against either General Briggs or Mistress Briggs."

Falco's sneering smile turned on Simon. "Lord Chancellor, I called upon you last night."

"To make inquiries regarding mythology and history. You made no mention of charges."

Falco's sneer increased. "I *did* speak to your legal expertise."

"Then I will need time to review the *evidence* related to these charges."

Falco jowls tightened, and his gaze narrowed. "You will see the evidence soon enough."

"Stand down, Lord Chancellor." Pekka waved for Simon to move aside.

Jayson clenched the report until it wrinkled as he watched Simon confront Pekka and Falco. He went to speak privately when his father returned, but Simon motioned for silence.

Falco accosted Winnie. "You left Highburn to complete the rebellion he started. These companions prove your betrayal."

"What?" said Winnie, dubious. "They have nothing to do with my task."

"Ah!" said Falco, with glee. "So, you admit, you had a task."

"I already said my task—to learn what really happened to my father."

"Sire!" Simon strenuously objected, only to be given another dismissive wave by Pekka.

Falco ignored Simon. "By conspiring with the enemy?" He approached Zoe and Zane.

"What enemy? Children?" asked Pekka.

"Not children, Sire. Piskies!" Falco ripped the sash off Zane's head then Zoe.

Audible gasps of astonishment echoed through the room. Words such as *devils, demons,* and *villains* came from the crowd. Jayson and Simon watched with both sympathetic concern for the Piskies and annoyance at Falco. The Queen bit her lip to contain her rising emotions. Eleanor placed a supportive hand on Rona's shoulder.

Winnie shouted to argue over the rising tension. "No! They are kind and compassionate creatures. They saved my life when I became wounded by a splintercat!"

"Silence!" the herald shouted and pounded the staff. "Come to order!"

When the room finally grew quiet, Pekka spoke. "Piskies are mortal enemies of men."

"No, Sire!" Winnie rebuffed. "They saved my life. What mortal enemy would do that?"

"So, as a result of their *kindness,* you enlist them to help foment rebellion against me."

"There is no rebellion!" Winnie cried, on the verge of tears.

"Conor would not betray you!" Rafe spoke for the first time. "Although others might." He cast a sideways glare at Falco.

"Words of a delinquent ranger are not to be trusted, Sire," Falco countered.

"As opposed to what? An ambitious charlatan?" Rafe snapped. Falco's backhand came hard and swift across Rafe's face. He staggered slightly but remained standing. Blood oozed from a split lower lip.

Simon and Jayson flinched at the assault of Rafe. Simon seized Jayson's arm. "They don't remember him. Let's keep it that way," he harshly whispered in Jayson's ear.

Rona felt Eleanor's grip on her shoulder tighten at the assault on Rafe and heard a low gasp. She took hold of Eleanor's hand in mutual support to endure the interrogation.

Falco seized Rafe's leather tunic. His face inches from the ranger. "Keep your words behind your teeth if you want to keep your head!"

Fearful of the threat, Winnie held Rafe's arm in warning. Zoe whimpered in fear and buried her head in her hands. Zane placed a protective arm about his sister's shoulders.

Falco roughly released Rafe. "There is proof enough, Sire."

"Proof?" questioned Rona, aghast at what she witnessed. "What proof? A ranger and two Piskies?" She immediately turned to Pekka, not allowing Falco to answer. "How does this prove Winnie guilty of betrayal?" Seeing Pekka squirm in his seat at her question, she continued. "What will these witnesses say about the King's justice if you pass judgment on such flimsy evidence?"

"There is more evidence involving Piskies," said Falco.

"Oh?" asked Pekka, intrigued.

Falco motioned. "Master Jayson. Tell the King what you discovered about Piskies."

"Stay professional," Simon hastily said before Jayson stepped forward.

Jayson avoided Winnie's angry questioning glare. "Prior to the Great Struggle, Piskies were divided into three major tribes with Morgrath being the supreme tribe of Piskies kings. To this tribe, the Almighty charged them to guard the secrets of Thorndel—"

"Thorndel!" shouted Pekka. His attention immediately returned to Winnie. "Is that where you were heading?"

Stunned, Winnie hesitated to answer.

"It is where *you* sent Conor," Rafe bravely replied.

Tolbert clouted Rafe on the back of the head, which sent him to his knees. "You speak too freely, ranger!"

"It's true!" Winnie loudly affirmed.

Pekka's eyes widened with outrage. "Briggs told you where he was going?"

"No! I inadvertently saw a map next to his saddlebag with the word *Thorndel* on it." Tears swelled. "My father did not betray you. Nor have I. But something awful happened to him on his way to Thorndel on your behalf."

"*Scrutern!*" said Rafe to Pekka.

Irate, Pekka pushed himself up off the throne. Despite being unsteady on his feet, his face reddened with fury. "Out! Everyone!" He tripped while descending the platform. He pushed Rona away when she helped. He shouted, "Falco!"

Falco barely contained his rage at Winnie. "Take them back to the dungeon!" he told Tolbert before he hurried after the King.

Tolbert jerked Rafe to his feet and pulled him from the room. Winnie, Zoe, and Zane also received rough handling.

Rona managed to discreetly intercept Jayson during departure. In hasty words, she said, "Be careful what you say to the King should he require further answers." She left with Eleanor.

Simon leaned close to Jayson. "You *do* need to be careful about many things. Especially if it involves the Queen." He nodded toward the departing Rona.

"My concern is for Winnie and *him*."

"So am I. But we can't let that concern lead to foolhardy actions."

Jayson looked crossly at his father. "Would you renege on your promise to help?"

"No. You heard my objections. Knowing the charge, we must proceed to refute it—tactfully with legal precision!" he stressed when Jayson began to object. "Come. We mustn't be too far from the King's study if Lord Falco wants your report."

"How do you know he's gone there?"

"Pekka always retires to his study after a Council meeting."

As they made their way down the hall, a female called, "Lord Chancellor."

Simon softly smiled. "Lady Eleanor." Her smile grew shaky, so he took her hand. He spoke with tender sympathy. "Say nothing. I understand."

"Thank you." She flashed a shy smile and left.

The cryptic exchange puzzled Jayson. "What was that about?"

"Nothing you need to be concerned about right now. Come." Simon nudged Jayson up the grand staircase.

Back in the dungeon, all were thrown into the cell. The shackles remained on Rafe and Winnie while Zane and Zoe set loose.

"I'm sorry," Winnie whimpered. Tears rolled down her cheeks.

"No need to apologize. Discovery of our kind was bound to happen," Zane lamented.

Winnie noticed Rafe rotated his neck with a grimace of pain. "Are you badly hurt?"

"No," he said with a reassuring smile. "But I gave them something to think about."

Baffled, Winnie asked, "What was that word you said to make the King so angry?"

"The object of why anyone would go to Thorndel," he discreetly replied.

She frowned in annoyance. "That's hardly a clear answer."

Rafe stepped beside Winnie. "I dare not speak for fear of being overheard. Yet know this: *you* possess the answer." His eyes lowered to her skirt.

Winnie's eyes grew wide with dreaded understanding. Her knees weakened and forced her sit. Rafe immediately knelt. Watery eyes looked at him. Her voice was a breathy whisper. "If Papa knew, I could have prevented him from being killed …" She burst into tears.

Rafe held her as best he could with the shackles. He spoke in her ear. "*Shhh.* No. There is more beyond that." He tilted her head. "When was your birthday?" She sniffled back tears to think, but found it difficult, so he continued. "Before or after he left?"

This question began to quiet her discomposure. "After."

"Afterwards is also when you received the gift, correct?"

She nodded and wiped the tears from her face. "But if …"

Rafe placed two fingers over her mouth. "Speak no more of it to anyone." At her scowl, he added, "If you can't trust me, then trust the Almighty that there is a reason for silence. For Conor's sake. For *all* our sakes." He nodded toward the twins.

Chapter 17

SINCE PEKKA WALKED MORE SLOWLY DUE TO ILLNESS, Falco caught up with the King at the top of the Grand Staircase. No words spoken as he followed Pekka to the King's study. Once inside, Pekka sat at his desk to catch his breath. Several times he cast irate glances to Falco, who patiently waited on him to recover.

When Pekka found his voice, he demanded, "How does a ranger know about *Scrutern?*"

"That I could not say for certain, Sire. However," Falco added in hopes of forestalling further outrage. "It is a well-known legend associated with Thorndel. The jewel of kings."

Pekka's eyes widened with a disturbing thought. "What if Briggs isn't dead like you said? Could he have told the ranger?"

"My sources were quite certain regarding the general's demise."

"But the girl left to find him!" Pekka loudly rebuffed.

"A misguided notion on her part."

Emotions caused Pekka to become short of breath again. This made speech difficult. "Your *source* should have sent Briggs' body back to allay all this uncertainty!"

Falco made no comment to the outburst. Instead, he watched Pekka deal with breathing issues. After a moment, the King asked another question.

"And the Piskies? What is their involvement in this?"

"Master Jayson was attempting to explain when interrupted."

"Then get him! I want answers."

Falco instructed a royal page to fetch Jayson. Impatient anger made Pekka shift in his chair. Once the young scholar entered, the King accosted him.

"Tell me about the Piskies."

Jayson fought to maintain his composure at the royal outburst to answer. "As I was saying, Sire, prior to the Great Struggle, Piskies were divided into three major tribes with Morgrath being the supreme tribe of Piskies *kings*. To this tribe, the Almighty charged them to guard the secrets of Thorndel. Including the safekeeping of Scrutern. Although, it is now considered the jewel of kings, it was not always so."

"What do you mean?"

"In the Piskie tongue, *Scrutern* means *Guardian of Knowledge*. Divine knowledge, to be specific. It is believed the Almighty created the jewel as a symbol of his *divine* appointment of the Piskies as guardians of Thorndel. They not only protected the citadel but also ensured that knowledge of the Almighty was properly disseminated. Tutors in divine law and life, if you will. Hence the name *Scrutern* given to the jewel. Once the Piskies were defeated, *Scrutern* came into possession of your family while Thorndel hid by supernatural means. With such a precious jewel, the symbolism changed due to the oath your ancestor Danior swore as Thorndel faded from the realm of men. Whoever possessed *Scrutern* would become the rightful king of Orrin. As if binding Danior to the oath, the jewel glowed in blinding hot brilliance that burned Danior's hand before the light faded. Since then, it passed through Your Majesty's family."

"Until my foolish uncle lost it!" Pekka complained. "The fool became so demented in mind that he couldn't remember what happened."

"It doesn't lessen the oath, especially in the absence of an heir," said Jayson matter-of-factly.

Pekka sat forward. "Impertinent, youth! Don't you think I know that? To break the oath means forfeiture of both my life and reign."

"I'm certain Master Jayson did not mean it as an insult, Sire," said Falco.

"No! Of course not. Forgive me, Sire. My scholar's tongue spoke out of turn." Jayson bowed at the waist in submission.

Pekka sat back. His eyes momentarily closed as he heaved in several deep breaths.

Falco addressed Jayson. "You spoke of a kingly tribe of Piskies called Morgrath. Could those creatures with Winnie Briggs be from that tribe?"

Jayson shrugged in consideration. "It depends upon how she came to fall in with them."

"And that impudent ranger!" Pekka curtly added.

"Sire, the only way to know is to interview the girl," Falco said.

"That's what I was doing!"

"Perhaps she would be more forthcoming in private. When given the proper incentive."

A dastardly smile appeared on Pekka's face at Falco's suggestion. "Indeed."

"What of legal counsel?" asked Jayson.

Falco's sly glance shifted from Pekka to Jayson. "Since you are her friend, you can provide that counsel."

"Friend?" asked Pekka in a piqued tone.

"We know each other, just like everyone else in Highburn," said Jayson, defensively.

Pekka suspiciously eyed Jayson before making a wave of dismissal. "Fetch her."

Jayson lowly bowed. His father waited in the hall but did not approach when Jayson shook his head and continued his appointed course. Not what he expected when asked by Falco to prepare a report on Piskies. He fought discouragement and fear on Winnie's behalf during her interrogation. When confronted about being *her friend*, he balked. Was it fear for himself or the scholarly caution mentioned by his father? He didn't have time to consider which before being ordered to fetch her for a private interview.

This time, the jailer proved more cooperative when Jayson requested entry to the cell. For a moment, he stared at Winnie. "You're to come with me," he said, a hint of regret in his voice.

"Without a guard?" the jailer asked.

Jayson wouldn't suffer the question and scolded the jailer. "No need with the shackles."

The jailer jerked Winnie out of the cell and locked the door. In a gentler manner, Jayson took hold of her arm to leave the dungeon.

"Where are we going?" she asked, which prompted him to signal for silence.

Unlike earlier with Tolbert, Jayson boldly brought Winnie through the main entrance and up the grand staircase. His father noticed their approach, but again Jayson shook his head.

Fearful, Winnie drew back at the door to the King's study. "Why did you bring me here?"

"Courage," Jayson said. "I'll be with you." His mind instantly argued *what good will that do since you balked at being her friend?* He pushed the thought aside to knock. They entered when told by Pekka to do so.

The King and Falco both wore grim expressions.

"Winnie Briggs. On Lord Falco's advice, you are graciously given a second chance to explain yourself," said Pekka.

"What more can I say than to again deny betrayal or rebellion?"

"Tell me how you came to be in the company of Piskies and that ranger."

"Sire, I already said they saved my life when I became wounded by a splintercat. If not for their healing arts, I would have died."

"Where were you when this happened?" asked Falco.

"The forest of Morgrath."

"Ah!" said Pekka, with glee. "So, they are from the tribe of Piskie kings!"

Winnie shrugged ignorance. "I don't know."

"Jayson," prompted Falco.

"It is a proper assumption, given what I discovered."

"What?" asked Winnie, confused by Jayson's response.

"Never mind." Falco dismissed her inquiry. "What of the ranger?"

"He was in the village when they brought me there for healing."

"He became the Ranger of Morgrath," Jayson muttered under his breath.

"What did you say?" asked Pekka.

"The Ranger of Morgrath is the protector of the forest. I ran across a description during my research, but uncertain of the connection to the Piskies since they were believed extinct."

"It appears both are real!" scoffed Pekka.

Falco approached Winnie. With hauteur, he glared at her. "Tell me about *Scrutern*."

Intimidated, she took an impulsive step back. Jayson held her waist in support.

"Well?" demanded Falco.

"I … I don't know," she stammered.

"Don't know or won't say?" The calmness in Falco's voice was more frightening than his towering presence.

Winnie trembled to withstand Falco's interrogation. "I don't know," she repeated.

"My lord, she answered that question," Jayson said.

Falco ignored Jayson and remained focused on Winnie. "But you were going to Thorndel."

"To learn what happened to my father." Her voice cracked with fear. She lowered her head to regain her composure.

Overcome by guilt, Jayson blurted out, "She doesn't know the way. But I do."

This admission brought Pekka to his feet and Winnie to look at Jayson in astonishment.

"How do you know this?" demanded Pekka.

Jayson swallowed back a twinge of anxiety. He had spoken, and now he needed to continue. For Winnie's sake. "I learned its whereabouts from the research requested by Lord Falco for this morning."

Curious and hopeful, Pekka asked, "Could you find Thorndel and recover Scrutern?"

"Aye."

Gleeful, Pekka said the Falco, "Do you hear that? All could be made right!"

Falco didn't appear convinced. "Perhaps, Sire."

Pekka waved aside the pessimism. "Name what you need," he told Jayson.

"It is a dangerous journey, Sire. I can't do it alone."

"You mean the ranger?"

"Ay, Sire. Along with Piskies and Winnie."

Pekka grew skeptical. Royal ire rising. "Why?"

"My knowledge is geographical. Being of the kingly tribe tasked with guarding Thorndel, they would know what secrets it holds. Winnie can learn about General Briggs, whom you sent to find Scrutern. Thus, return with evidence that neither betrayed you."

Falco flashed a mocking smile. "Simon taught you well."

Jayson bowed his head in acknowledgement. He then said to Pekka, "I will need Your Majesty's signature to release the prisoners into my custody and for the armory to provide what is needed for the journey."

"Done!" Pekka steadied himself to resume his seat. He wrote out the orders. Once signed, he handed them to Jayson. "Leave at first light tomorrow."

Jayson and Winnie bowed to Pekka.

Falco waited until the door closed upon their departure. "Sire, I believe Captain Tolbert should accompany them. To guard against any treachery of wanting another king should they succeed in finding Scrutern."

"Make it so. And send for the royal physician. I need my tonic." He wearily sat back.

Falco stepped into the hallway where he found Tolbert. The captain resumed his duty after returning the prisoners to the dungeon. He motioned for Tolbert to accompany him to his chamber down the hall from the King's study. Once in private, he spoke. "The King has entrusted young Clarke with an expedition to Thorndel to recover the jewel."

"I wondered why he looked pleased when leaving with the girl and Simon," said Tolbert.

"The girl planted seeds of doubt, as Pekka also questioned the report of Briggs' death."

"Balor risks a great deal by a false report."

Falco scowled in brooding consideration. "The group going with Clarke includes her, the ranger, and Piskies." His expression grew deadly. "Go with them. Take whatever steps are necessary to secure the jewel. Once I have it in my possession, I can use it to convince Pekka to name me his heir."

"What of Clarke and the others?"

"Leave no witnesses."

Winnie walked between Jayson and Simon as they crossed the courtyard from the main building to the dungeon. Earlier, she wondered if Jayson would keep his word. He had, yet in a way she never expected. He volunteered to find Thorndel. "Jayson," she began in a tone of admiration.

"Say nothing at present. We'll have time enough to speak once we're away."

The jailer smiled after he read the King's order. "I never thought you capable of what they said. Not the general's daughter. I'm sorry for such rough treatment. Doing my duty, Lord Chancellor."

Simon merely nodded for the jailer to remove her shackles before releasing the others.

Emerging from the dungeon into the rear courtyard, Rafe grinned at Jayson. "I knew wisdom would turn into resolve."

"When you hear what we're doing, you might not think it wise," Jayson bantered in reply. "For now, we go to the armory."

"Armory?" Rafe repeated.

"To fetch supplies for our *continuing* journey," Winnie said.

Rafe widely grinned with approval.

"In the meantime, I shall prepare a defense should Falco wish to press further charges," said Simon. With brotherly pride and affection, he regarded Rafe. "Take care of them. And yourself."

"I will."

Simon smiled at Jayson and Winnie. "The Almighty go with you." With that said, they parted ways, Simon for the main building, the others to the armory.

Tolbert met them at the armory entrance. "I'm coming with you," he stoutly said.

"Why?" Winnie asked.

"To prevent treachery." He took a step toward her. She resisted the impulse to move back. "Others might believe Briggs infallible and feel sorry for you. I'm not one of them." He looked at Zoe and Zane. "Nor am I easily swayed by myths." His arrogant gaze shifted to Rafe. "I can best any ranger and certainly not gullible enough to be fooled by scholarly words. So, all of you, mind yourselves, and you might survive to return."

When no response came, Tolbert said, "We shall order what is needed and spend the night in the stable to leave at first light."

Chapter 18

ALL LEFT HIGHBURN CASTLE WELL EQUIPPED WITH WARMER cloaks, blankets, and saddlebags filled with supplies for the journey north. Each were also given flasks of water while the men and Winnie had pouches that contained flint and matches for fires. Instead of scarves, the Piskie twins wore coif hats to cover their ears that tied under the chin for security. Even their clothes were changed to appear more childlike for a boy and girl. Jayson shed his scholar's suit for traveling clothes and knee-high boots. Rafe, Jayson, Tolbert, and Winnie rode normal-size horses. Since no ponies were available, Zoe sat behind Winnie while Zane rode double with Rafe.

Once out of the city, Jayson took the lead with Tolbert riding beside him. Winnie and Rafe followed.

"I'm surprised you're not riding rearguard to keep us in line, captain," Rafe snidely said.

"Be glad you're even making this journey, ranger! If I had my choice, you would rot in the dungeon," Tolbert curtly replied.

"Being antagonistic toward each other won't help," said Jayson.

"So speaks the diplomatic scholar." Tolbert made a scoffing chuckle.

Jayson kicked his horse forward and made a sharp turn to come face-to-face with Tolbert. This forced the captain to stop, as did the others. "You have made it quite clear why Lord Falco sent you. Yet, know this, we all want this journey to succeed. So, let's at least be civil."

Tolbert's jowl tightened at the rebuke. "I could cut you down at any moment."

"Then how will you find Thorndel since there is no map? The knowledge I possess is memorized," Jayson brazenly replied.

"You know the *scholar* is right, *captain*," Rafe spoke with deliberate emphasis.

Tolbert stared at Jayson. The latter withstood the intense scrutiny. "Lead on!"

Jayson caught Winnie's gaze. She looked at him with a sense of curious wonder. He grinned before correcting his horse to continue.

Tolbert's presence made discussion difficult; thus, speech was limited to directions, weather, and meals. They paused for an hour at midday to eat from the packed supplies. The rest of the day and into the evening, they switched from riding to walking the horses. Any other stops were only long enough to let the animals drink.

Shortly after sunset, Winnie felt Zoe slump against her back while the Piskie's hold grew loose. "Zoe?"

Zoe's head jerked up, and eyes snapped open. "Are we there yet?"

"No. I just didn't want you to fall off."

"Oh." Zoe yawned. Again, she leaned against Winnie's back.

"Jayson!" Winnie called.

He slowed enough to turn in the saddle. "What?"

"When are we stopping for the night? Zoe keeps falling asleep."

"Another hour and we'll reach an inn," Tolbert said.

"You know this place?" Jayson asked.

"Ay. Soldiers use it frequently when heading north."

"Did you hear that, Zoe? One more hour. So, hang on," said Winnie.

Zoe muttered a sleepy reply.

Over the course of the next hour, Winnie frequently woke Zoe. Finally, they arrived at the inn. Rafe helped Zoe down from behind Winnie before a teenager came to tend the horses. Once inside, the place didn't appear too crowded.

"Gilley!" Tolbert shouted.

Gilley, the innkeeper, happily greeted them. "Captain, welcome. Your usual?"

"Aye." Tolbert led them to a table in the front corner of the inn, away from other guests.

Gilley paid special attention to the captain and his companions. The meal proved hearty and warm. The Piskies picked at the human food, which comprised pork and lentils.

"Would your children prefer something sweeter, Captain?" asked Gilley.

"They are not my children," Tolbert said. At the innkeeper's bewildered reaction, he added, "They belong to the ranger." He motioned to Rafe.

At Gilley's questioning glance, Rafe said, "Vegetables, please. They are not partial to pork."

"First time I heard children want vegetables instead of sweetmeats," he chuckled, yet left to fetch the vegetables.

"They should eat what they are given," Tolbert chided.

"Pork makes us sick. I don't think you want that," Zane said.

Tolbert scowled at the response but said nothing as Gilley returned with a plate of cooked carrots, onions, and potatoes.

"Thank you," said Zoe.

He smiled at her. "How many rooms?" Gilley asked Tolbert.

"One. Your largest."

"Oh, captain," he said with a twinge of disappointment. "That would be the loft over the stables. A damp, smelly place not fit for a family." He indicated Winnie, Rafe, and the twins.

Jayson fought a smile when Winnie blushed. Rafe too smirked at her abashed reaction, but covered it by eating.

Tolbert didn't hide his amused grin at the mistaken identity. "It will serve for tonight."

Jayson added, "We must get an early start and don't want to disturb the other guests."

"Before breakfast?" asked Gilley.

"I'm afraid so."

Gilley scratched his scrawny chin. "I can pack a couple of today's sweetmeats, three loaves of brown bread, and sausage—

beef, not pork—cheese, and bring it over to the loft before closing for the night. Wouldn't want you leaving on an empty stomach."

Jayson smiled in agreement. "That will suffice. Thank you."

After they finished eating, Jayson paid Gilley, who provided a lantern for the trek to the stable loft.

True to the description, the loft was cold and smelled of horse. The room consisted of four beds with pillows and blankets, two chairs, but no stove for warmth. A small, dirty window overlooked the stable yard.

Jayson examined the window. "Can't be opened to help lessen the stench."

"I've been in worse places," said Tolbert.

"After twelve hours riding, it's best to get a good night's sleep. Winnie, you and Zoe take that bed. I'll share with Zane, leaving the others for Jayson and Tolbert," said Rafe.

"What? You don't want to share a bed with the mother of your children?" Tolbert heartily laughed at his own coarse joke.

Angry, Winnie threw a pillow at Tolbert, which struck the captain in the head. Tolbert's initial surprise turned into more laughter. He tossed the pillow back. Winnie noticed Zoe smile.

"Don't you start," she warned.

"It was funny." Zoe climbed into bed.

Rafe chuckled. "Keep your cloaks on. It's going to get colder tonight without heat."

"Should we take turns on watch?" Zane asked.

"Only if the captain suspects treachery."

Tolbert took off his scabbard. The sword remained sheathed and propped up beside the bed. "I suspect everyone all the time. It's what keeps me alive."

"What a sad way to live," said Zoe.

Tolbert's brow wrinkled with some discomposure under the gaze from her innocent green eyes. "A soldier's life is hard. Disciplined and dangerous."

"So, you truly have no children?" Zoe asked.

Hesitant to answer, Tolbert got into bed. Again, her eyes compelled a reply. "No. I'm not married. I pity the man who does. Soldiering is no life for a woman." He lay down in a huff.

With Tolbert's back turned, Rafe moved close to Winnie and whispered, "Is it still safe?"

She patted her leg and nodded.

When Tolbert moved, Rafe spoke aloud to Winnie. "Go to sleep. I'll stay awake until Gilley arrives with the food." He took a chair to sit beside the door.

Winnie lay snuggled beside Zoe. She turned to where Jayson slept. "Jayson," she spoke in a hushed tone.

"Aye?"

"Thank you."

"For what?"

"Taking such a risk to help me. I didn't think you would."

"I made a promise." He tenderly smiled. "Now, get some sleep." He watched Winnie until certain she fell asleep. Tolbert also appeared to be sleeping. Carefully, Jayson rose to join Rafe. He whispered, "Can I ask you something, Uncle?"

"*Shh!*" Rafe lowly hissed. He pulled Jayson close. "Tolbert doesn't recognize me. Let's leave it that way." Both glanced back to where the captain slept. When Jayson started to leave, Rafe snatched his arm and pulled him close again. "Are you certain you know the way?"

"Aye," came the confident reply.

A soft rap came at the door. Rafe quickly opened the door to find Gilley with a basket. "Much obliged. Goodnight." He then said to Jayson, "Let's both get some sleep."

Jayson returned to bed, but sleep eluded him. His mind a whirlwind of images from the past few days; Winnie's capture, the discovery of Piskies, and becoming reacquainted with Rafe. Why did Rafe leave and never let them know he was alive is the question he wanted to ask. He understood Rafe's concern regarding Tolbert. Having the captain along already proved a deterrent to speaking freely and hindered interaction. Mostly his mind warred about his boast to find Thorndel. Could he really do it? After all, he was just a scholar, learned in books and not a soldier or ranger. He rarely ventured outside Highburn.

Jayson turned to a sleeping Winnie. Her body silhouetted by the dim moonlight piercing the small dirty window. He heard her heartfelt gratitude when she thanked him for helping her. True, he promised, but sheer impulse made him volunteer. Or was it guilt? Although younger than him, she possessed the courage to leave and face the unknown. Whether driven by impulse or a promise, he could not back down with her life at stake, with the fate of Orrin at stake. He looked up to the ceiling and softly prayed. "Lord, help guide me for the sake of all. Help us learn the truth."

Chapter 19

OR TWO NIGHTS AFTER LEAVING GILLEY'S INN, THEY managed to find shelter in barns of farmers willing to accept payment. However, the further north they traveled, the less populated the countryside. At the last farm, Tolbert convinced the family to provide some potatoes, carrots, onions, and sausage. Of course, no one would refuse a King's officer. On the fourth night of the journey, they made camp just off the road.

Rafe poked the fire over which hung a guinea fowl. Zoe and Zane used sticks to cook potatoes. Winnie and Jayson sat close to the flames to warm their hands. Tolbert kept watch beside the horses just in the rim of firelight.

"Ready to eat," Rafe announced. He removed the fowl to place on a rock and used his knife to divide the portions. He placed them in Piskie bowls to serve. "Watch out. It's hot," he told Winnie and Jayson. He rose to give Tolbert a bowl.

"Surprised you trapped a fowl so quickly," said Tolbert.

"I am a ranger." Rafe returned to the fire to eat his portion.

Zoe and Zane ate the potatoes.

"Scholar," began Tolbert. "How much further?"

Since Jayson couldn't answer due to eating, Rafe spoke. "It's fifteen days from Highburn to Norwood. So, that leaves eleven days."

Jayson shook his head. He took a drink to swallow. "No need to enter Norwood. I know a path to circumvent the city that leads us straight to Shadowspire. It will save three days."

Disturbed, Rafe asked, "You don't mean the Pass of Katkova, do you?"

The question surprised Jayson. "You know it?"

"I've heard of it. A narrow, treacherous valley that few dare take."

"Why? Is it haunted like Shadowspire?" Zoe nervously asked.

"No. It is said to be the lair of splintercats," said Rafe.

Winnie shivered and impulsively touched her wound. "That's why we traveled the main road before."

"Aye." Rafe then spoke sternly to Jayson, "Norwood is safer."

"If we go to Norwood and leave by the north road, people will know our destination."

"Better that than facing splintercats or worse!" argued Rafe.

Tolbert moved to the fire. "If it will shorten our journey and keep our mission secret, the scholar's route is the best. These two have already caused too much interest," he said of Zoe and Zane. "Keeping their identities secret in barns and an isolated inn is one thing, but taking them to a large city is risky."

Rafe rose to confront Tolbert. "Have you ever faced a splintercat, captain?" When Tolbert's jowls tightened in a scowl, Rafe continued. "The claws are this long! And capable of killing with just a scratch. Winnie can tell you. She barely survived."

"You're a ranger. Surely you know how to avoid such creatures," Tolbert countered.

"Aye. Go through Norwood!"

"Jayson. Are you sure Katkova is the only option besides Norwood?" asked Winnie

Jayson took her hand. "Winnie, placing you or anyone in danger is not what I wish. However, going to Thorndel is dangerous regardless of which way we take. We must pass through Shadowspire to reach the citadel. Ancient legends tell tales of how Shadowspire tests the hearts and minds of all who pass and proves a greater threat and challenge than either path." He looked at Rafe. "You know I'm right about this."

Rafe nodded, which prompted Tolbert to declare, "We take the Pass of Katkova."

"It should take a full day to travel the valley. I suggest we make camp before entering the pass to begin at first light," said Rafe.

"Fair enough," Tolbert agreed. "So, we stay on the main road for eight more days—"

"No," Jayson interrupted Tolbert. "Four days to the Shonta River, where we turn west outside Bramdon. Then three days due west through the river basin, which ends at the pass."

Tolbert stared with admiration at Jayson. "Indeed, you memorized the map. But you just told me the route."

Jayson returned Tolbert's stare. "Can you tell me the legends and lore of Shadowspire and Thorndel that could alter our journey?"

Tolbert huffed a sarcastic laugh. Instead of answering, he gave the empty bowl to Rafe and returned to stand watch by the horses.

The weather grew colder the further north they traveled. Some trees already shed their leaves. Several rainstorms forced them to take shelter off the road and wait. Farms and settlements became sparse as the terrain grew too hilly and rough for crops, with little grass for livestock. Each night, they either camped in the open or in a ravine just inside the tree line.

As they neared the Shonta River, the land flattened into a fertile basin. Although prone to flooding, the town of Bramdon took advantage of the rich soil for farming and the river for metal smithy. The day's rain made for a beautiful sunset reflecting off the clouds.

Tolbert stopped where the road turned into Bramdon. "We need supplies. The scholar and I will go into town while you take the rest and find a suitable place for camp," he told Rafe.

"I don't think that's a good idea."

"Your opinion doesn't matter." Tolbert turned his horse.

Jayson heaved a hapless shrug and said to Rafe, "Stay along the river's edge." He kicked his horse's leg.

"Tolbert is the type of human we Piskies try to avoid," Zane scoffed.

"He's not too pleasant for us to deal with either." Rafe moved his horse west.

"Do you think Jayson is safe with him?" asked Winnie.

"Tolbert would be a fool to harm any of us." Rafe drew rein after a hundred yards beside a small rocky outcrop. "This will serve. They can see us from the bend." He helped lower Zane down before dismounting. "You and Zoe fetch wood for a fire, but don't stray into the forest," he instructed Zane. "I'll try to catch some fish."

"Why? They are getting supplies," said Winnie.

"*If* they return with supplies, it will be for the remainder of the journey. Prepare a fire ring for when the twins return."

Rafe knelt and moved the moist soil to find a worm. He withdrew a hook attached to a string from his pouch and baited the hook. He tossed the hook into the water and held the end of the string. He threw it several more times before he felt a tug. Swiftly, he pulled the string and hooked a fish. Twice more he repeated the action to catch a total of three fish. During that time, Winnie started the fire. Rafe used thinner branches to skewer the fish for cooking. By the time they were ready to eat, Tolbert and Jayson returned.

"Were you successful?" asked Rafe.

"A bit," replied Jayson. "We just reached town before a grocer closed for the night. All he had left were four potatoes, three apples, some cheese, and two loaves of bread."

With a self-satisfied grin, Rafe looked at Winnie. "I told you we dine on fish tonight."

Jayson handed a potato to Zane. "You and Zoe will have to split a single potato each night until we reach our destination."

"We can manage," said Zane.

Once everyone finished eating, Winnie excused herself.

"Don't wander too far!" Tolbert warned.

"Leave her some privacy," chided Rafe.

Winnie walked far enough to be out of view, yet close enough to see the fire. She needed only a moment for privacy but really wanted to be alone. She sat on the other side of the rocky outcropping. Moonlight filtered through the clouds to dance upon the water. Nothing was turning out as she expected. She prayed for discernment, especially since Tolbert joined them. His presence brought a foreboding darkness to the journey. Prayer helped to bolster her courage to withstand him. Still, many unanswered questions remained. The only clear direction she felt during prayer was to continue to Thorndel. Would she find the answers there? If she did, could she accept them? Rafe and the Queen added to the mystery. Rafe suggested a connection between the necklace and

Thorndel. Why give her the necklace? Merely a coincidence between the jewel and her birthstone month? *No. Everyone tells me there is more to this than I realize.*

"Oh, father. I need your wisdom and advice like never before." She sniffled back tears.

"You shouldn't stay away too long." Tolbert appeared.

Winnie slightly shrunk back, first startled by a voice then cautious upon sight of him. She said nothing in reply rather return to stare at the river.

He stood in front of her. "What drives you? A misguided belief that Briggs is alive?"

Winnie refused to look at him. Her jowls tightened in resolve to remain silent. She jerked up in defiance when Tolbert grabbed her arm. "Let go!"

Tolbert flashed a mocking smile and released her. "You have courage. However, that will be of little use against what is to come."

"You mean Lord Falco's plan? The one he used my father to try and achieve?" A gasp of fear escaped when Tolbert seized her.

"Be warned, girl."

"Captain!" Jayson shouted in command.

Tolbert immediately changed his demeanor to calm. He stepped away from Winnie. "I was just going to help her down." He then said to her, "You shouldn't stay away so long." He left.

Jayson watched Tolbert leave before he approached Winnie. "Did he hurt you?"

During Tolbert's departure, she regained her composure. "No."

Jayson appeared unconvinced. "Are you sure?"

She grinned. "I'm fine." She shivered and rubbed her hands together for warmth.

"He frightened you," Jayson said with certainty.

"No. I'm cold."

He held out a beckoning hand. "Come back to the fire."

When he helped her down from the rock, she felt the necklace in her pants pocket hit her leg. She paused and wondered if she should tell him about it.

"Something wrong?" he asked at her hesitation.

At his question, warnings from the Queen and Rafe about keeping it hidden instantly flashed through her mind. "Eh, no. My legs are cold and not easy to move."

"Come." He placed an arm around her waist to guide her back to the fire.

Rafe noticed Jayson supporting Winnie. "Are you hurt?" he asked.

"She's cold," replied Jayson.

Rafe tossed another log on the fire to stoke it for more heat. Jayson fetched the blanket from behind the saddle of her horse and placed it about her shoulders.

"The scholar forgot one item we bought." Tolbert went to his saddlebag and fetched a corked pottery bottle. "Cider." He held the bottle near the fire and swirled the contents to warm the cider. "This should help." He gave it to Winnie. He turned to Jayson. "Tell me, scholar, what legend will we find at Thorndel?"

"It was once a place of knowledge regarding the Almighty. A citadel of beauty and magnificence before Balor seized it."

"You know about Balor?" asked Zane, surprised.

"Naturally. The Ancient manuscripts speak of him and his pact with Danior, Pekka's ancestor." Jayson grew thoughtful. "Shadowspire concerns me. The tales of it are harrowing."

"Before we find out, it is best to get some sleep. We still have three days to reach the pass. I'll take the first watch," said Tolbert.

Chapter 20

D AWN BROKE. RAFE HELD THE REINS OF HIS HORSE AS HE stared at the Pass of Katkova. A creek ran through the base of the valley with steep grassy mountain slopes on either side. Despite the idyllic landscape, Rafe's eyes narrowed with trepidation. Trees grew higher up the slopes, capable of providing cover for anything lurking above the valley floor. Water flowed down to the creek and gouged out gaps in the mountainsides. Another place for predators to hide. He ignored the sounds of stirring behind him. The others prepared for departure.

Thus far, the trip proved uneventful. At least danger-wise. Tolbert's misgivings about Zoe and Zane began to wear on Rafe. Frankly, Tolbert's entire attitude grated on his nerves. Now, they stood on the verge of entering a very hazardous part of the journey. Could the others handle it? Only he and Tolbert were trained in combat. Winnie had courage, yet was unskilled in arms, with minimal survival knowledge. Jayson's scholarly training wouldn't be much use against splintercats or other creatures between here and Thorndel. Piskie power may provide some aid, but it was barely enough to help escape their earlier encounter with the werebear.

Tolbert led his horse to join Rafe. "See something, ranger?"

"No. And that concerns me." He tossed the reins over the horse's head in preparation to mount. "Be ready to act on my warning."

"I'm always ready for action."

Rafe stopped Tolbert from mounting. "Not like this," he spoke in deadly earnest.

Tolbert's brow wrinkled in wariness at the warning. "Very well, ranger."

Rafe released Tolbert. When Zane approached, Rafe said, "Ride with Jayson. If action is needed, I want to be unencumbered." He continued while Zane complied. "Jayson, did you distribute the food as I instructed?"

"Aye."

"Good, because there will be no stopping. We eat while riding."

Winnie paused in helping Zoe mount behind her. "You said it would take all day to cross the valley."

"Aye. We need to do so quietly to draw as little attention as possible. There will be enough noise from the horses. This time, I take the lead. We'll follow the creek yet steer clear of the soft bed to avoid leaving tracks. Jayson will follow me to give instructions when necessary. Then Winnie. Captain, rear guard. Remember to be quiet! And let us pray the Almighty allows safe passage."

They entered the pass in a single file. Rafe's instincts focused on the ground in search of disturbance and tracks. Wearily, Jayson and Winnie looked from side to side. Tolbert sat in the saddle, alert, also scanning the terrain only with a more trained eye than either Jayson or Winnie. Zoe held on tight to Winnie, while Zane muttered in the Piskie tongue.

Jayson leaned back and asked Zane, "What are you saying?"

"A Piskie prayer to the Almighty for protection."

Rafe fully turned his torso in the saddle, face stern, and finger to his lips for silence. Jayson made a sheepish nod. Rafe returned forward to continue visual search of the ground.

Although the sun continued to its apex, clouds increased to spread a greyness over the valley. This decreased the chance of shadows on the mountain sides. Despite riding for hours, nervousness overcame Winnie's need for food. Jayson only took a few bites of cheese. Both Piskies refused to eat. Rafe didn't eat to concentrate on leading the group. With seeming disinterest in their lack of nourishment, Tolbert munched on an apple.

Rafe slowed the pace when the valley narrowed to create a gorge that stopped on the side they traveled. He raised a hand in signal to halt. He pointed to the other side, placed a finger to his lips, and proceeded to carefully move his horse into the creek. The others slowly followed. Being shallow at the bend helped minimize splashing from hooves. Unfortunately, this meant emerging on the far bank where tracks became imprinted in the soft earth.

Zoe held on tight to Winnie when the horse slipped upon exiting the creek. It neighed in panic, which caused Winnie to draw a quick rein for correction. The horse bucked and Zoe fell off. Tolbert kicked his horse to leave the creek, jumped down before the animal stopped, and scooped up Zoe. Winnie steadied her horse in time for Tolbert to place Zoe back behind her.

"Thank you," Zoe murmured in gratitude.

Tolbert made no acknowledgement. He fetched his horse and mounted. Rafe, Jayson, and Zane anxiously waited. Zane bit his lip to keep quiet when he saw Zoe fall. His worried glance found his twin. She smiled an *all is well*, and he relaxed.

Rafe's attention turned to the near-vertical slopes on either side of the gorge. Joined with the gray clouds of the afternoon, the narrowness of the mountains created long dark shadows.

"Do you think we were heard?" Jayson cautiously asked.

Rafe didn't immediately reply; his attention remained focused on the surroundings.

"All appears quiet," Tolbert said.

"Too quiet. But let us take it as a blessing." Rafe motioned to continue.

For two miles, they rode through the darkened gorge before the valley widened. Although the sun remained obscured by thick clouds, the valley was brighter. A sense of relief settled over the group for having successfully navigated the gorge.

An hour later, Jayson brought his horse beside Rafe and pointed forward with eagerness. The slopes decreased at what appeared to be the end. Rafe nodded in acknowledgment. Jayson pulled back to Winnie. He smiled and made the same eager indication to her. She sighed in relief.

Tolbert noticed Zoe continuously glanced backwards. She didn't look directly at him yet appeared nervous or maybe scared. He couldn't tell which exactly. Despite not being keen to Piskies, curiosity made him pull his horse alongside Zoe and Winnie on the opposite side from Jayson.

"What do you keep looking at?" he demanded in a low harsh tone.

"I sense danger. We are being watched," Zoe replied in a shaky voice of fear.

"Splintercats?" asked Winnie, nervously.

"I can't tell. But it draws near."

"Close ranks with the ranger," Tolbert told Winnie and Jayson. He pulled back to survey the surroundings.

They barely begun to close the gap when Tolbert pushed his horse past them in a gallop. He pulled to a hard rein beside Rafe. "In the gap!" he warned.

Rafe no sooner looked toward the danger when he saw a splintercat race up a boulder in readiness of an attack "Look out!" He shoved Tolbert from the saddle just as the splintercat leapt at them. It jumped over a falling Tolbert to knock Rafe from his horse. The full weight of the beast drove Rafe to the ground.

"Uncle!" Jayson shouted in fear.

Tolbert heard Jayson. He scrambled to his knees, unhurt. "Uncle?" he repeated.

Rafe lay dazed and winded, unable to move. Momentum made the splintercat pounce off him and turn for another attack.

Zane and Zoe spoke Piskie in unison. A whirlwind of dirt and rock engulfed the beast. It let out an angry roar. The splintercat emerged from the debris, still bent on attacking Rafe.

"Hang on!" Jayson said to Zane. He made his horse rear, which temporarily made the splintercat retreat from flying hooves.

Winnie's horse once again proved skittish, only this time, when it bucked, its hind hooves caught the splintercat in the head. The beast rocked sideways at impact.

Jayson saw the result and turned his horse's rear to the splintercat. "Hit the rump!" he told Zane.

Feeling the hard slap, the horse bucked. The second impact to the head sent the splintercat staggering, seriously wounded and bloodied. Tolbert arrived with his sword ready to strike when the splintercat fell backwards into him. Both crashed to the ground with Tolbert's legs pinned underneath the beast.

Rafe managed to get to his knees and arm his bow. When the angry splintercat rose to hiss at Tolbert, Rafe blinked back pain to shoot. The arrow pierced the beast's neck, and it fell dead. Dizziness made Rafe collapse to all fours.

"Uncle?" Jayson dismounted.

"I'm just stunned. No claw wounds or bites."

Tolbert limped slightly from a twisted ankle caused when he freed himself from the beast. He wore a mocking grin. "Rafferty Clarke. I thought you were familiar, but uncertain of how, until your nephew gave you away just now."

Irate, Jayson confronted Tolbert. "He saved your life. Twice *just now.*"

Rafe rose to restrain Jayson. "Easy, lad. It was only a matter of time before he recognized me." He then said to Tolbert, "I'm surprised it took you this long to remember."

"Raffety?" Winnie questioned.

"Rafe is my family nickname," he explained. He looked up when rays from the setting sun broke through the clouds. "We shouldn't linger. Other cats will come now that our presence is discovered." He caught his horse where it grazed. "At the gallop. The pass ends up ahead."

Jayson and Winnie's horses lagged due to carrying two. Despite the Piskies being small, the animals bore extra weight all day without stopping. By the time they reached the end of the pass, both horses were lathered and labored for breath.

Aware of the urgent need to rest the horses, Rafe steered them into a grove. He drew rein. "Down!" he urged Jayson and Winnie. "Captain, get Winnie's horse." He took Jayson's mount.

Rafe and Tolbert tended the exhausted animals. This required removing all tack, a few minutes of walking to cool down, followed by splashing them with water from the creek. Once the horses recovered their breath, they were allowed to drink. They were tethered beside the other horses with enough slack to graze.

Meanwhile, the twins collected firewood while Jayson and Winnie prepared camp. Once the horses were out of danger, they sat around a small fire to eat and rest. Rafe made a low groan as he rotated his neck and shoulders.

"Are you certain you suffered no injury?" Jayson asked.

"I wouldn't be standing if even nicked by a claw."

"A wound is that lethal?" asked Tolbert, skeptical.

"Aye!" Winnie emphatically answered.

Tolbert raised a surprised brow at her forcefulness.

"I told you she could have died from a splintercat claw wound if not for the Piskies," Rafe reminded Tolbert.

"Then I accept your affirmation." Tolbert spoke in an unusual respectful tone to Winnie.

"What of gratitude for saving your life?" Jayson demanded.

"Soldiers protect. That is our duty."

Jayson's ire grew at the dismissive reply.

Rafe took hold of Jayson's shoulder. "The captain is right. I only did what needed to be done. What we all should do—protect each other if we are to survive." He flinched in pain.

"I thought you said you weren't injured?" Jayson questioned.

Rafe cocked a sarcastic grin. "I'm sore. It does hurt being taken down from a horse by a splintercat."

Tolbert chuckled at the retort. "Rest. I'll keep watch," he told Rafe. "In the morning, the *scholar* can tell us which way to proceed."

When Rafe leaned back against a tree to rest, Winnie moved to sit beside Jayson. His narrow, angry eyes focused on Tolbert's back. She spoke quietly. "Do not let Tolbert upset you."

"Hasn't he upset you?" he countered.

"We both know he is a bully."

Jayson grunted in the affirmative. His glowering look returned to Tolbert.

"Trust your uncle."

"I do."

"Not entirely." To Jayson's quizzical glance, she said, "I, too, hesitated to trust him when we first met. But he has proven himself. There is too much at stake to let the past interfere."

For several moments, Jayson regarded Winnie. He noticed a growth and maturity in her eyes he hadn't seen before. "The compulsion you spoke of has become certainty."

She flashed a wry grin. "While the compulsion has grown stronger, certainty has been tested many times since leaving."

"Yet not enough to dim the desire."

"That is the Almighty's doing, not mine." She made a slight motion with her head toward Tolbert. "His presence is a challenge in more ways than I can count." She softly smiled. "But I'm glad you're here." She fought a yawn.

"Sleep." Jayson nudged her to lay down. "I will rest too," he added when she hesitated.

Chapter 21

THE FOLLOWING MORNING, JAYSON LED THEM DUE NORTH from the grove. On this day, he chose to ride alone. Zane went with Tolbert. The trek was wide enough to ride side-by-side. Rafe spoke little and this concerned him.

"Are you certain you are well?" Jayson asked.

"Soreness and a headache prevented me for sleeping last night. That is all."

"You would tell me if needed?"

"Aye, lad. I suffer from nothing a good meal and night's sleep in a soft bed won't cure." Rafe wryly grinned.

Jayson felt some relief, yet a twinge of regret remained. "I'm sorry my slip of the tongue revealed your identity to Captain Tolbert. Fear made me react."

"Take no blame. As I said before, it was only a matter of time before he remembered."

Jayson screwed his lips with consideration. "Now that he does know, can I ask the question you silenced at Gilley's?"

Rafe somberly sighed. "You want to know why I left and didn't tell you I was alive."

"I think I'm owed an explanation."

Rafe cocked a rebuking brow at the statement. "Oh, you do?"

Jayson backtracked. "I mean no disrespect. I mourned for years. I'd like to know why?"

Rafe carefully glanced back. Winnie, Tolbert, and the Piskie twins rode about ten yards behind them. His voice deliberate in reply. "Full explanation must wait for a more opportune time. Yet," he said to forestall any objection. "Know the reason is for the future of Orrin. I never meant to hurt you. Sadly, such pain proved a regrettable part of a necessary decision. Pain for both of us. Now, let us speak no more of it until I judge the time is right."

"Scholar!" Tolbert called.

Jayson drew rein to allow the others to catch up.

"You said eight days. It has been that long. How much further?"

"From my recollection, we should reach the foothills of Shadowspire sometime this afternoon. Providing there are no hindrances."

Fretful, Zoe muttered in Piskie.

"What did you say?" Tolbert demanded.

"A prayer for protection from whatever haunts Shadowspire," she timidly replied.

"You believe in ghosts?" he scoffed.

Rafe came to Zoe's defense. "Piskies are very sensitive to nature. They can perceive forces humans cannot."

"My sister told you about a presence before the splintercat attacked, which is why you warned Rafe," Zane reminded Tolbert.

"And we created a small whirlwind to protect Rafe from the splintercat," added Zoe.

"Ah, that was you," said Tolbert. "Why fear Shadowspire if you possess such abilities?"

"Legend tells of strange things happening to those who travel through the pass in hopes of reaching Thorndel," replied Zane.

"The Ancient manuscripts also mention such encounters," confirmed Jayson. "Now, if the captain is satisfied, I suggest we resume or risk not arriving until nightfall." Not waiting for an answer, Jayson kicked his horse to continue.

Rafe grinned with approval as he rode beside Jayson. "Well done. Tolbert can be a bully."

"I'm aware of that. Although I never confronted him at Highburn, this journey is different than anything I've ever experienced."

"Yet you volunteered. That takes courage."

Jayson cocked a sardonic grin. "No, impulse. Just like with you, when I saw Winnie in danger, I blurted out that I knew the way. Such impulsiveness is unusual for me."

"Don't underestimate yourself, lad."

Jayson brazenly retorted, "Aren't you underestimating me by remaining silent?"

"No! I'm keeping you alive. Now, enough! We need all our faculties to face what is to come."

The rest of the trek continued in relative silence, only interrupted by an occasional remark from Jayson about direction. They ascended into the mountains. Some places steep and narrow while others a gentle sloping meadow. At midday, they paused beside an icy mountain stream to eat and water the horses.

Continuing further up the mountains, the landscape grew rockier with large boulders protruding from the earth. Scrub brush, mountain heather, and sporadic groves of towering pine trees lay before a sheer stone precipice. Jayson drew rein to stare in wonder at the massive stone peak rising across the alpine meadow. The others joined him.

Intimidated, Winnie asked, "Is that …?"

"Shadowspire," Jayson finished her question with the answer. He then quoted: *"It rises from the earth as a stalwart sentinel, gray and foreboding. Its peaks jagged and sharp. Chill upon sight drains the courage of the most stouthearted men who are not easily deterred."*

"It is impressive. But I don't consider myself a coward," boasted Tolbert.

"No one does until their courage is tested by the unknown," Rafe warned.

"You admit fear, ranger?"

"I would be a fool if I didn't. It is said the deep dark shadows of the spire tests the hearts of all who enter. Are you ready to face that test and reveal your heart?"

Tolbert's answer was to spur his horse and head toward Shadowspire. Upon nearing the saw-tooth peak, the horses became unsettled. Another hundred yards and the animals stopped, breathing hard and trembling. No amount of coaxing could make them move.

"We'll dismount, tether the horses, and proceed on foot," said Rafe. "Take only what you can carry. Leave the rest."

The massiveness of Shadowspire proved frightening up close. Vertical rocky cliffs created an opening so narrow that only one could enter at a time. Dark shade from the cliffs made seeing what lay beyond the entrance nearly impossible.

Winnie drew her arms about her in fright. "Now, I know why my father looked fearfully at me when leaving. There is a cold dread." She blinked back tears.

Tolbert's brow wrinkled in discomposure at her statement. "Briggs knew what he was doing." His voice of forced bravado twinged with regret.

Rafe placed a comforting arm about Winnie's shoulders. "Conor was no coward."

"We can proceed and learn the truth if you wish to wait here," Jayson graciously offered.

"No!" Winnie declared, then softened her tone. "Your uncle is right. My father was not a coward. Nor will I be. I've come too far to quit now."

"So, will you take the lead?" Tolbert asked Winnie.

"No, I will," Jayson firmly said. "Remember, I know the map. She can follow me." He looked up. "Lord, you know why we are here. May your spirit guide us and show us what to do."

"Amen," said Rafe, Winnie, Zoe, and Zane. Tolbert remained silent.

Jayson compassionately gazed at Winnie. "For the general." He entered the pass.

Winnie quickly followed, then came the Piskie twins.

Rafe delayed Tolbert from proceeding. "Be warned, captain. I will not let any scheme you or Falco have planned to harm Winnie, Jayson, or the Piskies."

Tolbert's eyes narrowed. "Mind your words, ranger! Your threats will not stop me from making certain all is recovered according to Lord Falco's wishes."

"Then let the Almighty and Shadowspire decide who will prevail." Rafe entered the pass.

Jayson warily eyed the cliff walls. The deeper he traveled into Shadowspire, a dark dread welled up inside him. From the pit of his being, the dread rose to invade his mind. At first, he thought he heard the whisper of human voices. They grew loud, although the words were indistinct. Visions began to accompany the words. Was he really seeing ghostly images or just his eyes playing tricks? Then a single male voice spoke clearly.

"Jayson, why are you here?"

"To find the general," he replied.

"Look beyond the reason you believe to what truly lies in your heart." The voice ended in maniacal laughter.

The images suddenly turned into scenes from his life. His mother's death, his uncle's disappearance, and his father's urging him to become a scholar despite wanting to be an artist. Then came his friendship with Winnie during childhood. More recent memories: learning about the general's death, and his promise to help Winnie. The discovery of Rafe being alive, the Piskies, and all the knowledge gained from research about the royal jewel. The dread of Shadowspire became real as the images were accompanied by emotions of fear, grief, and uncertainty that challenged his courage and questioned his motive.

"No!" he cried in defiance. "I mean to help her! She is my friend."

"Just a friend?" asked the voice from earlier.

"I love her!" Jayson admitted through tears.

"And if what you seek costs that love? What then?"

Jayson regained his resolve. "If it restores the general and gives her peace, I will be content."

The images suddenly vanished, and the voices ceased. Jayson found himself on the other side of Shadowspire. No signs of anyone else. "Winnie?" he questioned, fearful. When he moved forward to return into the darkness, a force repelled him. He tried twice more only to be repeatedly repelled. He staggered back and sat upon a boulder. He could do nothing more but wait.

Chapter 22

THE GLOOMINESS OF SHADOWSPIRE ENGULFED EVERYTHING in a nameless fear. The cold dread Winnie felt before entering the pass intensified. She forced herself to keep moving in defiance of the icy terror threatening to debilitate her. She held her cloak tightly closed to stop the shivering. Mumbled voices grew louder. Visions of ghostly shapes suddenly surrounded her. She shrunk back against the cliff wall to inch past the shapes.

"Winnie," a male voice called. "Why are you here?"

She paused to catch her frightened breath enough to answer. "To find my father."

"Look beyond the reason you believe to what truly lies in your heart." The voice ended in the same maniacal laughter.

Shadowy images turned into familiar faces.

"Mother?" she gasped in surprise.

"You are special," her mother said.

"Father!" She impulsively reached out to touch him.

"My little ruby," he said.

Through tears, she watched events from her life. She wept anew at her mother's death, the dread on her father's face the day he left Highburn. She screwed her eyes shut against the visions, but they remained in her mind. The voices of Lord Falco and Master Simon telling of her father's death. Opening her eyes revealed the Queen giving her the necklace and again hearing her father say, *My little ruby.* She felt for the necklace in her pants pocket. It remained hidden. She jerked back when a large face of the King came towards her and exploded in a puff of smoke. From the clearing smoke emerged the throne, crown, and necklace. The Queen appeared beside the throne. With outstretched hand, she said, *"Come, my child."*

Winnie shook her head, befuddled. "I don't understand."

"Come, my child," the Queen repeated.

Winnie gasped with comprehension, and her knees gave way. She fell hard to the ground, where she clenched the hidden pocket. "I have seen the future!" she muttered in awe. "This is to save a royal child. Not my father." She wept.

"You know the Almighty brought you here. What will you do?" asked the voice.

Winnie fought to regain her composure. "As father would have and aid the Queen."

She heard the voice of her father. *"Trust the Almighty with your souls. Do not fear the outcome or your fidelity. Providence works in mysterious ways to aid us when we need it most."*

"Aye. For the sake of Orrin, let Providence guide me." She bowed her head.

In a flash, the images vanished, and the voices ceased. Winnie found herself on the other side of Shadowspire.

"Winnie!" Jayson shouted in relief and embraced her. "I thought I lost you."

"Jayson?" said Winnie, confused. "Are we safe?"

"For the time being. We made it through Shadowspire." He tenderly touched her face.

Winnie looked about. "Where are the others?"

"I don't know."

She bit her lip, sheepish to even ask. "Did you see or hear anything?"

"Oh, aye! Images of my life, along with a voice challenging me about what I saw and why I'm here. You?"

"The same. Yet more." She wrapped her arms about as if warming herself from a chill.

"More?"

She looked at him through moist, tearful eyes, once more debating what to tell him.

"Winnie?"

Again, she chose discretion. "Do you think the others will experience what we did?"

"I believe so. All we can do is wait." He no sooner spoke then Zoe and Zane emerged from the pass. "Here!" He waved them over. "Are either of you hurt?"

"No, we're fine," Zane casually replied. He then became concerned. "You both look pale. Are you well?"

"Did you see or hear anything?" asked Winnie, anxious.

"No. There aren't any ghosts," Zane teased his sister. Zoe smirked in annoyance at him.

Jayson and Winnie appeared perplexed. "Why did they not experience what we did?" she asked him. He shrugged.

"What *did* you experience?" asked Zane, curious.

Jayson took a deep breath to recover before he replied. "Images from our lives and a voice challenging us about those images. When we answered correctly, we found ourselves here. Safe on the other side of Shadowspire."

Winnie shook her head, still befuddled. "I don't understand how you experienced nothing like we did."

"We thought we would," Zoe began, yet added when Zane laughed, "Very well, *I did*. We heard so many stories."

Jayson listened with due consideration. "You are from the royal Morgrath tribe tasked with guarding Thorndel. Perhaps that makes you immune to testing."

"But Balor is a Piskie," argued Zane.

"Who rules Thorndel as the Piskies once did. Or at least, you guarded it," Jayson added when Zane attempted to dispute. "It is why the Almighty created Piskies."

"It sounds reasonable," Zoe said to Zane.

"What of Rafe and Captain Tolbert? Did you see them?" asked Winnie.

"They were behind us," replied Zoe.

"We can go back and look for them," offered Zane.

"No. There is a force that prohibits returning. I tried," said Jayson. "We wait."

Rafe believed he saw the end of the pass and made a sprint for it. Overcome by a stifling force, he stumbled sideways into the cliff face. Murmuring voices and misty images appeared.

"What trickery is this?" he demanded.

"Rafe, why are you here?" questioned the voice.

"What manner of specter are you? Show yourself!" Rafe reached for his bow, but it was knocked from his hand by an unseen force.

"Weapons are useless here. Now, answer the question."

"To serve my sovereign and protect Orrin."

"Search for your heart for the truth."

The images sprang to life, beginning with a young Jayson. It was followed by his encounter with Conor and the Queen at Highburn, his fake argument with Simon, and his relationship with the Piskies. The necklace hovered in the air before it dropped into his hand to place around Winnie's neck. Quick flashes of Thorndel, Pekka, Falco, and the throne ended with a loud bang. The deafening sound brought Rafe to his knees. He gritted his teeth against the pain.

"No! By what strength the Almighty provides, I won't let them win! Orrin will be restored, and the Piskies freed. To my pledge I hold!"

A brilliant flash of light blinded Rafe. When he was able to see again, he found himself lying on the ground beyond Shadowspire. His bow beside him. He heard his name and sat up.

"Uncle!" Jayson dropped to his knees beside Rafe. "You made it! Thank the Almighty."

In wonder, Rafe regarded Jayson and felt the young man's arm. "You're not a specter. And unharmed." He hugged Jayson in grateful relief.

"Aye. So are Winnie and the twins."

Rafe smiled and took Winnie's hand in reassurance that she, too, was real. "It is good to see you both, also," he said to the twins.

"They did not experience what we did," said Winnie about Zoe and Zane.

"That's not surprising. They are Piskies." Rafe stood and took a drink from his flask. After a moment of recovery, he asked, "What of Tolbert?"

"No sign of him. He may show up yet," replied Jayson.

Tolbert drew his sword upon sight of the apparitions swirling around him. "I fear no mortal or ghost!"

"What do you fear, Tolbert?" asked the voice.

"Nothing!"

"Oh, but you will." The voice ended with a maniacal laugh.

What began as bravado turned into anxiety, as Tolbert watched images of his life flash before him. Clandestine meetings, dishonorable betrayals, Falco's voice speaking; *Let none return alive* followed by an exploding throne.

Tolbert gritted his teeth against being confronted. "I follow orders like a good soldier."

"Really? Shall we see if that is true?" challenged the voice.

A scene materialized of his argument with Conor before the general left for Thorndel. Conor reluctant, but Tolbert unrelenting when he threatened, *"You don't want Winnie to suffer Arabella's fate, do you?"* Conor's anguished face at the deadly threat loomed large before him. The shadow of death seized Tolbert with bone-chilling reality.

"You were not under orders when you uttered those words. You took it upon yourself to approach Conor. The blame belongs to no one else," said the voice. "What will you tell Winnie when she discovers the truth? That you sent a man to his fate under such a threat. Will you follow through on orders and kill them in cold blood to maintain your proclaimed duty as a soldier? Honor stained with blood."

Overwhelmed by the profound unmasking, Tolbert's sword fell from his grasp. The clinking of metal hitting the ground echoed loudly. He barely had voice to speak, and when he did, the words forced. "I had no choice. Not from Falco or the king."

"There is always a choice between right and wrong. Good and evil. By the grace of providence, a choice still lies before you that could change the course of your life. Choose wisely."

The force of blinding light and thunderous sound threw Tolbert face-first to the ground. When all faded, he noticed his sword beside him and feet standing around him. Looking up, he recognized his companions.

"Are you injured?" asked Rafe.

Made mute by the supernatural encounter, Tolbert couldn't reply.

"You saw them too," Winnie said with confidence. "Images along with a voice."

Tolbert sluggishly nodded. Words difficult.

Zoe knelt and held a flask to his lips. "Drink."

He took a greedy gulp. "Give me a moment."

"I think more than a moment," began Jayson. "Twilight is fading. It's best to make camp and proceed to Thorndel in the morning."

Stunned, Tolbert stammered. "You want to camp here? Beside that?" He motioned to Shadowspire.

"We can all use the rest." Rafe held out a hand to aid Tolbert to his feet.

"I don't think I can rest until this is over."

"We all must try."

Tolbert took a moment to straighten his clothes and sheath his sword. He used the time to regain some of his composure. Still, the unnerving encounter is hard to totally dismiss.

"There is no wood for a fire, but that shallow cave can serve as shelter," said Zane.

Jayson escorted Winnie to the cave. "Sit close to the back. I'll sit in front of you."

Tolbert entered last. He cast a look of regret to Winnie but quickly turned aside before she noticed. He sat nearest the opening. He wrapped the cloak about him and sat with legs up to rest his chin on his knees.

Rafe pulled out the remaining whole sausage and an apple to distribute. Tolbert shook his head in refusal of food. The twins accepted the apple, while Jayson and Winnie took some sausage. Rafe sat opposite Tolbert at the opening to eat his portion of the sausage. He studiously watched Tolbert. The once arrogant and defiant captain was strangely subdued. In grim silence, Tolbert met Rafe's regard. No words passed between them.

Chapter 23

As early morning light rose over Shadowspire, a wispy mist brushed upon their faces. "Wake!" commanded a breathy female voice. "Wake!"

Startled, Winnie sat up. Jayson, Rafe, and Tolbert also jerked up with Rafe and Tolbert ready to make defense.

Zoe and Zane stood at the cave entrance. "The Mist of Shadows!" said Zane. His voice a mix of excitement and trepidation.

"What?" Winnie pulled back at seeing a misty shape just outside the cave.

Zane explained. "The Mist of Shadows is a Piskie legend about a mystical being surrounding Thorndel."

Rafe lowered his bow. "Why are you here?" he asked the mist.

"I am to show you the way to Thorndel," came the reply.

Skeptical, Tolbert hesitated to sheath his sword. "Is this specter to be trusted?"

"It can embody both evil and good depending upon its motives," replied Zane.

The voice took no offence in speaking. "This is your reward for successfully navigating Shadowspire. Without my guidance, you will neither find nor enter Thorndel. Is that not what each of you want? To learn the answer to your challenges?"

"It is," said Rafe. He removed the arrow and placed the bow over his shoulder. He signaled for Tolbert to put away his sword.

"Then come." The mist turned east from the cave.

Jayson followed with Winnie. Rafe accompanied the twins while Tolbert took up the rear guard. Through winding narrow passages, they followed the mist for hours until they lost all sense of direction.

"This can't be the way!" Tolbert shouted in dispute.

"Do not question the Mist," began Zane in rebuff. "If you do, we will be lost forever in the labyrinth of Thorndel."

"Strange the scholar failed to mention this labyrinth," scoffed Tolbert.

"I didn't know. The Ancient manuscripts made no mention of it. I only found descriptions of Shadowspire and a harrowing journey."

"Another test?" Winnie wondered aloud.

"It said leading us to Thorndel was our reward for passing Shadowspire. So, why another test?" said Zoe.

Suddenly, the female voice turned into a deep wicked male laugh and disappeared. From the fading mist, two splintercats charged at them.

"Balor! It's a trap!" Rafe armed his bow while Tolbert drew his sword.

Jayson turned Winnie aside to shield her from the beasts. Tolbert landed a glancing blow on the hindquarters of one cat. Rafe shot the other in the body when it passed him. Both cats headed toward Winnie and Jayson.

Zoe and Zane spoke Piskie. A wall of rocks formed in front of Jayson and Winnie in time to prevent the splintercats from reaching them. This also allowed Rafe and Tolbert to strike the beasts again. Rafe launched three more arrows into the one he initially hit. Tolbert slashed at the other, landing deep gashes to its head and neck. Both cats fell to the ground, mortally wounded.

"Quickly!" Rafe urged them to flee.

Zane waved his hand, and the rock wall crumbled to free Jayson and Winnie. Jayson winced in pain when a rock struck his left shoulder and tore through the skin. He ignored the injury to usher Winnie to follow Rafe.

"You don't know where you're going!" Tolbert shouted at Rafe.

"Does it matter?"

Rafe pulled to a stop when the passage ended on a grassy plateau. In the middle of the plateau, stood an enormous structure. The massive stone walls rose thirty feet and stretched for nearly a mile. Twenty towering turrets rose skyward from the wall at equally spaced intervals. Between the turrets, arched windows once brilliantly made of colored glass now appeared smoky black. In the center of the structure, an immense gabled and arched keep dominated the view. The intricate stonework and carvings of the keep degraded overtime. The gable roofs of smaller buildings rose just above the walls.

"Thorndel!" Rafe said in awe.

Tolbert surveyed the wall. "I see no gate on this side."

"According to legend, the main gate is hidden." Jayson bit back pain.

"You're hurt." When Winnie reached to inspect his shoulder, he pulled away.

"A scratch. Caused by a falling rock, not a splintercat," he clarified to her concern.

"If the gate is hidden, how do we get in?" asked Tolbert.

"An ancient password." Jayson withdrew a piece of paper from his pouch and read: *"Await the rays to light the way. Speak the word for all to hear. Take heed to what you say, for careless will make you pay."*

"Wonderful! A blasted riddle," chided Tolbert.

"Piskies always speak in riddles to hide secrets. It's part of our defense," said Zane.

"Do you know what it means?" Jayson handed Zane the paper.

"Well, if the *rays* mean sunrise, we arrived too late. But if sunset, then we wait on the west side."

"So, the *word to speak* is the password?" asked Rafe.

"I believe so."

"And what would that *word* be?" Tolbert asked with impatience.

"I don't know. At least not yet," Zane hastily added at Tolbert's irate scowl.

Rafe observed the sun's position. "I reckon two hours until sunset. We head for the west side. We'll use the labyrinth's shadows to avoid being spotted in the open."

Carefully, they began to circumvent Thorndel by staying close to the jagged walls of the labyrinth. Hearing an echoing screech, Rafe looked up. A massive bird with black and white feathers and red head circled the meadow.

"Take cover!" Rafe grabbed Winnie to pull her under an overhang.

Nervous, she peeked out. "What is that?"

"A vulture eagle," he whispered then placed a finger on her lips to stop further questions. They waited for nearly ten minutes before the vulture eagle flew off.

"I wonder if we'll make it to the west side," Tolbert complained. "First splintercats and now a vulture eagle. Balor knows we're here."

"Then turn back if you're afraid!" Winnie chided.

Tolbert scoffed at her bravado. "I don't understand your determination since Lord Falco told you Briggs is dead."

Winnie's eyes narrowed in pain and tenacity. "I don't believe that!"

Her forceful reply caused words to echo in his mind; *What will you tell Winnie when she discovers the truth?* He flinched, as if in pain.

Rafe noticed the drastic change in demeanor. "Tolbert?"

"Nothing!" he roughly dismissed concern. "Let's continue."

Although, skeptical about Tolbert's attitude shift, Rafe again took the lead. Without further mishap, they reached the west side of Thorndel.

"Now what?" Winnie asked Zane.

"We wait to see what the sun's rays reveal."

Tolbert studied the citadel. "Strange, there are no guards posted."

"Why?" inquired Rafe. "Shadowspire is enough of a deterrent. If anyone gets this far, they need to find a way in. Which they wouldn't know unless blessed like we are with a *scholar*." He purposely spoke the term Tolbert used in an unflattering manner toward Jayson.

"And Piskies," Jayson added.

"There!" Zane drew attention to a gate, now illuminated by the fading sun's rays.

With nervous excitement, Winnie asked, "What does it say?"

"It's too far to read." Zane moved toward the gate.

"Be careful," Zoe warned.

The cry of a vulture eagle sounded as it dove toward Zane.

"Zane!" Zoe cried in warning the same moment he noticed the vulture eagle. He dove behind a boulder in time to be missed by the vulture eagle's talons.

Rafe took aim to shoot when the eagle turned for a second attempt to snare Zane. It banked to avoid being struck in the body. The arrow pierced its wing, which caused the eagle to veer off. By the time Rafe looked to locate Zane, the Piskie reached the gate. No one heard what was said, but rather saw the gate begin to open.

"Quickly!" Rafe urged them to run. They slipped inside before the gate closed.

"What did you say to get it open?" Jayson asked Zane.

"I simply read the inscription and spoke Piskie."

"Where would Balor keep my father?" Winnie asked Zane.

The Piskie shrugged with some uncertainty. "Maybe a dungeon or tower room."

Tolbert studiously regarded Winnie. "You really believe he is alive."

"I pray to the Almighty to know for certain because without a body, there is a possibility."

He saw in her eyes an unshakeable faith. "Very well." He turned to Jayson. "Scholar, have you memorized a map of this place?"

"I found none. However, most citadels and castles have a basic structure."

"We split up to make a search," began Rafe. "I will take Winnie and Zane to find a possible dungeon. Captain, you take Jayson and Zoe to look for a tower room."

"And the jewel?"

Rafe stared intensely at Tolbert. "The general first! If it is here, he will know." Before Tolbert could speak, he ushered Winnie and Zane toward the rear of the citadel.

Uneasy, Zane glanced about as they moved in the shadows. They paused at the end of an alleyway to survey a small courtyard.

"There is foul coldness to this place. Evil has caused its decay from its famed splendor."

"You're not old enough to know," said Winnie.

"My father described Thorndel of his childhood. A place of wonder and splendor. He would be dismayed to see it now."

"*Shhh!*" Rafe pointed across the courtyard. A splintercat paced in front of a door. He whispered, "That may be the dungeon."

"How do you get by it?" Winnie mimicked his tone.

"Leave that to me." Zane focused his attention on the beast. He began speaking Piskie under his breath. The splintercat stopped to sniff the air.

Zane continued speaking. His words coming faster and more intense. The splintercat growled and then bounded towards them. Rafe and Winnie retreated deeper into the shadows. Instead of launching at them, it leapt up the nearby stairway to the top of the wall where it disappeared over the rampart.

Amazed, Winnie asked, "Where did it go?"

"To hunt for a meal. I made it think a hare is nearby."

Rafe grinned in approval. "To the door." He led them in a sprint across the courtyard. The door was unlocked. He grabbed a torch off the wall before they proceeded inside.

Winnie shivered. "It's colder in here than outside." She gathered her cloak about her. Her nose wrinkled in disgust. "What is that smell?"

"Wait outside." Rafe began to push her toward the door.

"No! I want to know if he is here."

Rafe held her gaze. "It is the smell of death."

She flinched slightly at his words, yet her speech fearless. "I will go with you."

Rafe made a curt nod. "Hold this." He gave Zane the torch to arm his bow. He motioned for Zane to move forward.

The damp, dark passageway led them deeper into the dungeon. There were no steps to descend, only a narrow passageway. It ended in a circular room lit by three torches. Four cells lined the room in a semi-circle. The light illuminated the cell bars, but darkness shaded the rear part of the cells, making it difficult to see the occupants clearly. A goblin sat at a table eating raw meat. The emergence of torchlight from the passage brought the goblin to his feet, spiked club in hand, to confront the new arrivals. Rafe's bow was up and fired. The arrow struck the goblin in the right side of the chest. It raised the club to strike. Another arrow pierced its neck. It gurgled, unable to breathe. A third arrow finished it.

"I'm surprised it took three shots," spoke a human male.

Winnie gasped at hearing the voice. She grabbed the torch from Zane and moved in the direction of the speech. The torchlight silhouetted a person in the back of a cell. "Who are you?"

"Winnie?" He moved into the light. His light brown hair unkempt, clothes filthy, while his scruffy features pale. He squinted in avoidance of the torchlight.

"Papa!"

With urgency, Conor reached through the bars to take her hand. "What are you doing here?"

"We came to get you," said Rafe.

"Why did you bring her? You know it's dangerous!" Conor scolded Rafe.

"There is much to explain." Rafe examined the lock. "We need to find the keys." He waved for Zane's help in a search.

Winnie touched Conor's face through the bars. "Papa. You look ill."

"Weeks in a dungeon will do that. But you should not be here!"

Rafe discovered the keys on the belt of the dead goblin. "Move aside," he told Winnie. He tried three keys before one unlocked the cell.

Conor emerged, weak and a bit unsteady on his feet. Winnie took his arm in support. "We must get her to safety," he told Rafe.

"Easier said than done. Falco sent Tolbert with us."

"Indeed, he did." Tolbert arrived with Jayson and Zoe.

Conor immediately shielded Winnie. "What foul business does Falco want this time?"

"The same thing he wanted when sending you here."

Conor's eyes narrowed in anger. "So, you brought Winnie to coerce me?"

"Actually, it is the other way around. I came with her. But enough of this! Where is the jewel?" Tolbert reached for his sword.

The action prompted Rafe to aim his bow at the captain. Conor put up his hand to stop Rafe as he answered Tolbert. "I don't have it! I was captured before discovering its location."

They heard the echoing of a roar from outside.

"The splintercat has returned!" Zane warned.

"We need to leave before it can trap us here," Rafe said.

Tolbert grabbed Conor when he tried to pass. "If you're lying about the jewel—"

Conor punched back in defense, which made Tolbert lose his grip. Conor awkwardly urged Winnie to hurry outside with the others. Tolbert hastened after them.

Once in the courtyard, Conor snatched the torch from Zane and shoved it into a water barrel to extinguish the flame. The full moon provided enough light to navigate. Rafe stood with his bow ready for any sign of the splintercat.

"You, Piskie!" Tolbert jerked Zane around. "Do you know of a treasure room?"

Intimidated, Zane said, "I've never been here before."

"But the citadel belongs to the Piskies."

"Centuries ago!"

"More than likely, there is one in the keep," said Jayson.

"You better be right, scholar." Tolbert shoved Jayson to move. He then grabbed Zane by the shoulder to pull him along. Zoe haplessly went with them.

Conor delayed Winnie and Rafe from following the others. His voice urgent and determined. "Whatever happens to me, you must leave with Rafe. Ask no questions. Just go."

"But, Papa," she began to object. He seized her shoulders to face him.

"You must obey me in this! For Orrin."

In distressed befuddlement, she gaped at him. Tears swelled. She found him, and now he ordered her to leave him.

"She will," Rafe assured Conor.

Unable to speak, Winnie nodded.

"Come, before Tolbert places the others in danger," Rafe said.

They moved slowly to accommodate Conor's weakened state. They paused at the corner of a building.

"Papa?" asked Winnie with concern.

He waved her off. "I'll be fine. I just need to get my legs back after long inactivity."

Rafe took the last hunk of sausage from his pouch. "Eat this to regain your strength."

Conor shoved the entire piece in his mouth. While Conor ate, Rafe observed the citadel's main courtyard. Torches and moonlight helped visibility. This made lurking in the shadows of vital importance. The others hid behind a broken wagon opposite the keep. He pointed them out to Conor. A nod from the general, and they moved to join them.

"Report," snapped Conor.

Tolbert pointed as he spoke. "Two goblins guard the entrance. Vulture eagles are perched on the towers. I hear splintercats but can't spot them."

Winnie tapped Zane's shoulder. "Can you distract the goblins like the splintercat?"

"I don't know. Goblins are unpredictable creatures that we rarely encounter."

"Let them capture us. You and me," Conor said about him and Tolbert.

All eyes quizzically turned to Conor at the statement.

"And why should I agree to that?" Tolbert's sarcastic tone broke the stunned silence.

"Because, *captain*, they will take us to Balor. He will know where the jewel is located. Only we do this away from the others to ensure their safe departure." Conor spoke Tolbert's rank with authority.

"Pa—" Rafe's heavy hand on her shoulder stopped Winnie from speaking.

Neither Conor nor Tolbert heard her beginning objection. Both focused intensely on the other. Finally, Tolbert nodded. "Very well, general."

Rafe kept Winnie in her place, as they watched Conor and Tolbert return to the corner leading to the dungeon. Once there,

Tolbert held Conor in a manner of escorting a prisoner. When they neared the keep, the goblins accosted them and pulled them inside.

"Time to go." Rafe tugged on Winnie.

"No." She jerked away.

"You promised," he insisted.

Her tear-filled eyes stared expectantly at him. "You once told me that when given a mission, you complete it. Will you leave him to die without completing this mission?"

Rafe winced at the reminder, yet hesitated. "He gave new orders," came the weak rebuttal.

"He can't stand against Balor in his weakened condition," she continued her argument.

"She's right, uncle. Nor can we trust leaving him alone with Tolbert."

"And there is the jewel," Zane added.

Rafe's vacillation lasted only a moment when he spoke to Jayson. "Compromise. You and the twins take Winnie and wait near the labyrinth. I'll help Conor." He then waved a finger at Winnie and sternly said, "Go, as promised."

Chapter 24

THE GOBLINS BROUGHT CONOR AND TOLBERT INTO THE great hall. Numerous torches lined the hall. Even with so much light, the room appeared grimly dark. Frescos on the walls muted by greyness; the mosaic floor weathered. The interior of the arched, colored glass windows just as bleak as outside. The figures and events meant to be vibrantly celebrated in glass were barely seen in outline. At the end of the hall stood the elevated throne backed by a magnificent window of stained glass trimmed in gold. Moonlight showed this also muted by the hall's gloominess. The gold-gilded throne aged and worn. The being who sat upon it appeared ancient, his wrinkled face pale, a sign of many years passed. The bright green Piskie eyes dulled by centuries of toil. Heavy black and silver robes too large for a Piskie hung over his feet so the hem touched the floor. The left sleeve appeared empty and tucked into a belt around his waist. A splintercat lay beside the throne. It stood and growled when Conor and Tolbert appeared.

"Easy, my pet." Balor stroked the beast's head. The splintercat sat yet kept a close eye on Conor and Tolbert. "Well, well, Captain Tolbert. This is a surprise. I wonder what scheme Lord Falco has hatched this time."

"I could ask you the same since you haven't held up your end of the bargain. He is still alive." Tolbert jerked a thumb at Conor.

Conor's brows knitted in rancor. "Why rescue me if you thought to find me dead?"

"Rescue was not the intent," Tolbert chided. "An exchange."

Conor's face briefly showed confusion before he said, "Me for the jewel."

Balor laughed. He bent forward to speak. When he did so, a chain hung from his neck. Attached to the chain was a large ruby encased in silver. "Oh, general. Only at the end, do you become aware of your role in this."

Conor forced himself to curb any reaction to the necklace. He cast a quick side glance at Tolbert. The captain appeared unfazed by Balor's movement. Still curious about the reason for the exchange, he asked Balor, "Why me?"

"Revenge for your ancestor depriving me of my arm during battle."

A puzzling answer to wait hundreds of years for revenge, but Conor made no comment.

"I'm here to collect the agreed item," said Tolbert.

The statement told Conor that Tolbert was ignorant of the jewel's proximity.

Balor calmly sat back. "The terms have changed."

Tolbert grew red-faced. "Lord Falco will not accept any alteration to the agreement. You have Briggs. Now give me the jewel!"

The splintercat stood and snarled at Tolbert's perceived threat. The goblins grunted in warning and held spears ready.

"Temper, temper, captain. My pet and guards could kill you instantly."

Tolbert pressed his lips together to contain his outrage. He forced words from his mouth. "What are the new terms?"

"I know you did not come alone. There are two young Piskies with you." Balor sneered. "I want them!"

Tolbert heaved an indifferent shrug. "Why risk the agreement for them? They are inconsequential. Briggs is more valuable."

"They are the future of the Piskies. In them lies the blood of our kings. Their demise in exchange for the jewel."

Conor closely watched the negotiations regarding this new, unexpected twist. He flinched at feeling something hit the top of his head. A second small object hit him. It came from above. He carefully glanced up. He caught a glimpse of Rafe. Conor quickly resumed his posture of watching Balor and Tolbert. They continued to debate, unaware of Rafe's presence. True, he didn't anticipate Rafe rather hoped he left with Winnie, but something needed to happen soon.

Irate, Balor again leaned forward, which again revealed the necklace. Green eyes focused heavily on Tolbert. "You have no choice, captain! Give me what I want or die this instant!"

Conor noticed Tolbert staggered as if struck by something. Yet not a blow was landed. In fact, the captain's whole demeanor shifted to stunned. A surprising reaction considering Tolbert's blustery bravado. But he didn't have time to comprehend why the change when Tolbert droned a docile response.

"As you wish, my lord." Tolbert bowed in submission.

Tolbert subdued, Conor shouted, "Come and get me!" He knocked Tolbert sideways into a goblin and willed his legs to move quickly toward the main entrance.

An arrow whizzed through the air when the splintercat leapt from the platform. Struck deep in the chest, it fell dead. Balor gaped, shocked at the cat's swift demise. The goblins moved to seize the humans. Conor ducked to avoid being caught by a goblin. Another arrow, and the goblin attacking him fell, seriously wounded. Conor picked up the spear for defense and braced his legs to remain standing.

Age and long robes made it difficult for Balor to rise from the throne. He pointed to the balcony. "Up there!"

Tolbert drew his sword and parried a goblin's spear. His thrust pierced the goblin's body. The creature squealed and backed off, wounded.

"Guards!" Balor moved sluggishly as he tried to get to safety.

Tolbert intercepted Balor at the foot of the platform. "Where is the jewel?"

"Look out!" Conor yelled a warning when another splintercat charged Tolbert.

The captain fell backward in avoidance of the cat. It turned to pounce on Tolbert. Conor threw the spear and impaled the cat. In his attempt to roll away from the beast, Tolbert's head struck a pillar. He became dazed upon impact. Hearing nearby commotion, he pushed himself to his knees. He blinked back dizziness to ascertain the situation.

Outraged, Balor drew a dagger and charged Tolbert from behind. An arrow struck him in the chest. He staggered backward and collapsed against the foot of the platform.

Ignorant of Balor's demise, Tolbert stood. He just got to his feet when pierced through from behind by a spear. He fell to his knees and slumped to the floor.

Conor grabbed Tolbert's fallen sword and finished the goblin who skewered the captain. The still, pale face told him that Tolbert was dead. Conor hastened to the platform and ripped the jewel from Balor's neck. "Get out!" he shouted up to Rafe.

Conor didn't wait for a reply. He shoved the necklace in his pants pocket and ran in staggered steps for the door. He flattened himself against a wall when two more goblins entered the hall. They passed him unnoticed. He hurried outside. He kept to the shadows as he made his way toward the citadel's gate. Winded, he paused to catch his breath and get his bearings. He jumped to make defense when a hand grabbed his shoulder. Rafe. Conor took a quick breath of recovery from fright before confronting Rafe.

"I told you to get her out of here!"

"The others are doing that. They should be waiting for us at the labyrinth entrance." He balked when Conor nudged him to leave. "What about—?"

"I got it." This time, when Conor pushed, Rafe moved.

Forced to evade splintercats and goblins, they made slow progress to the gate. The pauses also allowed Conor to catch his breath. Near the gate came a *hissing* sound. Both made ready for defense. Zane appeared.

"What are you doing here? You were supposed to leave with Winnie," Rafe chided.

"I waited to open the gate. It closes as soon as anyone passes through."

"Be quick! We can't be caught," Conor said.

Zane spoke the Piskie password, and the gate slowly opened. Once wide enough, they slipped through. The shadow of the labyrinth wall served as cover to avoid detection. They would have passed the others save for Zoe's quiet call from behind a large boulder.

"Papa!" Winnie embraced Conor. Several sobs escaped as she held on tight.

"Where is Captain Tolbert?" asked Jayson.

"Dead," Conor somberly replied. "So is Balor."

"What about the jewel?"

Rafe spoke the same time as Jayson's second inquiry. "We must navigate the labyrinth quickly. Can you make it?" he asked Conor.

"No need for that. There's a more direct entrance further on."

"Will we reach it before dawn?"

"Aye. Follow me and stay close." Conor used Tolbert's sword to steady his pace.

Winnie walked beside Conor for support. After a mile, he began to falter and paused beside a boulder. "You need to rest," she quietly insisted.

"No need. The passage is behind this boulder. I just needed to catch my breath."

Zoe scanned the ground. "Ah! *Elueth!*" She picked a small plant growing in the shade of the wall. She placed the leaves on the boulder and used another rock to grind them. Once satisfied, she put the green mess in his flask. She shook the flask and handed it to Conor. "Drink. It will help restore your energy. Sorry about the taste. Mama usually puts in honey to lessen the bitterness."

Conor coughed down the herb mix. "How much should I drink?" he asked in a voice strained in recovery.

"That's enough for now. Keep the flask and take a swig each time we stop."

Conor placed the flask over a shoulder and waved to continue down the new path. Winnie continued beside him, alert for any sign of weakening. Within the hour, they found themselves back at the cave where they spent the night after traveling to Shadowspire.

"Well, that was easy," Zoe commented.

"There is still Shadowspire," warned Jayson.

"Do you think we will experience the same as before?" Winnie sounded worried.

Jayson shrugged uncertainty. "I don't know."

"The pass is the only way in or out." Conor took another drink and grimaced. "That's the last of it. I don't know whether to be grateful or come to tolerate the taste."

Rafe chuckled at the comment. "Best put up our weapons before we start, and pray the Almighty allows us safe passage before nightfall."

Conor tucked the sword in the belt of his uniform. "I'll take the lead. Rafe the rear." He glanced up and prayed, "Lord, we commit our path to you."

The narrowness forced Winnie to follow Conor. The twins walked between her and Jayson with Rafe at the back. The sheer cliffs of Shadowspire prevented sunlight from reaching the path. Eyes forced to adjust to dim shade.

"How now, general," the male voice spoke.

Conor stopped. "What do you want?"

"Papa?" asked Winnie, confused. He spoke to no one that she could see.

"The Almighty awaits your obedience," said the voice.

"What makes you think I will waiver?"

"Papa, who are you talking to?"

"Hush!" he harshly warned her.

Zane tugged on Winnie's arm for her to lean down. "A voice from the Almighty," he whispered.

Winnie straightened and shivered slightly due to remembrance. She still heard nothing.

The voice continued speaking to Conor. "Love is a powerful human emotion. Sacrifice is hard."

Conor rose to attention. "I made a solemn pledge. To that I hold."

A misty face appeared that only he could see. "Then go. The future of Orrin lies before you." It disappeared.

Conor bowed.

"Papa?" she asked upon seeing his reverent action.

He tenderly smiled at her. "My little ruby." He kissed her forehead. "Come."

They continued through Shadowspire without another encounter or mishap. To everyone's surprise, the horses remained where tethered.

"Ride Tolbert's horse," Rafe told Conor, yet delayed Conor mounting to whisper, "Rona gave Winnie *Scrutern's* broken piece."

Conor's stunned gaze shifted to Winnie, then quickly back to Rafe. His face was a mix of excitement and dread. "That is what the voice meant when questioning me. It is time. Finn must be told."

Rafe allowed a small smile of agreement before he aided Conor to mount.

"We're ready, uncle." Jayson and Winnie were mounted with the Piskies behind them.

Once Rafe was mounted, he spoke to Conor. "We ride as far as you can manage."

After only an hour, Conor's fatigue overcame him. Rafe led them to take cover in a grove sheltered by foothills. The twins fetched wood while Rafe and Jayson left to snare supper. Winnie watched over Conor as he slept.

It overwhelmed her to see him alive! Yet saddened by his weakened state. So strong in faith, personal convictions, and physicality that his appearance came as a shock to her. He said it was due to nearly two months in a dungeon. His soiled clothes showed weight loss while his face haggard, hair unkempt, and shaggy beard. She had never seen him with a beard before. Clean-shaven matched the meticulously groomed appearance of a renowned general. Streaks of gray hair invaded the brown. She hadn't thought of him as "aging."

Winnie didn't move from vigilance when the twins prepared a fire. Rafe and Jayson returned with two hares and one grouse. Zane spoke of finding berries and mushrooms for Zoe and him. Not until the food was cooked, did Conor wake.

"Papa?"

He stretched. "I'm well. Do I smell meat?"

"Aye. Rabbit and grouse," said Rafe. "Thought you could use some sustenance."

"Indeed!" Conor sat up against the tree trunk.

Rafe cut the grouse into manageable pieces, placed it in a Piskie bowl, and gave it to Conor. "The grouse is for you. We'll eat rabbit," he said of himself, Jayson, and Winnie.

When Conor began to devour the bird, Rafe said, "Slowly! No need to rush."

"I haven't eaten meat in weeks," Conor replied with a mouthful.

"You know better, *general*," Rafe spoke in a half-teasing tone. "Starving men eat some now, then rest, and finish the remainder later."

Conor nodded and placed the bowl aside. He finished chewing and drank some water. "I heard you received an unexpected birthday gift," he said to Winnie.

The statement surprised her. "Who told you?"

"I did," said Rafe.

"May I see it?" asked Conor.

Winnie put down the bowl to withdraw the necklace from her pants pocket. "I was told you would approve since ruby is my birthstone."

Conor smiled with a hint of melancholy in his pleasure. "I do. Although I hoped to be present when you received it. Why was it in your pocket and not around your neck?"

"Rafe told me to hide it when we were captured by Sergeant Cadel." When she motioned to Rafe, she noticed Jayson's dejected expression. He shied from her.

"Cadel?" Conor's voice was rough with disapproval.

"Following orders, he claimed." Rafe proceeded to explain all the events leading up to their arrival at Thorndel.

Conor's features hardened at the mention of Cadel, Falco, and Tolbert. The chain became clenched in his fist. "The Almighty repaid Tolbert for his treachery."

Troubled by his declaration, Winnie said, "Papa, he is dead."

Stirred to compassion, Conor took her hand. "Child, I do not rejoice in the death of anyone. However, Tolbert posed a great danger to me, you, to all here. His sole aim was to fulfill the wish of his master, Lord Falco, and claim the ancient jewel of Thorndel for himself. Tolbert would have killed all of us once he had it. Just like he did Arabella." His voice pained in speaking of his beloved wife.

Stunned, yet uncertain of what she heard, Winnie asked, "Papa, what do you mean like Mama?"

Jayson spoke the same time as Winnie. "He threatened Winnie during our journey here."

Conor flushed with anger and immediately shifted his attention from Jayson to Winnie. "How did Tolbert threaten you?"

"He mocked me about believing you were alive. I withstood him. Yet, sad to learn of his death. But what did you mean about Mama and him?" She repeated her earlier inquiry.

Conor ignored the question. "Life and death are determined by the Almighty. What matters is you and the jewel are safe."

Zoe sat up, excited. "You found the jewel?"

"Aye. And before more harm can happen, we will return it to the Piskies." Conor smiled.

"Then we're going home!" Glee radiated from Zoe's face.

Conor grinned at the enthusiasm. "I'm certain Finn and Burdock will be pleased with its recovery." He flinched in pain. His face became pale.

Winnie felt his forehead. "No fever. However, we've talked too much. You need to rest."

"Let me put this on you first." Conor placed the chain around her neck. "Keep it hidden under the collar."

"I've done that before." She tucked the jewel underneath. "Now, rest."

Conor lay down to sleep.

Disturbed, Winnie quietly asked Rafe, "Will he recover?"

He smiled with reassurance. "Aye. Mora will make sure of it with Piskie remedies. Same as with you."

Winnie noticed Jayson's hurt expression. He again averted his gaze when their eyes met. She sat beside him, but he continued to look at the ground. "There were many times I wanted to tell you about the necklace. Only Tolbert's presence made it impossible. He couldn't learn I had it, as he would have told Lord Falco." She touched his hand. "I'm sorry I disappointed you."

"Lad. She was given charge of it by a *great lady* to keep it safe," said Rafe.

The term *great lady* made Jayson look up. "You mean the Queen." Neither Rafe nor Winnie answered. They didn't have to. By their expressions, he was right. "It makes sense. She wanted me to tell her everything I found in my research about Piskies and the royal jewel."

"Again, I'm sorry," said Winnie, sheepishly. When she rose, Jayson grabbed her hand.

"One apology is enough." He softly smiled.

Chapter 25

AFTER JAYSON LEFT, SIMON MADE CERTAIN ALL HIS SON'S illustrations and research notes were safely hidden. He thought best to keep them out of view from the straying eye of Lord Falco, who visited the scholar's office every day. The Prime Minister asked the same pointed questions about the jewel and Piskies. Although Simon could read Jayson's shorthand, he gave vague answers. And when he didn't know, he assured Lord Falco he would find out.

In truth, the atmosphere at Highburn Castle became tenuous since the group's departure. The King's mood soured with each passing day. Soldiers snapped to attention while servants desperately tried to avoid interaction with the King. Pekka frequently summoned Simon to reiterate Jayson's information. No matter what answers he gave, neither Falco nor the King was satisfied. The constant inquiries came at all hours of the day and night. Lack of sleep began to wear on Simon and caused more frequent headaches. Rodney aided Simon by providing headache remedies to help alleviate the stress.

Despite being after midnight, Simon sat up in bed reading Jayson's notes. Arrival of the Piskies turned legends and myth into reality. The harrowing accounts of Shadowspire and Thorndel sent a chill through him. His son would face unimaginable horrors. Could he survive? What of Winnie? Her fate could be sealed. He rubbed tired eyes and leaned back against the pillows.

"Oh, Lord," he sighed with a sense of helplessness. His eyes snapped open at hearing a knock on the door. He quickly gathered the papers to shove in a satchel.

"Master?" Rodney cautiously called.

Simon didn't immediately answer for rising and placing the satchel in a hidden compartment of his desk. "Come," he finally said. "The King or Falco?" he grumbled.

"Neither. The Queen."

Simon's momentary surprise was replaced by haste. "My robe and shoes!"

Once properly attired, he accompanied Rodney to the Queen's antechamber via the private entrance. After the signal knock, Eleanor admitted Simon.

"Majesty." Simon bowed.

Rona made a gesture of dismissal to Eleanor. She waited until the antechamber door closed. "The King's irritation is almost unbearable."

"Indeed. His Majesty is rather demanding these days," he spoke with unusual sarcasm.

Rona's voice barely audible. "I summoned you because I can no longer keep this safe." She held out the folded and sealed piece of paper Ennis placed under the necklace.

Simon balked in recognition.

"You know what this is." She spoke with certainty at his reaction.

"I took the dictation from him."

"I thought as much. I place it in your charge, for you are the only one left I can trust."

Concerned, Simon paused in accepting the paper. "Eleanor?"

"She is too close to me, thus constantly watched. By his actions, Jayson has shown loyalty to Pekka."

"He would not betray you, my lady," Simon reassured her.

Rona kindly smiled. "I know. But appearances are what matter at present. Your son's action reflects favorably on you as Lord Chancellor." She again offered him the paper.

He tucked it inside a pocket of his robe. "Upon my life, I will keep it safe."

Rona became startled at hearing voices from the main chamber. She seized Simon's arm. "If anything should happen to me, you must see it done. Tell her everything!"

"It shall be done."

"Now, go!" She nudged him to the private entrance. After his departure, she momentarily held onto the door to gather her courage. Upon entering the main chamber, she found Pekka speaking harshly to Eleanor. "My lord? What brings you here at this hour?"

"There is a reported intruder in your chamber."

"My lord?" She asked with fake surprise. "There is no one here."

"Then why were you in your wardrobe rather than in bed at this hour?" he demanded.

"Since Winnie is gone, Eleanor and I were selecting my clothes for your birthday celebration tomorrow. Winnie has a talent for choosing the best dresses and accessories."

Pekka scowled in disbelief and moved past Rona to enter the wardrobe. She watched him throw open doors and drawers during his heated inspection. Although the private passage was hidden from casual observance, Pekka knew the location. All royals had escape routes.

"Did the intruder leave this way, madam?" He flung open the passage door.

Rona clenched her hands together to maintain her composure. "There is no intruder."

Thwarted, Pekka slammed the panel shut. "Be warned, madam, do not incur my wrath!"

"I would not dare. My duty is to serve you, Sire." She bowed her head.

Pekka stormed out of Rona's apartment.

"Is all well, Majesty?" Eleanor asked.

"Aye. All is well. Let us retire for the night and trust to Providence and our friend."

Simon hastened back to his chamber and placed the sealed paper with Jayson's satchel in the concealed compartment. He locked the dresser and hid the key.

He sat in front of the hearth to stare at the embers of a dying fire. The turn of events happened so fast that he barely had time to comprehend it all. In truth, everyone involved knew this day would come. How and when were always the questions. He closed his eyes against the regret of not revealing everything to Jayson before his son left. Of course, there wasn't time to speak in private, which served as a small consolation. Before then, he discouraged Jayson when Winnie's first departure drove Jayson to dive deeper into research. However, what he learned from that research is what made Pekka dispatch Jayson to Thorndel.

Simon sighed at another prick of pain upon remembering that Falco sent Tolbert with Jayson and Winnie. Tolbert's ruthlessness was well known. "Rafe," he said with a twinge of hope. "Oh, Lord, you prepared my brother for his part. May you strengthen him to see it through."

Rona's words echoed. *I place it in your charge, for you are the only one left I can trust.* Followed by: *If anything should happen to me, you must see it done. Tell her everything.*

The recollection spurred his legal instinct. Simon moved to his personal writing desk. Quill in hand, he wrote two lengthy documents over the course of several hours. When finished, he applied his seal and hid them in the dresser. Exhausted, yet satisfied, he again sat before the hearth. By now, the embers had cooled. He took no notice of them, nor the rising sun peeking through the windows. Only when he heard a rooster did he look up.

"Hope comes in the morning," he quoted. "May it be so."

A knock at the door followed by Rodney's voice. The assistant entered upon instruction. He carried a tray with a teapot and a cup. "I brought your headache remedy before we leave for breakfast with the Queen."

The statement briefly perplexed Simon. "Breakfast with the Queen?"

"I've been instructed to bring you to Her Majesty for a private informal breakfast." He gave Simon the cup of warm soothing tea. "Bolster for the day before celebration, so I am told."

Simon paused in drinking. "Oh! Ay, the King's birthday. I forgot. Lay out a new robe for me while I finish this. Less formal. Save the courtly one for later today."

Once ready, Simon went with Rodney to the Queen's apartment. Both bowed to Rona. She wore a simple day dress with her hair partially pinned back. "Majesty."

"Lord Chancellor, welcome." She indicated for him to sit at the table with her and Eleanor. She motioned Rodney to a sideboard to serve food. "I see by your face I'm not the only one suffering from lack of sleep," she commented.

"A natural response to the current situation."

Rona grinned. "Would you do the honors, please?"

Simon spoke a simple blessing before partaking of breakfast. Halfway through the meal, there came a knock at the door and the voice of a maid. At the Queen's nod, Rodney admitted a maidservant. She carried a tray containing a silver platter covered with an ornate lid.

"Compliments of His Majesty from yesterday's successful hunt," she informed them.

"Thank His Majesty," said Rona in a tone of dismissal.

Rodney took the tray from the maid, who made a quick curtsey and hastily departed. He approached the table and lifted the lid to reveal stuffed venison rolls.

Rona frowned with disgust. "He begins the day with a slight!" she complained. When Simon appeared confused, she clarified. "Pekka knows my dislike of venison, especially the way he orders it prepared, highly spiced with juniper berries." She softened to make a polite offer to her guest. "But please, help yourself."

"I'm afraid juniper berries give me a headache." Simon courteously declined.

"Eleanor, you like venison." Rona motioned to the platter.

"Thank you."

Rodney held the tray while Eleanor helped herself to two small venison rolls. He then placed the tray on the sideboard alongside the rest of the food.

Rona resumed the conversation. "Now, Simon, about Jayson. What have you told him?"

Simon sighed. He suspected more than a casual meal. "Not as much as I should have, considering the circumstances. Although he knows more about Thorndel than I—" He stopped when

Eleanor suddenly began to choke. A look of terror overcame the lady.

"Eleanor?" Rona fearfully gasped when Eleanor fell from the chair to the floor. She struggled to breathe. Froth began to spew from her mouth. "No!" Rona got to her knees beside Eleanor. Simon joined her. "Rodney! Wine, quickly!"

Rodney ignored the spilled wine in his haste to fill the goblet. "Should I send for the physician, Majesty?"

Rona didn't answer as she tried to get Eleanor to drink wine. Unfortunately, Eleanor began to vomit. Rona turned Eleanor onto her side. With a loud exhale, Eleanor became still. "No! No!"

"Majesty?" Simon tried to comfort her. "Was it a seizure?"

Rona urgently gripped his arm. "No. Poison. Like Arabella."

Simon understood the deadly reference. He threw open the door and shouted, "Guards!" Two soldiers immediately appeared. "Someone tried to poison the Queen, only Lady Eleanor intervened! You!" he said to one, "go to the kitchen and find the one who prepared a tray of venison rolls! You," his tone turned mournful. "Fetch the undertaker."

Simon aided Rona to resume her seat at the table. She tightly held his arm. Her words choked by tears. "You know what this means, don't you?" She leaned toward his ear. "Someone knows." She bitterly wept.

Rodney gave Simon another goblet of wine for the Queen.

"Take heart. Hope is not lost. Not while I have what is needed." Simon's consolation became interrupted at hearing activity in the hall. "What is that noise?" he chided.

Rodney opened the door to investigate. Curious servants and nobles gathered in the hallway. "Be still and quiet lest you disturb the Queen!" he told them and slammed the door. "I fear word has already spread," he spoke with regret.

In the time it took to fetch the undertaker, Pekka and Falco arrived. "What's this I hear about poison?" asked Pekka.

Rona turned her face away, lips pressed together to keep from speaking.

Simon replied on her behalf. "Poisoned venison rolls, Sire. Supposedly, a compliment from you for Her Majesty's breakfast."

Pekka grew red-faced. "And just what are you doing here, Lord Chancellor?"

"I asked him to breakfast," Rona said sternly.

"Why?"

"Because you heartlessly sent his son on a mission with no thought to the possible deadly consequences!" Passion brought her to stand. "Now this!" Her breath caught in her throat as the undertaker prepared to remove Eleanor. "Have you no compassion for those who serve you?"

Pekka trembled with rage, yet a hint of pity in his expression as the undertaker left with Eleanor's body. "I never sent you venison rolls! I know your disdain for them."

"Someone did! And in your name," Rona bravely countered. "A poison meant for me! But, sadly, Eleanor …" She couldn't finish for new tears of grief. Simon helped her to sit.

Pekka's jowls flexed between anger and indecision. "You are excused from duty today, madam." He left.

Falco lingered. His usual hauteur masked by sympathy. "My condolences, Majesty."

Rona sneered. "I have no stomach to deal with your false empathy."

"Majesty …"

Rona bolted to her feet. "Get out! Guards," she shouted.

Falco's façade crumbled at her command. He left just as the guards arrived. Simon signaled for the guards to remain.

Once certain of Falco's departure, Simon instructed the guards, "The Queen is not to be disturbed. She needs to rest."

Grateful, Rona held Simon's hand. "You must be very careful, my dear Simon. I cannot bear to lose anyone else."

"I shall keep you company today. Tomorrow, I will instruct Lieutenant Kincaid to assign soldiers to guard your quarters."

Chapter 26

THE MURDER OF LADY ELEANOR SENT SHOCKWAVES through the court. With Captain Tolbert absent from Highburn, Falco ordered Sergeant Cadel to investigate the crime. Naturally, this put a damper on the King's birthday celebration. Under the dire circumstances, Pekka managed to stem his attitude toward Rona, the initial objective of the attempted poisoning. However, servants and soldiers suffered royal wrath as Pekka viewed everyone with a suspicious eye. He ordered the remaining venison given to the hounds. Not a scrap was to be found in the kitchen.

Rona took full advantage of Pekka's leniency and kept to her room for several days. The only exception came when she attended the funeral for Eleanor. Simon remained at the Queen's side, offering comfort during a time of mourning. He also escorted her to the funeral. After four days, Rona graciously dismissed Simon to resume his duties. Both knew Pekka's patience would not last much longer.

Simon returned to the scholar's office. "Rodney," he casually spoke upon entering. The office was empty. Perhaps Rodney was in the antechamber. None of the low-ranking scribes had seen Rodney. "Strange," he muttered.

Despite the unusualness of Rodney's absence, Simon went to his desk. A pile of papers and books awaited him. He heaved a huff of frustration and tossed off his hat and robe. He did not begrudge serving the Queen, rather disturbed at the amount of work undone. Rodney was usually more efficient in assigning tasks during his absence. He pulled the bell cord located beside the hearth to summon Rodney from the assistant's personal chamber.

Simon began sorting through the papers while awaiting Rodney's arrival. Normally, it took five to ten minutes. He used the time to prioritize the work. When the mantle clock chimed the bottom of the hour, he realized thirty minutes had passed, and Rodney still hadn't arrived.

He pulled the bell cord again. Before he reached his desk, there came a knock followed by a man saying, "Lord Chancellor."

Simon recognized Pekka's page. "Come. Marvin. Have you seen Rodney this morning?"

Marvin avoided the question; instead, he stated his purpose. "The King requests your presence."

Simon's shoulders sagged in exasperation. The constant summons proved exhausting and disruptive. "Very well," he grumbled. He grabbed his robe and hat to accompany Marvin to the King's private study.

"The Lord Chancellor," Marvin announced to Pekka.

Simon lowly bowed to the King and gave Falco a formal nod of acknowledgement. He also noticed a soldier standing to one side of the room. Although the soldier looked familiar, the name escaped him. "You sent for me, Sire?"

"What do you know of Rodney Wilson's activities?" demanded Pekka.

The question confused Simon. "Sire?"

"Are you deaf, man? Must I repeat the question?"

"No, Sire. I'm simply baffled by the interest in my assistant."

"We know he's your assistant. That's why you're here. To explain his treachery!"

Simon stood dumbfounded at hearing the word *treachery*. He needed to reply, but struggled to find his voice. "Sire, I ... I am at a loss. What treachery?"

Pekka's eyes narrow, skeptical. "Are you claiming ignorance of his actions?"

"Truly, Sire, I am totally befuddled."

"Falco!" Pekka motioned toward Simon. A sign for needed clarification.

In an unnervingly calm voice, Falco spoke. "Rodney Wilson is accused of being complicit in the poisoning of Lady Eleanor."

The stunning news made Simon rock back on his heels. He steadied himself on a nearby chair as Falco continued.

"Sergeant Cadel," he indicated the familiar-looking soldier, "uncovered Wilson's treachery during interrogation of the kitchen servants."

Pekka sneered at Simon's posture, "Stand up straight, man!"

Simon released the chair to stand with feet apart for balance. This made no sense. "Forgive me, Sire. The news shocked me."

"Then you have no knowledge of his activities?" Falco asked, deadpan in voice and expression.

The shock abated, and Simon's legal mind took over. "No, my lord. In fact, I find it impossible. Rodney served us breakfast. Not to mention the venison rolls were brought by a maidservant. He never touched the venison rolls, only lifted the lid to reveal the tray's contents."

"It was said he had accomplices," Falco pressed.

Simon understood the veiled meaning. "Who said? The same kitchen maid who brought the poisoned food? So, by her tainted word, you accuse Rodney and now me of being her accomplices?"

Falco curbed a smile at the brash retort. "No one accused you, Lord Chancellor."

"Then why bring me here for interrogation if not to find fault? Or do you claim guilt by association without solid evidence against either of us?"

"You are impertinent!" Pekka chided.

"Maybe, Sire. But I am certain of Rodney Wilson's innocence. He has served me faithfully for twenty years. Not one mention of scandal or disrepute has tarnished our time in Your Majesty's court. Furthermore, both you and his lordship saw Rodney in Her Majesty's chamber that fateful day. He was nowhere near the kitchen during the preparation of the food."

Pekka turned red-faced at the vigorous defense. "Why were you with the Queen at all?"

"Her Majesty informed you that she graciously invited me to breakfast, where later the maid arrived bearing a tray of venison rolls supposedly brought to Her Majesty at your request. Could that implicate you, Sire?"

Pekka's outrageous fury prevented him from replying.

"You go too far, Lord Chancellor!" Falco hotly warned.

This time Simon calmly spoke. "Merely an example of how *guilt by association* can be misused. Not a true accusation against His Majesty. Nor should hearsay from a kitchen maid be considered enough evidence to convict a man of treason and murder." He turned to Pekka. "If you wrongly execute an innocent man, the stain of injustice will haunt your reign."

Pekka threw up his hands. "Get out!" he shouted at Simon.

Simon bowed and withdrew. He made his way back to the scholar's office. Emotions don't often get the better of him, but this revelation shocked him to the core. Rodney served him for two decades. He knows secrets … Simon screwed his eyes shut against what torture his loyal servant might have endured.

First, Arabella, Conor's mission, and now poor Eleanor. Few remained. Simon stared out the window. His eyes were misty with regret at the thought of Jayson. "I should have told you."

He hastened to his desk and shoved aside several books to clear an area for writing. He wrote a few quick words, folded, and sealed the paper. He stuffed it in his robe pocket before making his way to Jayson's bedchamber. After a quick search, he found the key to Jayson's secret document compartment. He placed the sealed paper inside the compartment. Once locked, he returned the key and headed back to his office. To his surprise, a soldier stood beside his assistant's desk.

"Lieutenant Kincaid?" When Simon stepped further into the room, he saw Rodney sitting at the desk with his head down." The clothes were dirty, yet intact. When Rodney lifted his head, Simon balked at the grim paleness. "How badly did they torture you?"

"I told them nothing, master," Rodney weakly spoke.

Simon kindly smiled. "I never thought otherwise. Are you whole?"

"He's as whole as can be. He's tough," said Kincaid.

Rodney nodded. "Just sore and tired."

"Come, man. I'll take you to your chamber." Simon gently aided Rodney to his feet. "Lieutenant." He indicated for Kincaid to accompany them.

"Why did they let me go? I thought I'd be hanged for sure."

"Your presence in the Queen's apartment was witnessed by the King and Lord Falco. That counters any false statements from a kitchen maid."

Once in Rodney's chamber, Simon carefully treated Rodney's wounds. Kincaid aided by fetching water or whatever Simon needed. True enough, mostly bruising and some small gashes, but overall, mild compared to others. In his capacity, Simon served as legal defense for a noble prisoner. For security, Simon locked the door to Rodney's chamber.

"Place a guard to watch him. He needs to rest undisturbed," he told Kincaid.

A maid intercepted him on his return to the scholar's office. She quietly handed him a note, made a quick curtsey, and departed. Rona! Simon changed course to the Queen's chamber. Since Eleanor's death, his being seen with the Queen became commonplace. After a brief knock by the guard to announce him, Simon was admitted.

"You wanted to see me, Majesty?"

Rona waved for Simon to sit with her on the sofa. "Is it true about your assistant? Did Rodney poison Eleanor?"

"No. The word of that kitchen maid put them on his scent, but I managed to convince Pekka otherwise." His eyes narrowed in consideration. "In fact, I'm not certain the maid even mentioned Rodney. He may be a scapegoat. An attempt to cover for the real perpetrators."

"Surely you don't suspect Pekka of wanting me dead?" Anxiety made her voice shake.

Simon shook his head. "Doubtful. He became disturbed by Eleanor's death and denied sending the venison rolls. Falco, on the other hand ..." He didn't finish, seeing that she understood. He then noticed they were alone. "Have you no maid?"

"Pekka has not allowed a replacement to tend my needs."
Troubled by the answer, Simon made search of the room. Curious, Rona watched. "What are you doing?"

"Making sure all is secure."

"Lieutenant Kincaid's men are very efficient. The lieutenant is here each morning and evening to issue instructions to new guards. They inspect everyone who enters."

He sat back on the sofa. "What of food? Who brings it?"

"I have eaten little, save when we are together." She regarded his studious pondering. "You believe there may be another attempt on my life?"

He tried to soften his reply. "I'm afraid it can't be ruled out. Order the servant who brings food to test everything, including the drink. Leave nothing to chance."

She squeezed his hand. "I can say the same for you, my dear Simon. We both must survive until ..." She couldn't finish.

"With the Almighty's help, *all* of us will survive. In the Lord we must place our trust. Keep the faith, my lady."

Chapter 27

OVER THE NEXT THREE DAYS, CONOR'S ENERGY improved by eating nightly roasted meat provided by Rafe along with uninterrupted sleep. On the fourth day, they reached the outskirts of Bramdon, where they again camped beside the river. Rafe caught four small fish while the twins fetched mushrooms and berries for their supper. Jayson made a quick trip into the city to buy cheese, bread, and sausage.

Conor knelt beside the river to splash water on his face and hair. He tried to scrub the dirt from his cheeks and forehead.

"Isn't it cold?" asked Jayson.

"Invigorating is the word I'd use." Conor sniffed his clothes. "Perhaps I should submerge in the river to get the stench off."

"You'd freeze overnight," said Rafe in a light teasing tone.

Conor slicked back wet hair and sat beside the fire. "At least my hair feels better." He scratched his face. "I can't wait to shave."

"Neither can I." Jayson felt the two-week growth on his face.

"I think you look better clean-shaven," Winnie told Jayson.

He flashed a pleased grin, then frowned as he again scratched his face. "I can't stand the itching. How do you tolerate whiskers?" he asked Rafe.

Rafe shrugged. "I've grown accustomed to the beard. There is no need to shave when one lives in the wilderness. No ladies to impress." He winked at Winnie, who blushed at the meaning.

Jayson again grinned and continued the teasing questioning. "Doesn't it get lonely?"

Rafe inspected the fish before answering. Not done yet, so he returned it to the fire. "At times, perhaps."

"That's when he visits us," said Zoe, chuckling. "For food and company."

Rafe laughed. "My duties keep me busy." He again inspected the fish. "Finished. Hand me the bowls." He distributed the fish to Conor, Winnie, and Jayson and kept one for himself.

"Your uncle mostly comes for the black mead," said Zane.

Conor nearly choked on a fish bone from laughing.

"You, too, general. I've watched you both outdrink my father," Zane continued.

Although amused by the story, Winnie gave Conor her flask to help wash down the fish.

Jayson widely smiled. "Black mead sounds like something I'd like to try."

Rafe waved a parental finger at Jayson. "You're too young to drink."

"In case you haven't noticed, I'm a grown man of twenty-two," Jayson said, still smiling.

Rafe rolled his eyes. "Too young to hold your drink."

Conor laughed. "Save it, lad. Your uncle knows what he's talking about."

Jayson flashed a contrary grin. "We'll see once we reach Morgrath."

"Speaking of, how long will it take to get there?" Winnie asked

"About two weeks," answered Jayson.

"That long?" Winnie asked, surprised.

Jayson nodded. "From here, we go back the way we came."

"That means going through the Katkova Pass again," said Rafe, none too happy.

Zane moved to sit beside Rafe. "What about Aois Forest?"

The question made Rafe stop eating and toss a look of concern at the Piskie. "You know what danger it could mean for you and Zoe?"

"Aois Forest?" asked Jayson, intrigued. "I don't recall that name on any map."

Rafe ignored Jayson, his attention focused on Zane when the Piskie spoke. "Balor is dead, so we may be safe." Seeing Rafe still not convinced, Zane added, "My father needs to know Thorndel is exposed and the jewel recovered. *Time* is pressing. Going through Aois will cut almost a week off the journey."

Zoe added her voice to Zane's argument. "You said the general needs mother's remedies to completely recover. Why make him travel further than necessary?"

"Uncle?"

"Rafe?" Winnie spoke the same time as Jayson.

Rafe placed down his bowl. "Very well. We go through Aois. May the Almighty protect us as we go."

For two days, they traveled due east from Brandom. Late on the morning of the third day, Connor drew his horse beside Rafe to observe a large, dense forest across the meadow.

Jayson stood in the stirrups to survey the surroundings. "From my calculations of landmarks, this is Maidenhead Forest."

"That is the name in our tongue. The Piskies call it Aois." Rafe's brow deeply furrowed as he focused intently on the forest.

Zane rode behind Jayson. "*Aois* means *ancient* in our tongue," he explained.

Conor noticed Rafe's scrutiny of the horizon. "What is it about Aois that troubles you?"

"Aois is the home of goblins," said Rafe.

"Ah," said Conor with understanding. "Nasty creatures."

"Balor is dead," insisted Zane. "His control of goblins and Thorndel is finished."

"Father told stories of how the goblins were friends of Piskies before the war," said Zoe. "Maybe that, too, has changed with Balor's death."

Rafe pursed his lips in consideration as he continued to stare at Aois. "Not a risk I really want to take to find out."

"You said the Almighty will protect us as we go through," said Winnie.

"Aye," Rafe confirmed. "Stay close. Like Shadowspire, light is dim in Aois." He took the lead with Winnie following, then Conor, and Jayson.

Thick branches of large ancient trees created a canopy over the forest floor. Dim light streaked through the branches to expose mushrooms, moss, and ferns that thrived in the dark and damp environment. It recently rained, as told by the dripping of water from overhead.

Rafe carefully steered his horse through the tightly bunched trees. They rode single file.

Moaning and low howling noises made Winnie nervous. "What is making such noise?"

Zane glanced around. "The old trees creak with the wind."

"Creaking, aye, but not the howling." Rafe gently released the reins to ready his bow. "Watch for goblins," he warned.

As they rode deeper into Aois, the canopy grew thicker, further reducing the light. More low howling. Rafe raised his bow in anticipation of an attack. A sudden loud roar startled the horses. Rafe steadied his horse when it bucked. Winnie's horse reared, throwing both her and Zoe. Conor turned his horse in time to avoid trampling them. Jayson's horse bucked, which sent Zane falling off into a tree.

Goblins charged them with clubs raised. Several held torches as well. The bright unexpected light temporarily blinded Rafe. He turned aside to regain his sight when a club knocked him from the saddle.

Conor shook his head to avoid the light, squinted, and reached for his sword in time to deflect a club. Jayson called for Zane. The Piskie quickly stood and took Jayson's hand to remount. The horse shied again at the sight of a swinging club. Jayson managed to steady the animal, so he and Zane remained seated.

Winnie reached to help Zoe stand when, "Look out!" Zoe warned.

Winnie turned. As she did so, light from a goblin's torch struck the ruby necklace, which had slipped out from under the collar when she fell. A burst of red light came from the ruby and blinded the goblins. The beasts halted.

"Scrutern!" one shouted. It dropped the club and knelt with its head lowered to touch the ground. The other goblins mimicked the submissive posture.

Winnie stood frozen in confusion at goblins kneeling all around her.

Conor quickly dismounted, grabbed Winnie, and urged her to mount. He helped Zoe up behind Winnie. "Go!" he shouted at Rafe and Jayson. He slapped the rump of Winnie's horse to go! He hastily mounted to follow.

Rafe pushed his horse as fast as possible through the dense forest. Several times, they slowed the horses to navigate a steep gorge or narrow passage.

Winnie forced her mind to concentrate on steering her horse over the rough and dark terrain. Questions filled her mind about the startling sight of red light coming from the ruby and goblins falling to their knees as if paying homage. Unfortunately, the remaining journey through Aois did not allow time for conversation.

Just after twilight, they reached the end of the forest. Rafe led them to a stream where the exhausted horses greedily drank.

Winnie stood beside her horse. "What happened back there? The light. The goblins."

"They recognized Scrutern," said Zane in a simple answer.

Winnie smirked in annoyance. "I know that. I mean the light and them kneeling to me."

Conor and Rafe exchanged wary glances before Conor spoke in a neutral tone. "Jewels naturally reflect light. And as Zane said, the goblins recognized Scrutern, Jewel of the Piskies."

"So, they knelt because of it, not me?"

Conor softly smiled. "Be at ease. We are safely out of Aois. After a night's rest, we continue to Morgrath."

Preoccupied with thoughts, Winnie silently went about preparations for camp, then eating. Sight of the goblins' strange reaction stirred up images and conversations over the past several months. Somehow everything connected to the royal jewel— *Scrutern* to the Piskies. The visions she witnessed when passing through Shadowspire struck her to the core. She became part of Orrin's future. Yet something deeper made her wonder if *she* was connected to the jewel.

The others bedded down for the night. Winnie poked the fire for heat. She focused on the flames when Conor sat beside her.

"You're still troubled about the goblins, aren't you?" he said.

She glanced along her shoulder at him. Her voice was low so as not disturb the others. "It was not a reflection. Light came *from* the jewel."

He poked the fire. "Scrutern is not a normal jewel."

"The royal jewel. But why do I have part of it? And why go to Thorndel for the rest?"

Conor's face drew tight in deep consideration. Now, he poked at the fire to avoid replying.

Frustrated at being denied answers, she took the stick from him. "What are you not telling me? What is everyone not telling me?" He stared at her with compassionate regret. "Papa?"

"We can't speak in the open." He forestalled her objection. "I promise, once we reach Morgrath, I will tell you everything. Answer all your questions. Now, get some sleep. I am well enough to take the first watch."

Winnie snuggled under the bedroll with her back to Conor, yet still near the fire. She removed the jewel from the collar. She turned it in various directions to catch some firelight. At a brief spark, she covered the jewel by closing her hand. She waited, but no reaction. She slowly opened her hand to regard the ruby. Vision of the Queen with outstretched hand came to mind. *Come, my child*, the words echoed in memory. She clenched the jewel and screwed her eyes shut against the sudden wave of emotions brought on by those words. *It can't be! How could it?* She argued with herself. She managed an unobserved glance at Conor.

She held the jewel against her chest and silently prayed, *"Lord, show me the truth."* She muttered, as if answering herself, "Morgrath."

Chapter 28

ESPITE SOME IMPROVEMENT IN STAMINA, BY THE END OF each day's travel, Conor was exhausted. Dinner of fish, hare, or fowl provided some needed nourishment, but not enough to fully recover from weeks in a dungeon on bread and water. Humans also ate cheese, bread, and sausage, which Jayson bought at Bramdon. Zane and Zoe foraged for their food of pine nuts, chestnuts, berries, and mushrooms.

Rafe and Conor rode side-by-side in the lead. Rafe noticed Conor sag in the saddle. "We will reach the village shortly."

"Good. Because I can't go much further without good food and lots of rest."

"You've done remarkably well considering."

Conor took a careful glance back at Winnie and Jayson. Winnie related to Jayson the details of how she came to the village. Zane and Zoe added stories about defeating a werebear and nearly drowning in the river. Jayson posed questions about Morgrath that Zoe and Zane willingly answered. Seeing them engaged, Conor inquired of Rafe.

"Have you or Finn told Winnie why Rona gave her the necklace?"

"Only that she is the keeper because Falco cannot know of its existence." When Conor frowned with disapproval at the answer, Rafe added, "We did not think it our place. At least not until we knew your fate. She never believed you dead."

"Fair enough." Conor glanced back at hearing laughter. Facing forward, he said, "The goblin's reaction has brought up many questions. She knows I haven't told her everything. I promised to do so when we reach the village."

Rafe clapped Conor's shoulder. "You have mine and Finn's full support. And I dare say, Burdock, once he learns the facts."

"Will *she* accept it, is the question.

"I wondered that, too, at first. However, she proved her mettle by standing against Falco and Pekka when questioned about searching for you. At that moment, she found the courage she never knew she had." Rafe grinned and said, "And here we are."

They entered the village from the north bank of the river. Twilight shone through the bare tree limbs. Piskies recognized them and called a greeting. Zane and Zoe had Jayson and Winnie stop so they could dismount and receive a welcome. Rafe drew rein near the twins' home. The humans dismounted.

Jayson regarded the village in wide-eyed wonder. "What a lovely place."

"Piskies are master craftsmen, who incorporate nature in everything," Conor said.

"Words spoken by a voice I never thought to hear again!" Finn happily said. "Conor!"

Conor warmly smiled and embraced the Piskie patriarch. "And dear Mora." He embraced her too.

Mora wiped joyous tears from her eyes. "Conor! You look like a battered scarecrow!"

"Dungeons aren't known for the best food and accommodations."

Mora grabbed his hand. "Come! I know just what you need."

Winnie avoided bumping into Burdock when she followed Conor and Mora.

Finn firmly forestalled Burdock from speaking. "You will raise no objection to hosting General Briggs and his daughter. Is that understood?"

"I would not begrudge the general anything. But who is this other human male?"

Rafe placed an arm around Jayson's shoulder. "My nephew, Jayson Clarke." He then spoke to Jayson. "This is Elder Burdock. High Priest of the Piskies."

"Pleased to meet you, sir." Jayson made a short bow.

Burdock fought a frown. "Well, since you are Rafe's nephew, I bid you welcome." He spoke sideways to Finn. "They can't stay very long."

"They will stay as long as I deem necessary," Finn firmly countered.

Rafe nudged Jayson inside the front door. He spoke to Burdock. "There is news that affects all Piskies. Balor is dead. And the jewel recovered."

Burdock gaped up at the ranger in stunned silence. Finn, too shocked, yet found voice to speak. "Are you certain?"

"I shot him in defense of my comrades when he made a move to strike. Thorndel is free of his influence. There is more tell, but first rest and recovery are needed. Especially Conor. Who is in possession of the jewel?"

"Indeed," said Burdock in his most agreeable tone yet. "I must consult the scrolls and pray for wisdom on how to proceed." He bowed to Finn and Rafe before he scurried off.

Rafe chuckled. "That should keep him busy for a while."

"Soon, the entire village will know." Finn motioned him inside.

Zane and Zoe arrived and received instructions from Mora to fetch water for Conor's bath. Part of the main room sectioned off with sheets for privacy. The Piskie size tub was long but shallow. The hot water with healing herbs reached to Conor's waist.

Rafe took Winnie and Jayson on a tour of the village while Conor enjoyed a soothing soak. Piskies clamored for news about Balor's demise. Rafe retold his version of the battle inside the grand hall. Piskies gasped in awe at his captivating mannerisms. Even Jayson and Winnie listened with great interest since they were not present for the conflict. When he finished, a Piskie elder gave Rafe a large tankard.

"To quench your thirst after such a dramatic narrative."

Rafe drank half the tankard before he smacked his lips with pleasure. "Nectar of the forest."

"Is that black mead?" Jayson asked the Piskie.

"Aye, lad."

"My uncle told me there is nothing comparable to its quality in all of Orrin."

"Well then! You shall have some." The Piskie gave Jayson a tankard.

Rafe swallowed the remainder of the mead. "Oh, I don't think he handles it."

"Watch me." Jayson completely drained the tankard. He smirked in triumph at Rafe yet said to the Piskie, "My uncle is right. I've not tasted anything like this. It is delicious."

The Piskie beamed with pride. "Have another."

Rafe grew concerned. "Easy, lad."

Jayson's self-satisfied smile grew. "I proved my point. I intend to enjoy this tankard."

"Lassie." The Piskie gave Winnie a tankard.

They sat around a bonfire answering questions about their journey. Not until Zoe arrived to inform them that the food was ready did they leave the gathering. Conor was bathed, shaven, and wearing clean clothes that fit his human body perfectly.

"Where did you get the clothes? Those are too big for Piskies," asked Jayson, puzzled.

"The general is a frequent guest." Finn's reply did little to answer Jayson's confusion.

"I left some here. Never know when an article might become ripped or soiled beyond repair when traveling."

"Come, eat," said Mora.

"Fish. And quail?" said Winnie, somewhat amazed. "But Piskies don't eat meat."

"This is specially prepared to help Conor's recovery. You'll notice the abundance of root vegetables and bread," Mora replied.

"And roasted mushrooms," added Zoe with glee.

"The one that tastes like chicken. I've come to enjoy those," said Winnie.

After a blessing, the meal continued with casual chatter. Winnie kept looking at Conor. The camaraderie between him,

Rafe, and the Piskies was something she heard about. Witnessing the interaction raised more questions. He caught her eye.

"Enjoy and rest tonight. Tomorrow." He kindly smiled and winked.

She shyly grinned and returned to eating.

Curious at the cryptic exchange, Jayson leaned toward Winnie. "What about tomorrow?"

She gave him a reassuring smile. "I will share what I learn. No more secrets. Now, pass me another mushroom."

Hearing her mention the word *secret* made Conor and Rafe exchange wary glances. Finn also joined the clandestine visual exchange. He took the cue to speak.

"I'm certain you are all very tired. Zoe and Zane sleep in that loft. Jayson and Rafe can share with Zane while Winnie bunk with Zoe." Mora pointed. "Finn and I are in the other loft. However, we will vacate for Conor."

"Oh, no, that's not necessary. A pallet or small mattress will serve me," said Conor.

"Nonsense! You need a good night's sleep in a soft bed. And I'll take no argument."

"I yield to your judgement." Conor made a formal nod of submission.

Winnie laughed in amazement. "How did you get him to give in so quickly?" she asked Mora.

"Now, child, don't act so surprised," began Conor in a lighthearted tone. "I did the same with Arabella. And you know it." He waved a fork at her.

"Sometimes I wish you'd yield that quickly to me," she retorted in the same tone.

Conor sat back. His teasing expression changed to thoughtful. "I might just do that in the near future."

The abrupt change baffled Winnie. "Papa?"

He quickly reverted to jovial. "Nothing. A moment of parental reflection. Now, I think Mora is correct, and we all need sleep."

"Not before a cup of black mead to help you sleep." Finn rose from the table.

"None for me, thank you," Jayson politely declined.

Rafe nudged Conor. "I told you he couldn't hold his drink. Two tankards and he's done."

"No," said Jayson in sarcastic dispute. "I didn't want to publicly show you up in front of your adoring audience."

"Lad, that sounds like a challenge. Eh, Conor?"

Conor laughed and threw his hands up. "Leave me out. I don't have the stomach for more than a single cup right now."

"And you shouldn't until you are stronger," Mora advised. "Nor will you corrupt your nephew. At least not under my roof," she chastised Rafe.

"One cup for each," Finn told Mora. He poured and distributed the mead to Rafe, Conor, and Jayson. He raised his cup. "May the Almighty grant us success."

Rafe and Conor raised their cups. "Amen!" they echoed.

Jayson lifted his cup and made a quiet agreement. In one gulp, they downed the mead.

"Now, off to bed." Conor rose. "Good night." He kissed Winnie's cheek.

Zoe carried a lantern as Winnie accompanied her to the loft. Inside, the quaint room contained a single bed, chair, side table, trunk, and small brazier. Zoe used a match to take flame from the lantern to light the brazier for heat.

"The bed doesn't look big enough for both of us," said Winnie.

"You'll sleep on the bed. There is a small pallet underneath that I'll use." Zoe moved the pallet on the other side of the brazier and took a blanket from the trunk. She used a pillow from the bed. She spoke as she prepared the pallet. "We each keep an extra pallet in our rooms for company. Other Piskies." She paused. "Although, it's not very often other tribes visit. In fact, it's been years."

Winnie heard Zoe's remorse. "Maybe now that Balor is dead, life among Piskies will change for the better."

Zoe sat on the pallet. "Oh, a great many things will change for all of Orrin now that he is dead and Scrutern recovered."

Winnie grew thoughtful. "The how is what concerns me."

Zoe happily smiled as she nestled under the covers. "You don't need to worry about that. Not anymore. Goodnight." She extinguished the lantern.

Winnie lay with her knees bent so her feet didn't hang off the bed. Moonlight filtered in through the room's tiny window. She pushed aside the questions that plagued her mind since leaving Thorndel. "…*rest tonight. Tomorrow,*" she recalled Conor's smile and wink. "Tomorrow," she whispered to herself and closed her eyes.

Chapter 29

WINNIE WAS SURPRISED TO DISCOVER SHE SLEPT through the night undisturbed. In fact, Zoe had to wake her for breakfast. Daylight replaced moonlight coming through the window. Winnie took a few moments to prepare for the day before going downstairs with Zoe. Conor, Rafe, Jayson, Finn, and Mora sat at the table.

"Well, the sleepyhead wakes," Conor teased.

She smirked and took a seat beside Jayson across from Conor. "You know I rarely sleep late," she shot back, to which he laughed. "Are you feeling better this morning?"

"Aye. A soothing bath, good meal, and soft bed do wonders for one's health."

"Enough to talk after breakfast?"

Conor paused in reaching for bread to gaze directly at Winnie. "As I promised. Now, eat. Quail eggs." He passed her a plate.

"Jayson shaved," Rafe told Winnie in a light-hearted tone.

"I noticed when I sat down," she matched his tone.

"Impressive." Rafe winked at her.

She ate to cover a blush.

Zane entered the house. "The village is all abuzz with news about Balor and Scrutern's return. Mostly, they are interested in Winnie—"

Finn loudly coughed and sent a stern glare to his son. Zane balked upon realizing he spoke out of turn. Sheepish, he sat at the table to eat.

Finn's interruptions and Zane's timidity annoyed Winnie. "What about me?"

"I don't think you can wait any longer," Rafe told Conor.

Conor sat back to regard Winnie from under furrowed brows of contemplation.

"Papa?" asked Winnie, concerned by his expression.

Conor's eyes immediately swelled with tears. He lowered his head to regain his composure. "Lord, give me strength," he muttered in prayer.

In supportive sympathy, Mora squeezed his hand. "He has all along."

Conor raised his head to look across at Winnie. "You have called me *Papa* since you could first speak. But … I am not your father by blood."

Shocked, Winnie's face immediately turned pale. Jayson quickly placed an arm about her in support, yet his eyes stayed heavy upon Conor.

"What are you saying?" Jayson demanded.

"The truth."

"Hear him, lad," Rafe sternly said when Jayson grew angry.

"I … I don't understand," Winnie could barely speak.

"The day you were born, Arabella and I were tasked with raising you in secret. We lost our newborn daughter the same night the Queen went into labor."

Winnie's eyes grew wide with astonishment at the mention of the *Queen*. Conor continued.

"Pekka yearned for a son. Two stillborn daughters sent him into a rage against Rona, but her third pregnancy gave him hope. Alas, another girl, was born. Only this one alive."

"Me?" Winnie asked in a breathy voice.

Conor nodded. "Before Pekka could be told, Rona asked us to switch our dead newborn for you." He saw recognition on her face. "Aye. You are the rightful heir to the throne. My future queen." His voice cracked.

Rafe added, "If Falco discovered your identity, you would be dead. And if he possessed the entire jewel, he could negate any challenge, even from one of royal blood. What you wear is the fragment of Scrutern, Ennis broke to protect your claim."

"Balor also wore the remainder of Scrutern as a necklace. A clever way to hide it in plain sight. Fortunately, Tolbert didn't recognize it like I did. Now, it is returned to its rightful place." Conor motioned to Finn.

Overcome, Winnie shut her eyes. "That's why I saw her beckoning. She meant me!"

"What? Who?" asked Conor.

Winnie took several breaths to calm down. "In Shadowspire I saw a vision of the Queen standing beside the throne. She held out her hand and spoke *Come, my child.* She did this twice. I realized I saw the future of Orrin, but not that she called to me. Someone else."

Finn nodded with confirmation. "The Almighty uses Shadowspire to reveal the truth about each person who passes through. Only if they survive, can they approach Thorndel."

Winnie removed the necklace from under the collar. "The goblins *did* kneel in homage to me because of this."

Conor nodded. "And you were correct; light came from the jewel, not a reflection."

"Scrutern responds to the one it acknowledges as the rightful ruler," said Finn.

"That is why the villagers are curious about you," Zane told Winnie. He then spoke to Finn. "Burdock learned the truth from your entry in the ledger about Conor and Rafe."

Finn wryly grinned. "And from that, he surmised Princess Winifred's identity."

Seeing Winnie again overcome, Mora fetched a tankard of black mead. With a soft smile, she encouraged her to drink.

Winnie drank half the tankard before she could speak again. "Why did she wait until my eighteenth birthday to give me the necklace?"

"The time had come. You reached legal age," replied Conor.

Jayson appeared confused. "Why go to Thorndel for the jewel if Winnie had it all along?"

Finn answered. "The entire jewel is needed for the crown. Along with Piskie approval. For it is *our* sacred jewel, given us by the Almighty, to crown the next Monarch of Orrin and ensure unity among the races."

Conor clarified: "Pekka was never supposed to be king. He is the youngest of three sons, and the most volatile and ambitious.

Although never proven, it is believed he killed his two eldest brothers to assume the throne. As the youngest brother of Pekka's father, Ennis survived. Pekka never considered him a threat due to his limited mental state. Yet, we," he said as he nodded to Rafe, "knew different. Ennis pretended to save his life. He ultimately saved your life when he broke off a piece of Scrutern."

"He did that to stop Pekka's bargain with Balor," said Finn.

"He may not have known about Winnie at the time, but the Almighty used it to serve a greater purpose," said Mora.

"Aye," Finn agreed.

Conor continued explaining to Winnie. "It is also rumored that Pekka poisoned his first wife for failure to produce a male heir. He married Rona, believing a younger woman could provide a son. Alas, she suffered two stillbirths before you, and two miscarriages after your birth. What we didn't anticipate was that as you grew older, people remarked on your resemblance to Rona with such light-colored hair. Even Falco voiced suspicion. We tried to deflect it because Arabella was also blonde, although not as striking as you and Rona. So, when you turned six, Arabella brought you to help serve the Queen. This was done for several reasons, first, that by becoming a servant of the royal house, you would be protected from further scrutiny and Falco's machinations. Other reasons were for Rona to watch you grow and teach you royal etiquette. It also led to a broader plan to protect the crown and your future. Prince Ennis and the Queen recruited multiple people they trusted to facilitate this venture."

Hearing Ennis mentioned several times made Winnie hold up the necklace. "She gave me the necklace after returning from the prince's room. He had just died."

"After your birth, Ennis made the necklace from the broken piece. The remainder of the jewel was to be returned to Finn before either Falco or Pekka could learn your identity."

Rafe scowled in anger. "I never reached Morgrath. Balor intercepted me and took it!"

"You were tasked with returning it?" asked Jayson, astonished.

"Aye. Simon and I faked the argument so I could freely leave Highburn without arousing suspicion to my true mission."

Jayson's amazement increased. "My father is part of this?"

Rafe nodded. "Along with me, Conor, Arabella, and Eleanor. All bound by an oath."

"I found Rafe nearly dead from his encounter with Balor," began Finn. "It took months for Mora to nurse him back to health. To cover for his mission and keep our discovery secret, we convinced him to become the Ranger of Morgrath."

Rafe spoke to Jayson with a twinge of regret. "Although news of my death was exaggerated for security, I barely survived. The beard," he paused with a distressed sigh, "hides the painful remaining wounds from that encounter."

Conor looked directly at Winnie. "All our actions are done to protect Orrin's future queen."

Overwhelmed to the point of tears, Winnie hurried to leave.

"No!" Mora stopped Conor from following. "She must come to terms with this herself."

Jayson wrestled with the startling revelations. Angry, he slammed his fists on the table. "Why did my father never tell me?"

"To protect you," Rafe said.

"I'm a grown man!"

"Now. But you were four when Winnie was born. And a boy of ten when I left on my mission. So, save your outrage, lad. Simon has trained you to take his place. It is that training and learning Winnie needs to help deal with this." Rafe poured mead into a tankard and pushed it toward Jayson. "Drink and calm down."

Too annoyed to drink, Jayson left. Outside, he saw Winnie on the side of the creek surrounded by Piskies. He could tell by her posture and profile that she was uncomfortable. Small wonder after what she just learned. *After what we both learned!* The voice from Shadowspire echoed in his mind.

"And if what you seek costs that love? What then?"

He heard his answer: *"If it restores the general and gives her peace, I will be content."*

Conor is alive, and Winnie is thrilled to have him restored. But this? The change for her is immense, while he remains a scholar. The revelation also impacts the future of Orrin. Because of that, everyone involved must consider the ramifications personally and nationally.

He noticed Winnie leave the Piskies and disappear behind some trees. She needed time alone to think, as did he.

Winnie barely contained her anxiety in wanting to be alone while dealing with Piskies, excited about a new beginning for Orrin. Finally, she managed to reach a bend in the creek at the edge of the village. She sat on the bank with her back against an oak tree. In her hand, she held the necklace. The connection she felt to the jewel since Thorndel proved greater than she anticipated. Memories of childhood raced across her mind. She felt happy with her *parents*. A famed general as father and the queen's lady of the wardrobe as her mother. She remembered the first day of helping the Queen. Fear and nervousness made a six-year-old fumble some items. Yet even then, the Queen treated her with kindness and gentle encouragement. In all her years of service, the Queen never uttered a cross word to her. She even kept her very close after her *mother*—Arabella—died. Suddenly, their recent conversations at Highburn began to make sense. Tears swelled when she recalled the vision from Shadowspire. *Come, my child.* She pulled her knees up to her chest and wept. She cried until she had no tears left. Exhausted, she fell into a light sleep.

"Conor regrets there wasn't an easier way to tell you."

Winnie saw Rafe sitting beside her. "Why didn't you tell me?"

"It wasn't my place. At least not until I knew Conor's fate. We—Finn and me—had a plan should the worst happen. Conor is also hurting. He held the truth for so long knowing this day would come."

Winnie sat up. Her face showed understanding. "His challenge at Shadowspire!"

"What?"

"The voice spoke to him. That's what Zane said. I couldn't hear it, but I heard Papa ... *Conor's* response. *'I made a solemn pledge. To that I hold,'* he said. The oath you spoke of."

Rafe nodded. "I, too, was challenged in Shadowspire about the pledge we made that night." He sat up straight, a hint of pride in his tone. "Your acceptance of the truth shows that the pledge was worth taking. Your Highness." He bowed his head in reverence. He grinned when he looked above her head and stood to leave.

Curious, Winnie looked to her left. Jayson. "Don't you bow to me, too," she complained.

"I will if you command."

She scowled and made motion for him to sit.

"I know this was not easy to hear."

"Not easy? My whole world changed in an instant."

"No, your whole world has always been Highburn. True, a change in status, but not who you are in heart and character."

"Are those the words of a scholar or a friend?"

Jayson winced in sorrow at the question. "Both. For I am who I am. I'm sorry you see it as two different aspects of the same person." Hurt crept into his voice.

"I didn't mean it. I am grateful for your friendship."

"Friend," Jayson murmured.

Winnie heard disappointment. "You regret our friendship?"

"No!" Jayson took her hand. He visibly searched for words. "Your change in status may not alter your personality, but it does …"

"Does what?" She gently touched his shoulder. "Jayson?"

"I love you," he blurted out. "There I said it! Though now it cannot be." He quickly left.

Another prick to the heart! Winnie leaned back against the tree. "Oh, Lord!" she bemoaned. "Help me find the strength and wisdom to deal with all this."

Chapter 30

INNIE SPENT THE REMAINDER OF THE MORNING IN solitary contemplation beside the creek. So many thoughts, emotions, and conflicting conclusions swirled in her brain. She considered everyone she knew and how they impacted her childhood and current events. Silent tears fell when thinking about Arabella and Conor, her parents in heart. A change in status didn't alter feelings and strong attachments. Although they knew her identity, they embraced her as their own child. Never a hint of anything different about her or what lay ahead. She wiped away tears in recalling Conor's visible upset when telling her the truth. He wasn't a general obeying his sovereign in the performance of duty, but a man who deeply loved her. She always felt that love, now it became manifested in the most unselfish manner—yielding up a child to her future.

Suddenly, Jayson's admission of love echoed in her ears. Hearing those words again stirred feelings in her heart she didn't know existed. True, she considered him a close friend, one she went to for advice or just to talk. But love? The emotion became one among many she keenly felt during her introspection.

The Piskies entered her life in a most unexpected manner. Yet, in hindsight, she could see the Almighty's hand directing her path. Recalling conversations with them, she realized they knew her identity from the moment she spoke her name, and Mora discovered the necklace. All the sacrifices everyone made were to secure her destiny.

She heard the voice whisper the words spoken in Shadowspire: *"Look beyond the reason you believe to what truly lies in your heart."*

"Since Thorndel, I have sensed a deeper connection." She touched the necklace. Tears swelled. "She is my real mother."

"Now you know the truth. What will you do?" the voice whispered in her ear. She reaffirmed the answer she gave at Shadowspire. "For the sake of Orrin, let Providence guide me."

"The Almighty is with you." The wispy voice turned into an audible male speaking.

"I hope I'm not interrupting you."

Recognizing Conor's voice, Winne rose to embrace him. "I will still call you *papa* because I cannot give that endearment to anyone else. Not so wicked a man as the King!"

He tilted her head up. "In private, you may call me what you like. Yet once you are crowned, publicly, I must be General Briggs."

"Everyone at Highburn knows me as your daughter."

"Everyone also knows Jayson as Simon's son, but he still calls his father *Lord Chancellor* in public." He flashed a wry grin. "And you know court etiquette."

She made a small smile that did reach her eyes.

Conor closely regarded her. "Something still troubles you."

"I've spent hours considering everybody in my life and how all their actions surround me. Yet, there are details about Ma … *Arabella's* death you haven't told me. You even mentioned threats by Captain Tolbert."

Conor's face told of great sorrow. "I couldn't tell you the truth because you were only ten at the time. It is believed she was a victim of poison mixed with mulled cider that was meant for Rona. Only Rona felt unwell and refused food and drink. Arabella … well, it happened quickly."

"I thought food and drink were tested before the Queen ate."

"Aye. Arabella must have believed it was safe to partake of it."

Winnie thought back to the incident. "Ma … Arabella sent me to the laundry to fetch a specific dress for the Queen that the maid failed to bring. When I came back, there was so much commotion in the hall." She looked at him with tear-filled eyes. "You stopped me from going inside the room."

He held her. "It was not a sight for a child."

She sniffled. "You said the poison was meant for Rona. Why? She's so sweet."

"To prevent the birth of an heir. Those miscarriages she suffered after your birth showed her capable of having children. That wouldn't do for someone as ambitious as Falco. Protecting you became paramount should any future attempt succeed." He tilted her head. "That's when we enacted the plan to send Rafe with the jewel back to Finn. We only knew it failed when I came here in search of Rafe and found him nearly killed by Balor." Conor's face hardened in thought. "How Falco learned that Balor possessed the jewel is unknown. Since then, he dispatched various men to find Thorndel and retrieve it. When all those failed, he sent me." He gently wiped the tears from her cheeks. "I hope that answers your question about Arabella. She loved you." His voice slightly cracked.

"And I loved her."

"Now, if there aren't any more immediate questions, I came to find you, since the afternoon is upon us."

"Is it?" she asked in wonder.

"Aye. You've been away all morning."

"Oh, I hadn't realized the time. Where is Burdock's home?"

Conor took her hand to lead her through the village to another carved oak trunk. The house on either side of the trunk was considerably smaller than Finn's house. The men and Piskies stopped talking to acknowledge Winnie's arrival.

"Your Highness!" Burdock deeply bowed. "My sincerest apologies for my awful behavior. I had no idea I was in the presence of our future queen."

Winnie simply flashed a humorless smile at the awkward apology. "My fath ... General Briggs told me that you are making plans." She corrected herself in mid-sentence.

"In this company, you can call me what you like," Conor kindly said with a smile.

Finn began the explanation. "It requires boldness, as we must reveal ourselves to humans. Myself as King of the Piskies, and Burdock as our High Priest. Only by declaring our support of you as rightful heir can we hope to thwart Falco and confront Pekka with the truth."

"Our presence and confirmation are needed to establish a legitimate sovereign. It is why we were appointed guardians of Thorndel and Scrutern by the Almighty," said Burdock.

"This means returning to Highburn. You must be ready to confront them like before. Only this time, as heir and not mistress of the wardrobe." Rafe's resolute look matched his voice.

Winnie understood the reference. "Won't that be dangerous for Finn and Burdock to boldly walk into the castle? Pekka wanted to kill Zoe and Zane."

"Not if we use the secret lake passage," said Conor. "Remember how you used to sneak out to go fishing thinking I didn't know?" he teased her.

Jayson chuckled, to which Winnie said to him, "You came with me a few times." She then turned back to Conor. "You can't get to that side of the castle without a boat. That's why I left through the main gate."

Conor smiled, confident. "I have resources in town."

Jayson regained his serious demeanor to add his part of the plan. "Once inside, I will contact my father to learn what has happened since we left."

Winnie frowned in dispute. "I still think it's dangerous for the Piskies to be seen. Sergeant Cadel had Zoe and Zane wrap their heads with sashes to hide their hair and ears."

"Already considered," said Conor. "We will use one of the horses to travel in a covered wagon. I will drive with you and the Piskies inside. Rafe and Jayson mounted, while the fourth horse is tied to the rear of the wagon, should we need another mount."

For several moments, a heavy silence fell as Winnie considered the plan. The time to act came quicker than anticipated. Then again, nothing happened the way she thought it would since she originally left to search for Conor. *To search for the truth. And you have found it. Along with your purpose,* said the voice in her mind. Accompanying the voice came a surge of strength.

Winnie withdrew and lifted the necklace. After a brief glance at the jewel, she spoke with determination. "When do we leave?"

Conor lowered his head to hide a proud smile.

"General?"

He squared his shoulders at hearing her formal address. "We only need to gather supplies and fit our disguises, which should take a day or two to finish."

"What of you? Will you be recovered enough to proceed?" she asked, concerned.

Conor softly smiled. "Aye. There is no time to waste. Besides, riding in a wagon is much easier than traveling on horseback."

She felt their gaze of expectation. She gave an assenting nod. "Very well. We leave when ready." She grinned at Jayson. "Master Scholar, can I beg a moment of your time?"

"Of course." He followed her outside and into the shadow of the house, out of public view.

"Jayson," she began with tender regard. "I thought about what you said before you left—"

Jayson raised a hand to interrupt her. "Forgive me, Highness. I spoke out of turn."

"No! You spoke from the heart. I hadn't given my feelings towards you a name. First friendship, then affection, and finally love. With the situation changed, I'm uncertain of what do now that I have."

"The situation dictates what we must do. You will become queen, and I remain a scholar."

"That seems wrong!" she lamented.

He held her hands to curb her upset. "Hear me. There may come a time when our love can become public. But for now, we must guard our feelings. Nothing can interfere with the plan. The fate of Orrin depends upon our actions."

Winnie screwed her eyes shut against the truth of what he said. "I know! But changing my feelings towards so many in such a short time has been difficult."

"It has been challenging for all involved." He gently touched her face, which made her eyes open. "I swear by the Almighty, I will do all within my power to see you crowned, the Piskies freed, and Orrin saved for all to live in peace."

Winnie embraced him. They remained in each other's arms until Jayson spoke.

"I must return to finish the plans." He kissed her hand.

Winnie lingered a moment before she made her way to Finn's house. Along the way, Piskies bowed to her and gave friendly greetings. Mora was alone, busy in the kitchen area.

"Ah, Winnie, I mean, Highness."

Winnie sighed as she sat at the table.

Mora set a plate of food before Winnie. "I roasted mushrooms specially for you. Along with quail eggs and bread for breakfast."

"Thank you."

When Winnie hesitated, Mora encouraged her. "You must eat. Physical strength is required for what lies ahead."

"May I ask you something?"

"Of course." Mora sat opposite Winnie.

"How often did my fath … Conor visit you?"

"Frequently, after he found Rafe alive. At first, we were wary of him, but he bore a message from Ennis that placed us at ease. He told us everything about you and Rafe's mission. Rafe couldn't speak for a long time—until his jaw healed. Since then, both have been great friends to the Piskies and our family, Burdock's attitude aside."

Winnie chuckled. "Burdock apologized to me, but he's still a cranky sort."

Mora laughed, then grew serious. "Are you resolved to do what is necessary?"

Winnie paused in eating to reply. "I am."

Mora smiled, hopeful, and took Winnie's hand. "The Almighty will bless you. Now, eat. I need to prepare food and remedies for the journey."

Chapter 31

DAWN BROKE ON THE DAY OF DEPARTURE. THE ENTIRE Piskie village woke before the sun rose to help with last-minute preparations. Piskie workmen transformed one of their small open wagons into a covered one that appeared of human origin. The sides and roof were tall enough to accommodate humans. Before, the horse was too large for the harness, but now, the animal fit perfectly. Piskie seamstresses and tailors worked nonstop to create new clothes for the journey. They started with the basic articles of clothing for each human before creating new pieces.

Winnie and Conor waited with Finn and Burdock beside the finished wagon. She wore a simple green and brown dress that included a pocket in which to hide the necklace. Her cloak was repaired, and a broad-brimmed, flat cap matched the dress. Conor dressed as a servant to match Winnie, also complete with a broad-brimmed hat. Finn and Burdock wore coif hats to cover their hair and ears, and long robes to conceal their identity.

Conor inspected the harness. Like the other horses, the one in harness wore a saddlebag jam-packed with supplies.

Zoe and Zane arrived, also dressed for travel with long cloaks and coif hats.

Surprised, Winnie asked, "Are you both coming also?"

"A last-minute addition," said Conor.

"Why?"

"You may need small folk to fit in places humans and our elders cannot," said Zane.

"They're too old to move easily," said Zoe about her father and Burdock.

"But not too old to whip you when needed," Finn teased in return.

Winnie glanced inside the wagon. "Five of us can't fit."

"You'll ride with me in the driver's seat. They made it large enough for two," said Conor.

"Any other changes I should know about?" she wryly challenged.

"No," he said with a chuckle.

Rafe and Jayson led three saddled horses. Rafe exchanged his typical ranger clothing for the attire of a lesser human noble, complete with a feathered hat and cloak. Mora cut his hair to a more suitable court style. He thinned and groomed his beard along the chin and jawline, yet still covered the remaining wounds from Balor. Jayson's clothes were cleaned and repaired so he appeared the same as when they left.

"Certainly, no one would recognize you from last time," Winnie said of Rafe.

"I hardly recognize myself." He tied one horse to a ring on the back of the wagon. "That should do it," he told Conor.

"Then we should be leaving."

Burdock shouted in Piskie and waved all the villagers together. "Let us pray."

Humans and Piskies assumed a reverent posture, with males removing their hats.

"Almighty Lord, you told us in times past that this day would come. Of how you would restore what was lost to both Piskies and men. We ask for divine guidance in our mission. Go before us to prepare the way. May King Pekka be receptive to his true heir. May the enemy be thwarted. Protect those we leave behind. We commit all this to you. Amen."

"Amen," everyone repeated.

Mora kissed her children and embraced Finn. "Stay safe."

"Lord willing, we'll be back before you miss us," he spoke with bravado.

Finn, Burdock, and the twins climbed into the wagon. A thick piece of canvas covered both the front and the rear of the wagon to shield the inside from view. The canvas behind the driver's seat was already secured by straps tied at the corners. Both canvases could be rolled up and tied to the roof with more straps. Conor secured the straps of the lowered rear canvas before joining Winnie on the driver's seat. He took the reins. They waited for Jayson and Rafe to mount. Rafe waved to Conor for departure.

Piskies followed the wagon to the edge of the village, shouting words of encouragement.

Conor noticed Winnie held the part of her skirt where the necklace lay hidden. "Are you truly ready for this?"

"Aye. Why do you ask?"

"You appear nervous."

"Shouldn't you be nervous also? Everyone at Highburn believes you are dead. Showing up alive will cause quite a stir."

He flashed a sarcastic grin at her retort. "I've faced worse than coming back from the dead." She didn't respond to his humor rather faced forward. "I know something troubles you."

She heaved a sigh. "Can I ask you something?"

"Of course."

"If all this had not happened, when were you going to tell me the truth?"

"That's a fair question. We decided your eighteenth birthday would be the ideal time. You would be of legal age to assume your rightful place. Being dispatched by Falco and Pekka to Thorndel was unexpected and proved an interruption to our plan. Rona simply followed through in giving you the necklace. I assume she didn't tell you because the situation proved too hazardous with my supposed *death*. And let's not forget *you* left Highburn." He put up a hand to stop her dispute. "Granted, you didn't know, and the intent was to find me. However, your departure caused another wrinkle in the plan. It is only by the grace of Providence that you fell in with Rafe and the Piskies."

"I prayed all along for the Almighty to guide me."

"And He has." His tender smile also reflected in his eyes. "I'm proud of you. Undertaking a journey to Thorndel and the subsequent revelation hasn't been easy."

She shyly smiled. "There may not be blood between us, but you raised me. As a *general's daughter*, how could I do less than you?"

Conor sniffed back a rise of emotion. "Well, now we go to secure your true destiny. A day I anticipated with excitement yet also dreaded. Selfish dread, I suppose."

"No, not selfish. Besides, if all goes well, I will need a general."

Conor cocked a teasing grin and motioned forward to where Jayson and Rafe rode ten yards ahead. "And a scholar? Might you need him, too?"

Winnie flushed with embarrassment, then sighed, dejected. "I don't know if it can be in the *personal way* that we feel for each other."

"I assumed by that statement you have both expressed those feelings openly."

A lump caught in her throat, preventing words, so she nodded.

"Then why downcast? Establish your reign as queen, then marry whom you will."

Winnie sat up, a glimmer of hope mixed with confusion. "Do you truly believe I can? Royals marry other royals. Or so, I've heard."

"Traditionally, perhaps. Generals don't *traditionally* raise princesses. So, you have already set a new trend." He winked, which made her giggle. His tone changed to serious. "Yet, one step at a time. First, we need this plan to work before a wedding."

"A wedding we'd like to see!" came Zoe's voice from behind the canvas.

Conor heartily laughed when Winnie blushed. "You know they can hear everything."

Winnie struck the canvas.

"Ouch!" Zoe squealed, followed by laughter from Zane, Finn, and Burdock.

Hearing laughter, Rafe and Jayson turned in the saddle, curious.

"Why do I think they're talking about us?" Rafe sarcastically spoke to Jayson. He noticed Winnie smile at Jayson, then teased him. "Oh, no, it's just you they discuss."

Jayson frowned and faced forward. "Why tease me about something that can never be?"

"Who said it can't?"

"It's obvious! She will be queen while I remain a scholar."

"Anything is possible, lad."

"Not according to the Shadowspire voice," droned Jayson.

Rafe closely regarded his despondent nephew. "What did it say?"

"Two questions. *And if what you seek costs that love? What then? And I replied, If it restores the general and gives her peace, I will be content.*"

"You give up that quickly?"

"I'm not giving up, rather accepting reality."

"The reality is you love her. And from what I've witnessed, she loves you. What do you seek beyond that?"

"Nothing!"

"Then why should *it cost you love* if you seek nothing beyond her better good?"

Jayson grew frustrated. "What do you know of love? You've been off in the wilderness alone for over a decade."

Rafe's face hardened at the insult. "I know more than you think! Danger and sacrifice have been my companions these long years. So, take care, lad."

Jayson's shoulders sagged in regret. "I'm sorry, uncle. There are moments I find it difficult to consider anything past what has happened." He carefully glanced over his shoulder. Winnie and Conor appeared ignorant of the argument between him and Rafe.

"Simon taught you to apply logic and reason. For her sake, you must be prepared to face what is to come with scholarly precision."

Jayson straightened in the saddle. "I swore to her to do everything in my power to see her crowned, the Piskies restored, and Orrin saved. It is beyond that, I dare not hope. So, please, let us speak no more of it."

"As you wish," Rafe spoke in reluctant agreement.

Chapter 32

DIM LIGHT ILLUMINATED FALCO'S PRIVATE QUARTERS. He wore a dressing gown as he sat before a fire in the hearth. The dancing flames cast deep shadows on his brooding face. He held a goblet filled with the stomach remedy. He ignored the chiming clock that stuck one in the morning.

Since he sent Conor to Thorndel, the situation at Highburn had grown urgent. Dispatching Tolbert with the group helped minimize concern about Scrutern. He knew Tolbert coldly followed through on orders. Still, something more disturbed him than the retrieval of the jewel. The Council meeting showed the Briggs girl possessed a spirit and fortitude he had not expected. Beyond the physical resemblance to Rona, this display heightened his suspicion regarding her. True, being raised a general's daughter instilled a sense of worth and pride. Yet he sensed more to her than family traits. Of course, if Tolbert executed his orders, the girl would be dispatched and no longer of any consequence. Answers about her and Scrutern had to wait for Tolbert's return. For now, he concentrated on his master plan.

A knock on the door startled him from his contemplation. "Come!"

Sergeant Cadel arrived. He bowed to Falco.

"Well?" asked Falco, impatient.

"The maid has been silenced."

"And Rodney Wilson?"

"Clarke is keeping him close, even to the point of having Wilson sleep in his quarters. Any attempt to deal with him will cause trouble."

Falco leaned forward to stare into the fire. His eyes narrow and jowls taunt. "In the near future, Clarke will regret his interference. What of the physician?"

"He reports the King's health is deteriorating rapidly. He estimates a day at most."

To this, Falco showed surprised concern. "Did he say if Pekka spoke of a regent or heir?"

Cadel shrugged ignorance. "No, he only reported on the King's health."

"Then I must act quickly before Clarke can be notified of Pekka's condition."

"Before Captain Tolbert returns?"

"If Pekka has only a day left, it is doubtful Tolbert will arrive in time. So, my secondary plan is needed." Falco pulled Cadel to his wardrobe. He barked orders for the sergeant to help him dress.

Before he left his quarters, Falco grabbed his satchel. Cadel escorted him to the King's private apartment. Three physicians surrounded the King's bed.

"My lord!" said the chief physician.

"Master Herbert." Falco approached the bed. Pekka's face gaunt and pale. Indeed, he appeared dead. A slow rising of the chest in breath showed some life still left. "How is he?"

"Weak."

"Has he spoken? Did he ask for me or the Queen?"

"He asked for the Lord Chancellor. Just this moment, I dispatched a page to fetch him."

"Then I arrived in time."

"My lord?" asked Herbert, puzzled.

"The formalities of succession are discussed with the Prime Minister *before* any scholarly record is made. Now, wake him," Falco sternly spoke.

Herbert expressed misgivings about the order. "My lord, His Majesty's condition is very grave. He needs rest."

Falco stiffened at the brazen refusal. "The welfare of Orrin is at stake if the King cannot name his successor before he dies! Now, wake him."

Stunned into silence, Herbert only briefly hesitated before gently waking Pekka.

Weak and frail, Pekka tried to focus on the people surrounding his bed.

Falco motioned for a chair. Once seated, he spoke to Pekka. "Sire. Can you hear me?"

Sluggish, Pekka tried to focus. "Falco?"

"Ay, Sire."

Pekka licked his parched lips. "Clarke?"

"He will be here shortly. Before then, you must sign this to acknowledge your successor so the Lord Chancellor can officially enter it into the record. It is my duty as Prime Minister to witness the selection." He withdrew a document from the satchel. He placed the paper on Pekka's lap.

Pekka struggled to sit up. Two physicians helped elevate him against the stacked pillows. Bony fingers on a shaky hand lifted the paper to read. "The words are blurry. Who?"

Rather than a direct answer, Falco reminded Pekka. "I am certain Your Majesty recalls forbidding the Queen to be named Regent. So, naturally, it falls to the most qualified person."

Pekka's attempt at a scoffing laugh turned into a coughing fit. When recovered, he said to Falco, "That means you!"

"I am the logical choice to maintain order since you are without an heir."

Pekka's pale face sneered in anger at the reminder. "Impertinent, braggart!"

Herbert rushed to the bed. "Please, Sire! Do not upset yourself."

Although Pekka pushed Herbert away, his emotions exhausted him. He sank against the pillows, where his eyes closed.

Anxious, Falco touched Pekka's shoulder. "Sire?"

A groan told them Pekka was still alive.

"Sire, you mustn't delay. Sign the paper," Falco urged.

Pekka's eyes partially opened, and he waved. "Pen …" His voice was weak.

A nod from Falco, and Cadel fetched a portable writing desk with pen, ink, and wax. Falco took it from the sergeant to carefully placed within Pekka's reach. The King's hand shook so terribly that he couldn't grab the pen. Falco aided Pekka to take the pen in hand, dip into the inkwell, then guided his hand to the paper. In scrawling letters, Pekka signed his name. When Falco released Pekka's hand, the pen fell from the King's grasp. Falco used a candle from the nightstand to melt wax below Pekka's signature.

"Sire. The royal seal."

Feeble, Pekka raised his left hand, upon which he wore the royal ring. Falco turned Pekka's hand to press the signet ring into the wax. Falco's face relaxed with relief. He placed the paper in the satchel, then gave the writing desk to Cadel for removal.

"Rest, Sire. The kingdom is safe."

Pekka's eyes closed, and his breathing grew shallow.

Falco spoke to the physicians. "You three are witnesses that the King signed the order of succession."

None of them spoke rather bowed to Falco as he departed. Once the door closed, Herbert immediately felt for Pekka's pulse.

"It won't be much longer," he told his companions.

"Should we send for the Queen?" asked one.

The answer became interrupted by Simon's arrival. Rodney accompanied him and carried the official scholar's legal satchel. "The King sent for me."

"Ay, my lord, but he is in no condition to be roused again." Herbert no sooner finished speaking then they heard a loud inhale from Pekka followed by a lengthy exhale. He felt for a pulse. With a somber sigh, he shook his head. "The King is dead. May he rest with his fathers in the Almighty's hand."

Simon lowered his head to mutter a quick prayer. "Did he name a successor?"

"Lord Falco."

Simon stared with astonishment at Herbert. "He said Falco?"

"Not exactly. Lord Falco left a few moments before you arrived. He had the King sign a document naming him as successor. He said it was the logical choice since the King refused to name the Queen as regent."

"He forced the King to sign it," chided one in disgust.

"Hush, Mason!" the third scolded his companion. "Lord Falco said we are his witnesses!"

"Ay, we witnessed the King was too weak to even hold a pen."

"He's right, Brad. You cannot deny it," said Herbert, to which Brad nodded agreement.

The information heightened Simon's legal mind. "How did he force the King to sign?"

"He held the King's hand and guided it with each stroke," replied Mason.

Simon curbed his enthusiasm at hearing the misstep by Falco. "Then it was done under duress. The King did not sign by his own power."

"Herbert told Lord Falco His Majesty's condition was very grave, but his lordship insisted Herbert wake him." Mason said.

Simon assumed a rigid posture. His intense gaze locked on the three physicians. "Gentlemen," he began in a stern official tone. "By my authority as Lord Chancellor in all legal matters, I am placing the three of you under oath as to the testimony now given."

"What of Lord Falco?" asked Brad, fearful.

Simon allowed a friendly smile to appear. "Fear not, Doctor Brad. I shall see you are protected. My assistant will prepare your written testimonies while I summon Lieutenant Kincaid."

"What about the King's death? Should it not be announced?" asked Herbert.

"When we are done, I shall personally inform the Queen."

Despite the lateness of the hour, Simon and Rodney finished with the testimonies when Kincaid arrived. Simon moved to one side of the room to speak confidentially to Kincaid.

"I hope your wounds are fully healed, as our time has come. Falco tipped his hand and believed he has thwarted us."

Kincaid snorted a huff. "I'm ready. What must be done?"

"These men are witnesses to his scheme. I have their sworn testimonies, but they *must* be taken to a safe place, so Falco won't know they have spoken to me."

"Consider it done!" Kincaid approached the physicians. "Gentlemen, you have my word of safety. Now, quietly follow me and ask no questions."

A signal from Simon sent the physicians with Kincaid. The lieutenant grabbed a candle before escorting them through a secret passageway from the King's chamber.

Once Kincaid departed with the physicians, Simon spoke to the soldiers outside Pekka's chamber. "The King is dead. Guard the door and allow *no one* to enter. I go to tell the Queen before a formal announcement is made."

Rodney followed Simon a short distance to the Queen's chamber. The soldiers at the door snapped to attention upon sight of him. He paused to inform them about Pekka.

A soldier knocked on the door before allowing Simon and Rodney to enter. From the dying embers of the main room's hearth, Simon lit a candle and placed it in a holder. He rapped on the bedchamber door. "Your Majesty. It is Simon." He heard rustling from behind the door.

Slowly, it opened. Rona shielded her eyes from the candlelight. "What time is it?"

"Time to act, and swiftly. The King is dead."

Rona gasped and covered her mouth. "Has there been any word from the others?"

Simon shook his head. "I'm afraid not. But there is more to tell." He motioned for her to join him in the main room. Once Rona sat beside him on the sofa, he related the recent events.

Greatly disturbed, Rona asked, "Can he do that? Proclaim himself king without the jewel? And what of Winnie?"

"I will call a Council meeting to present legal evidence countering to his claim. Beyond that, her fate, and the fate of Orrin is in the Almighty's hands."

Chapter 33

After five days, the group reached Highburn at nightfall. The gatekeeper shouted for them to hurry inside so he could close the gate. Lamplighters continued their work of illuminating the streets. People rushed inside for warmth. Nighttime temperatures fell dramatically once the sun set.

Instead of heading toward the castle bridge, Rafe diverted the group to the west side of the city. Conor lowered the brim of his hat to shield his face, yet kept his eyes clear to drive the wagon. Winnie removed her hat in favor of a raised hood against the stiff breeze that added a chill to the cold evening. The Piskies remained hidden in the wagon. Jayson followed as rearguard.

The westside docks appeared empty. Rafe drew rein before a weathered shack at the dock. Jayson joined his uncle, and both dismounted.

"Which house?" Rafe asked Conor.

"I'll handle this. Stay with the wagon." Conor removed his hat, gave Winnie the reins, and hopped down. He approached a house two doors down from where they stopped. He knocked. A section of the door opened to reveal a pair of suspicious eyes.

"Who disturbs me?" he asked in a gruff tone.

"One who knows all about you, former *Sergeant* Quinn," replied Conor.

The section slammed shut, followed by the door opening. A slender man with a badly scarred, weathered face gaped. "General Briggs?"

"Hush!" Conor shoved Quinn back inside and shut the door. "Are you alone?"

"You know she left me," Quinn complained.

"Doesn't mean you don't keep company."

"With this face? Hardly." Quinn watched Conor inspect the one-room dwelling. No one. "Satisfied, gen—"

Conor grabbed Quinn's face to cover his mouth. "Quiet!" When Quinn nodded, Conor released him. "I need a boat. Now. No questions."

"Just you?"

"No, big enough for eight passengers."

"That's a tall order."

"I'm certain you can manage it. You are the dockmaster, after all."

Quinn studied Conor. "Where to?"

"I'll tell you that once we're all onboard."

Quinn put on a heavy coat and sailor's cap. "Dock three."

"I'll get the others and meet you there."

Conor stepped outside to watch Quinn head toward the dock. He then returned to the others, where he took the reins from Winnie. "Dock Three. Follow me," he told Rafe and Jayson.

They traveled four more streets from Quinn's house. The rowhouses stopped after two blocks at the large open market. Three docks protruded from the lakeside wall and could easily be shut by a gate that allowed access to the water. The docks could accommodate small to medium-sized boats for commerce, but were mostly used by fishing vessels. Dock Three was the last one before the western wall.

The gate stood open. By lantern light, Conor saw Quinn at the boat. He went to the rear of the wagon to open the canvas. Winnie, Rafe, and Jayson joined him.

"I've secured a boat to take us across to the castle, where we'll use the cover of darkness to take the fishing passage." Conor then told the Piskies, "Keep your heads down and don't talk."

Conor took the lead with Winnie beside him. The Piskies followed with Rafe and Jayson.

Quinn straightened from preparation. "Children? At this time of night?"

"I said *no questions!*" Conor moved threateningly close to Quinn. Intimidated, Quinn stepped aside so everyone could enter the boat.

Conor held Winnie's hand to steady her as she entered first. Then came the Piskies, who were nearly lifted into the boat. Zoe and Zane sat on either side of Winnie. Finn and Burdock huddled together so Jayson could sit beside them. Rafe and Conor squeezed into the smallest seat near the bow.

Quinn cast off the lines and used an oar to push away from the dock. He sat and fixed the oars into the oarlocks. "Where to?" he asked Conor.

"Douse the light! We don't need to be spotted on the lake."

"How do you expect me to see?"

"Such an experienced sailor should know these waters well enough to navigate," Conor spoke in sarcastic rebuff.

Quinn briefly stood to blow out the lantern. "Now, where to?"

"The castle's abandoned dock."

"Oh, gen—, you can't be serious?" he corrected himself.

"Get us there safely, and I might reconsider your past."

Quinn mumbled under his breath as he began to row.

Zoe blew on her hands for warmth. Winnie opened her cloak to wrap around Zoe.

Rafe leaned toward Conor to whisper. "Do you think the watch can hear the oars?"

"Quietly, Quinn!" Conor harshly whispered. "Unless you want to return to the dungeon."

Quinn's grumbling increased, yet he moved the oars more deliberately to lessen the noise and limit the wake.

The boat glided over cold, black water. Moonlight shifted in and out of clouds, giving brief sparkles to the waves before turning black again. Breath turned to wispy white vapor.

Anxious, Winnie strained to see the distant shore. She could make out her companions and Quinn but beyond that proved difficult. Moonlight only gave glimpses of what lay ahead. A black hulking shape made the horizon look like a void with stars above. Soon the faint glow of lights from the castle outlined the top of the horizon. She knew these to be torches and brazier for the night watch.

Quinn steered the boat west to follow the shoreline. After a half mile, the shoreline turned, and Quinn again steered on a parallel course. Once round the curve, he headed for shore. Soon, a dilapidated dock came into view.

"Be ready to exit and secure the line," Quinn told Conor and Rafe.

When the bow of the boat hit bottom, Rafe and Conor exited. Rafe slipped but caught himself on the dock to keep from falling into the icy water. He and Conor tied the boat securely for others to disembark. Conor helped them onto the dock while Rafe gave a hand from the dock to land.

"Be careful. The dock is broken in places," Conor warned everyone.

Once all were off the boat, Quinn asked, "Need a return trip?"

"No. And if the watch is not alerted by you to our presence, I will consider the matter closed."

"How can I be sure of that?" Quinn spat.

"You have my word," Conor stoutly replied.

"*His* word is enough surety for anyone," Rafe said.

Quinn nodded. "So, it is. Now, give me a shove off."

Rafe untied the ropes and pushed the boat away from the dock. For a moment, he and Conor watched until Quinn disappeared into the darkness.

"How can we find our way in the dark?" Finn asked

"Easy," began Winnie in a matter-of-fact tone. "There is enough light from the watchtower fires to see. I've used them before to find my way back in the dark."

"And I got a long lecture for being late," teased Jayson.

"If you followed more closely, we would have returned on time."

"She, too, received a lecture," Conor spoke sideways to Jayson. He chuckled and waved for Winnie to take the lead.

The Piskies stayed close to Winnie as she led them through the rough terrain of trees and thicket. Jayson kept the Piskies from wandering off course. Conor and Rafe covered the rear. Several times Winnie crouched down to hide and allow the soldiers walking the ramparts to pass. The others mimicked her actions. As they drew closer to the walls, Winnie moved more cautiously. Finally, they reached a neglected part of the castle.

"Let's hope the door still opens," she whispered. Winnie grunted and strained at trying to pull, but the door didn't budge.

"Is it locked?" asked Burdock.

She shook her head as she recovered her breath. "It wasn't this hard before. Of course, that was years ago."

"Stand aside." Conor and Rafe both pulled on the door. They too strained with effort. Slowly, it began to move. Jayson added his strength, and the door opened enough for a person to slip through. The men took several moments to recover from the exertion.

"Hopefully, you can find your way in total darkness," Jayson said in a light tone.

"The hallway is short." Winnie placed her hand on the wall to lead them inside. She balked at the wet slimy feeling of stone. After a hundred feet, the hall ended at another door. Light from the other side rimmed the frame. She looked through the keyhole.

"Where are we?" Zoe quietly asked.

"The basement servant's hall," Winnie softly replied. "I don't see anyone." She tried the doorknob. "It's unlocked." She gently pushed the door open but stopped at hearing the hinges squeak. She poked her head out. The hallway appeared empty. She pushed again to open it enough to slip through. "Quickly! Up those stairs." She ran to an old wooden staircase.

Rafe and Conor hurried the Piskies to follow Winnie. Once they reached the top, Winnie took a deep breath of relief.

"We can rest here. This is an abandoned storeroom," she said.

"I need to contact my father. How can I get to his quarters from here?" said Jayson.

"I can take you," said Winnie.

"No! You can't risk being seen. Not yet," Conor objected.

"Just tell me how."

Winnie instructed Jayson on the best way to the scholar's wing.

"We'll wait here for your return," Conor told Jayson.

Chapter 34

SIMON CHOSE TO SLEEP AND WORK IN THE SCHOLAR'S OFFICE. Too much was at stake to delay preparing the legal challenge. Falco wasted no time in establishing his reign. He only allowed two days of mourning. Once Pekka was entombed, he ordered Rona confined to her quarters until he decided how to deal with her. Falco had Cadel replace Kincaid's soldiers guarding Rona's chambers. Simon feared Rona's fate, as these soldiers forbade him entry. For three days, he tried to reason with them about the legal issues needing the Queen's signature, but each time they cited *King* Falco's orders of no admittance.

Surprisingly, Falco did agree to Simon's request to summon the royal Council and begin the procedure for coronation. According to Falco, *"All must proceed normally."* Everything needed to be ready by tomorrow.

Simon rubbed his temples in hopes of easing a headache brought on by fatigue. Rodney prepared hot tea with herbs to aid Simon. He sipped the soothing tea. He suddenly stopped at hearing a creaking sound. Both Simon and Rodney turned to investigate the origin. One of the panels across the room near the antechamber began to open.

Rodney grabbed the poker from the hearth for defense. "Stay behind me, master."

Dim light from the desk candles and fire in the hearth illuminated the room. A figure emerged from behind the panel carrying a small candle. Rodney raised the poker, ready to strike.

"No! It's me. Jayson," he hastily said.

"Jayson?" asked Simon in stunned wonder.

He stepped into the room so they could see clearly.

Simon's breath caught in his throat as he embraced his son. He silently wept.

"I am whole. No wounds or scars," Jayson assured him.

Simon wiped his eyes. "Thank the Almighty. Why did you come that way?"

"There is much to tell. Rodney, lock the door and stay near it to make sure no one overhears."

"Aye, sir."

Jayson escorted Simon to his desk, where both sat close to speak in hushed voices. "First, the general is alive and here with me."

Simon pursed his lips to stop a murmur of relieved joy concerning Conor.

"Also," Jayson's tone turned cross, "I know all about *her* true identity. And dismayed you didn't tell me before we left."

Simon closed his eyes and clenched Jayson's arm. "I deeply regret that fact. My intent was to protect you should the plan fail."

"Uncle told me the same, but it still hurts that you didn't trust me."

"Is Rafe whole?"

"Aye, and here. Along with *her* and Piskies."

Simon's eyes grew wide with fear. "She's here? No, no, that won't do. Or maybe it will," he spoke with consideration. "The Council will assemble tomorrow."

"Why?"

Simon's expression turned grave. "Pekka is dead." He then explained Falco's scheme. "I have all I need to present a challenge before the Council. So, it may serve that she and Conor are here. But why the Piskies?"

Jayson's voice lowered to where Simon leaned in to hear. "We found it. The jewel is now complete."

Simon tried to curb his enthusiasm. "Is Finn among them?"

Jayson nodded. "As is Burdock."

Excitement brought Simon to his feet. "Do you know what this means?"

"I do." Jayson waved for Simon to resume his seat.

"Then you also must realize the need to act is now! I can present the legal challenge to Pekka naming Falco, but Falco won't yield easily. Winnie and Conor's arrival will send a ripple through the proceedings. With Scrutern in her possession, we need witnesses to her birth and identity as Pekka's true heir."

"Are there witnesses beyond Conor and the Queen?"

"Aye. Leave that part to me also." Simon's brows furrowed in thought. "Yet, Rona's testimony is key. Unfortunately, Falco locked her in her quarters, and I have been denied access to speak with her."

"I can get to her. So, can Winnie and Conor." When Simon appeared skeptical, Jayson clarified, "Just like I did now. A secret passage."

"I should be present to incorporate what is said in my challenge."

"Then let me take you to the others."

Simon approached Rodney to relay quiet instructions. "Gather all the evidence for tomorrow and keep it with you. Let no one in. I will return later."

"Aye, master."

Jayson replaced the depleted candle with a new one. He led his father into the passageway and closed it from the other side. Simon held the back of Jayson's cloak as they navigated the darkness. Ten minutes later, they entered the storage room.

"By the Almighty! Conor." Simon embraced Conor.

"It is good to see you, too, old friend."

Simon chuckled at seeing Rafe. "You clean up well, little brother." He then bowed to Finn and Burdock in reverent welcome. "It has been many years."

"Too many. But let us not dwell on the past," said Finn. He smiled at Winnie. "Through Scrutern, the Almighty has made the choice, and we are here to see it fulfilled."

"It won't be easy to verify her lineage with Pekka dead," droned Jayson.

"What?" Conor questioned, shocked.

Simon explained all that transpired since Conor left, followed by Winnie's subsequent departure for Thorndel and Tolbert's inclusion.

"Tolbert died at Thorndel," said Rafe harshly.

Conor paced, deep in contemplation at the developments. "We must speak to Rona."

Winnie's face showed anxiety. "It will be strange meeting her again under different circumstances. I hardly know what to say to her. My real mother."

Conor comforted Winnie. "She is still the same person you have known all your life. Her love and concern for you guided all the decisions."

"The sooner the better," said Simon.

"Do think I'll be recognized?" Rafe asked Simon. His tone a bit mischievous.

Simon's gaze upon his brother turned somber. "Rafe. I'm afraid there is more grave news. Eleanor is dead."

Rafe's countenance fell from lighthearted to devastated. "How?" he could barely speak.

"Murdered."

Rafe's jowls tightened, and his body stiffened. "Who?"

"Unknown exactly, but like Arabella—poison. Although again, the intended person was Rona. Rodney and I were present when it happened. Venison rolls offered in Pekka's name, but Rona dislikes them, while I declined. Eleanor barely finished one ..." His voice trailed off, as they understood.

The news also struck Winnie hard. She covered her mouth to stifle a sob. In sympathy, Conor held Rafe's shoulder. The ranger's face shifted between sorrow and anger.

Tears swelled as Jayson suddenly realized the love and sacrifice Rafe made all those years ago. His voice broke the gloomy silence that followed the revelation. "I'm sorry, uncle." He recoiled slightly at Rafe's sharp gaze.

"As personally distressing as this news is, we can't let it alter our course," said Finn.

"We won't," said Conor. He then said to Winnie, "I suppose you know the back passageway to the Queen's chamber."

"If she doesn't, I do," said Jayson. To Conor's curiosity, he explained, "I used it frequently to keep her informed about my research regarding Piskies and Thorndel."

"Then take the lead."

They followed Jayson with the Piskies between the humans to hide their presence. Once at the secret door, Jayson didn't knock. Instead, he pushed it open to peek inside.

"The wardrobe is empty," he announced.

"Let me go first. It will lessen the shock." Simon nudged his son aside. He waved them in and shut the door. He carefully made his way to the main chamber.

Conor noticed Winnie's anxiety as she wrung her hands and bit her lower lip. He took hold of her hands and softly smiled. "Courage. She will greet you with open arms."

For Winnie, the few moments waiting felt like an eternity. Finally, Simon returned with Rona. The Queen's eyes moist with tears and her large smile quivered with emotion.

"My dear Conor! Thank the Almighty you're alive."

He bowed yet kept hold of Winnie's hand.

Rona's tearful, loving gaze found Winnie. "My little ruby." She opened her arms.

Winnie broke down crying as she ran for the embrace.

Rona stroked Winnie's hair. "You don't know how I have longed for this moment." She lifted Winnie's chin. "I'm sorry for all the years of secrecy, but necessary to keep you safe. And I could think of none better than Conor and Arabella."

"I understand that now."

"Majesty," began Simon, tactfully of interruption. "You remember Finn."

"Of course." Rona formally greeted the Piskie king. "My lord, you do us a great honor with your presence."

"My lady. This is our high priest, Burdock."

"Your Majesty." Burdock bowed.

"I bid you welcome, as best I can."

"We pray the Almighty bless our joint efforts to save Orrin, for we have been told of Lord Falco's treachery," said Burdock.

"We must formulate a plan in conjunction with Simon's challenge tomorrow," Conor informed Rona.

"Do you have the jewel?" she asked.

"We do. So far, Falco is unaware of our presence. And we must keep it that way."

"I can't leave my quarters while a servant brings meals to the door but doesn't enter."

"Good. The wardrobe can serve as our staging area," said Conor.

"Her Majesty's personal verification is required to support Winnie's identity and claim. Written testimony will not serve for the confirmation of a royal heir," said Simon.

Conor grinned at Winnie. "I'm certain our resident escape artist can guide myself and Rona through back passageways to the great hall closet."

Simon shook his head. "Winnie must present her claim in person before involving Rona."

When Conor frowned in disapproval, Winnie said, "Tonight I can take Zoe and Zane and show them the way. In the morning, they will escort my mother and keep her safe until needed."

Rona's lips pressed together with her joy when Winnie called her mother for the first time.

"Very well," said Conor in agreement. "You, Rafe, Finn, and Burdock can hide in the north alcove, you know the one servants use for waiting on guests at a banquet."

"I remember," said Winnie.

"If we get Winnie there early enough, I can block access," said Rafe.

"I already instructed Lieutenant Kincaid to bring the physicians there to await my summons during my challenge. He will have guards posted for security," said Simon.

"Excellent. Inform Kincaid of their arrival," Conor said. "The twins and I will leave first with Rona." Then to Rafe, "Wait at least ten minutes before taking Winnie to the alcove."

Jayson listened to the assignments without hearing his name. "What do I do?"

"You're with me, of course," Winnie replied. "Your father will confront Falco on legalities regarding events here, but you were with us at Thorndel and witnessed all that happened since. You can apply your scholarly mind to that end." She reached for his hand. "I depend upon your help."

Jayson straightened at her statement, a smile on his lips. "I am at your service, Highness." He kissed her hand.

"Let's try and get a couple of hours' sleep before undertaking our tasks," said Conor.

"There wouldn't be any food to eat, would there?" asked Zoe sheepishly.

Finn cuffed Zoe on the shoulder. "Mind your manners. Forgive my daughter, my lady."

Rona laughed. "No. I would be a poor host if I did not provide for my guests. Unfortunately, I only have a few apples, some bread, and cheese left from supper."

"That will do," said Zoe eagerly.

"I will send a request for an early breakfast. It might not be much to divide among so many, since I have eaten little of what is brought. But it should suffice."

"I must return to the office," began Simon. He smiled at Winnie. "I look forward to advancing your case as heir apparent."

"I can take you back," said Jayson.

"Just to the corridor. I can walk unhindered from there."

They left by the secret passage. When they reached the corridor, Jayson delayed Simon's departure. "Tell me about Uncle and Lady Eleanor."

Simon heaved a sober sigh. "They were betrothed before he left to seek out Finn. Word of his disappearance broke her heart. She never looked at another man, rather vowed to remain unmarried and devoted to Rona and our cause."

"What about when Rafe stood before the King? Surely, she knew he was alive then."

"Aye. And hopeful. You saw her when she spoke to me on our way to the King's study."

"Ah! I remember. Now I understand you both meant uncle."

Simon's face somber. "That's what makes it so tragic. Both sacrificed their love for a greater cause only to be denied by evil." Simon held Jayson's shoulder. "We are the voices of law and reason. Now, more than ever, we must utilize our strengths to save Orrin." He embraced Jayson. "Till the morning."

Jayson returned to the room. He quietly slipped beside Rafe, as his uncle drank from a tankard of cider being passed among the others. His voice barely rose above a whisper. "I'm truly sorry, uncle. I didn't know about Lady Eleanor."

Rafe paused in drinking. "There was no need to tell you. Only Simon and Conor knew of our private pledge to each other. There was too much at stake to risk Falco learning of it. Not until the plan succeeded would we be free to marry." He handed the tankard to Jayson.

"Still, I regret my harsh words."

Rafe patted Jayson's shoulder. "Take a drink and get some rest. You will need all your faculties tomorrow."

Chapter 35

After showing Zoe and Zane hidden corridors to the Great Hall closet, Winnie had difficulty sleeping. She gazed at the others. Each occupied a spot on the wardrobe floor. For weeks, Rafe and Conor told how Rona sacrificed by giving up her only living child to save the child's life. *My life! A life lived in the open for all to see, yet in the shadow of protection for my future.* The reality still felt a bit surreal, yet each of the sleeping individuals made a pledge that brought them to this hour.

The Piskies added a new perspective regarding her future. During the return journey to Highburn, she tried to envision what it would be like meeting the Queen, her real mother, and the challenge that lay ahead. The vision from Shadowspire of Rona standing with outstretched hand and saying, 'Come, my child,' replayed in her mind. What could she say in response? When she saw Rona's smile and open arms, all she could do was run into the embrace. She had no words.

Oh, she loved Arabella, the woman who raised her. Yet, that vision stirred a deep sense in Winnie about the Queen she couldn't grasp until learning the truth. Of course, she loved the Queen in a friendship sense during those years of service. Now, she understood those acts of kindness and charity held a secret yearning told by Rona's own words, *'You don't know how I have longed for this moment.'*

Winnie felt a jolt on her arm. Rona quietly knelt. She placed a finger to her lips and held out a hand for Winnie to rise. They walked a short distance to the door to the main chamber.

"I'm sure you have many questions. Only we don't have much time to talk."

"Conor answered any question I put to him. Including your motivation."

Rona tenderly touched Winnie's face. "I couldn't let Pekka discover your survival. Being raised at Highburn, you witnessed his cruelty."

Winnie's features hardened. "I can acknowledge you as my mother, but to accept him as my father …" She couldn't finish for anger.

"Imagine how I endured as his wife."

Winnie seized Rona's hand. "I know. I saw it many times when he belittled and humiliated you. I desperately wanted to defend you, but my station prevented me."

Rona kissed Winnie's hand. "The time has come for you to make that defense, only not for me, but for Orrin. Your destiny. Are you ready for it? Falco will not yield power easily."

Winnie's resolve showed on her face. "I have learned the true meaning of courage, love, and sacrifice from you, Conor, Arabella, Rafe, and others. For the first time in my life, I feel free to speak my mind."

Rona smiled with pride. She took Winnie's face in her hands to look directly into her daughter's eyes. "With the Almighty's help, we will stand united to confront what has kept us apart." She kissed Winnie's forehead. "Now, try to get some sleep. You will need a clear mind."

Winnie lay down. She silently prayed. *"Lord, I see your hand leading me to this day. Help us all."* With the deep breath of a settled mind, she slept.

Winnie stretched at hearing voices. Rona brought a tray of food. Portions were small, but enough to satisfy empty stomachs. The Piskies ate the vegetables and some bread while the humans consumed the meat and cheese.

Rona graciously smiled at Winnie. "You must not appear as a simple servant. Allow me to dress you as befits your station."

Winnie widely smiled. "I know your wardrobe well. There is a dress I admire."

When Winnie and Rona finished dressing for the occasion, they departed for their various positions at the appointed time. First, the twins left with Conor and Rona.

Zoe and Zane followed the path Winnie showed them. Rona wore a long-hooded black velvet cloak over her regal gown, complete with a crown hidden beneath the hood. When revealed, she needed to make a stunning impression in support of her daughter. During the night, Kincaid managed to bring Conor his general's uniform. He also wore a long black hooded cloak.

By sounds from the other side of the wall, they reckoned servants rose before sunrise in anticipation of the Council meeting and coronation. They paused to peek through hidden peepholes in the wall. Garlands of holly and ivy along with pine branches hung around the Hall and guest passageways. Arrangements of mums and winter roses with sprigs of witch hazel and pinecones filled large vases. The air alive with the scent of winter greenery.

When they reached the end of the hidden passage, Zoe carefully opened the door.

"Where are we?" asked Rona.

"This corridor runs behind the great hall. We need to cross the hall to that small door." Zoe indicated a door on a diagonal path from where they would emerge. "It is best we run."

Rona picked up her skirt and followed Zoe from the passage and into the open corridor. Conor came behind Rona. Zane watched the rear. Zoe and Rona just entered the closet while Conor stood in the threshold to wait for Zane.

"You! Stop!"

Two soldiers appeared at the far corner hallway.

"Quickly!" Conor went to grab Zane when the Piskie stepped back.

"No! I'll distract them. Keep the Queen safe." He nudged Conor inside and pulled the closet door shut before he ran down an adjacent hallway.

Zane had no idea where he ran; he simply wanted to draw the soldiers away from the others. Soon, he saw humans and changed course. Women shrieked in surprise at his sudden appearance while men cursed the reckless interference of preparation.

"Watch where you're going, boy!" a man angrily shouted.

To them, Zane appeared a lad since he still wore the coif cap that covered his ears and hair. Zane noticed the soldiers continued in pursuit. Up ahead, he spied a stone stairway. From the banister hung garlands with flower arrangements flanking the bottom step.

He spoke Piskie as he ran toward the stairs and waved his hand. He slid under the stairs just as the garlands came to life and detached from the banister to ensnare the soldiers. Maids who witnessed the strange sight screamed, and one fainted. The soldiers struggled against the garland that wrapped around their torsos and pinned their arms against their bodies.

Zane swiftly crawled out from under the stairs and raced back the way he came. He dodged male servants and maids. One man managed to grab him, but Zane kicked him and the man dropped to the floor. An older woman cursed at him. Zane hissed at her, and she backed away, yet threw an apple at his head. Zane ducked and snatched up the apple as we continued his retreat.

By now, other soldiers were alerted to an intruder. They ran on an intercept course near the back corridor from where he came. Zane noticed more elaborate greenery in a large vessel at the corner filled with pinecones. He spoke Piskie, and pinecones flew from the decorations to strike the soldiers in the head. Unfortunately, this only served as a momentary distraction. One soldier clouted Zane and knocked him unconscious.

"What do we do with him?" asked one.

"I don't know. Orders are to keep the peace and not let anything interrupt the proceedings." He looked around and spied a small door. "Let's put him in there for now." He picked up Zane.

Approaching the door, they heard a noise behind it.

"What was that?" asked the first one.

"Probably rats. Vermin tend to invade during the colder weather," replied the one carrying Zane.

"Are you sure?"

"Aye. It's just a storage closet." He motioned for the other to open the door. Light from the hallway penetrated halfway into the deep, narrow closet. Dark shadow lay beyond the light line. A rat scurried out. "See, I told you. Rats." He dropped Zane inside and shut the door. "I'll get the key from the steward."

Conor carefully glanced over his shoulder. He stood in deep shadows with his back to the door, shielding Rona, who held Zoe inside her cloak. Zoe emerged to kneel beside her brother.

"Zane?" She carefully touched him. "He's alive."

Zoe and Rona balked at hearing a sound at the door. Conor made ready to draw his sword. The jingle and click told them the door had been locked from the outside.

"That will keep him from causing more trouble until he can be dealt with," said a soldier.

Concerned, Rona said, "We're locked in! How do we get to the great hall?"

"Through the door at the other end. It's where I allowed Winnie to watch banquets from the peephole," said Conor.

Zane moaned and stirred. He became startled when hands touched him.

"Easy!" Zoe said. "By chance, they put you in the closet with us."

Zane took a deep breath of recovery. "I guess my distraction didn't work as I hoped."

"It did to a point. The closet is deep and dark, so they didn't discover us," said Conor. "If you can stand, we need to move into position."

Zane accepted Conor's help to his feet. Conor carefully led them through the darkness by placing a hand on the wall. A soft glow of light up ahead outlined the paneled door.

"Why did I never recognize this closet?" Rona asked Conor.

"It is hidden among the painted panels with the peephole cleverly concealed as a pair of eyes. The top of the cane is carved in relief as a knob." Conor's hand hovered over a section of the back panel. "I push a lever, and it opens from this side. The other side is unlocked by pressing the buckle on the painting before turning the knob. Pekka ordered it installed as a security measure, should he need a quick escape. Only Lieutenant Kincaid and I are aware of its location. The workers were well-paid and sent to live elsewhere on pain of death should they divulge its existence. That is why no one suspected Winnie was here. When needed, we will slip out and emerge from the crowd."

Sounds grew louder in the hall. Conor carefully opened the eyes of the painting for a quick glance. He closed his eyes before speaking. "The Council is gathering. And I saw Simon arrive." He then instructed Zoe and Zane. "You both must remain unnoticed. No matter what we do or what happens to us, keep quiet."

"We can help," Zane said.

Conor grinned and patted the young Piskie's shoulder. "You already have."

Troubled by the commotion, Rafe carefully looked out of the hidden panel.

"What's going on?" asked Winnie. She wore a long hooded dark green cloak that hid her face and totally covered her body.

"Not sure. I'll get to the alcove first, then find out from Kincaid."

"Where are we?" asked Jayson.

"Rear servant's corridor." Rafe peeked out again. He noticed Kincaid and two soldiers near the alcove. He placed two fingers in his mouth to make a low whistle. Kincaid turned. Rafe made a hand signal. Kincaid nodded and spoke to a soldier. The soldier hastened to the corner to keep watch. Once he was in position, Rafe opened the panel and ushered the others to the alcove. He held Winnie's arm. Jayson helped with Piskies, as the large cloaks made it difficult for them to see clearly. The three physicians were already there. Kincaid recalled the soldier.

"What was all that ruckus?" Rafe asked Kincaid.

"Something about a boy running wild and silly talk of magic garland."

"Sounds like a few maids nipped at the mulled wine too early," laughed a soldier.

Rafe rejoined the others and explained what happened.

Finn shook his head in parental disapproval. "Zane."

"I'm sure he had a good reason. Perhaps to keep *her* safe," said Winnie.

"You taught your children well, my friend," began Rafe to Finn. "They know what is at stake and are ready to make whatever sacrifice is needed."

Finn glanced up at Rafe, his eyes held a hint of sorrow. "Not too soon, I hope. Zane is to replace me as king when my time comes."

Burdock's eyes grew wide with surprise in regard of Winnie. "Scrutern!"

The necklace she wore glowed in the dimness of the alcove.

Finn withdrew the rest of the stone from his inner pocket. It too glowed.

"It is time!" announced Burdock.

"We must wait until my father has made the first challenge," Jayson spoke in warning. "Until then, keep both parts hidden."

Rafe sternly warned the physicians. "You saw nothing!"

"We don't even know what we saw," said Herbert. "Or who they are," he motioned to Finn and Burdock. "Although I recognize Winnie and Jayson. You, too, look familiar."

"Who they are and who I am is none of your concern right now. All you three need to do is confirm the testimony given to the Lord Chancellor. For the sake of Orrin."

Herbert stiffened at the threatening tone. "That is why we are here."

"Quiet!" Kincaid harshly whispered. "The Council is arriving."

Chapter 36

SIMON STOOD TO ONE SIDE OF THE RAISED PLATFORM, Rodney behind him. He watched the Council and nobles assemble. He had never felt nervous before a royal session, but this time was different. The fate of Orrin hung in the balance between two choices: allow Falco to reign under false pretense or install the rightful heir. Two soldiers guarded the draped alcove entrance. Kincaid carefully emerged from behind the curtain. When their eyes met, Kincaid made a short nod. The signal helped to calm Simon's nerves. If Winnie was in place, he felt certain Conor and Rona were also ready. He jerked slightly when the herald pounded the staff to call for order.

Lord, your will be done, Simon thought in silent prayer.

"Give heed. Curate Bennet, come forth," said the herald.

A distinguished looking man in his fifties in red and gold clergy robes moved to stand in front of the platform. He carried a gold-gilded, ornate staff.

To this announcement, Simon's brow leveled in suspicion. "What game are you playing, Falco?" he spoke under his breath.

"Master?" asked Rodney, confused.

Simon leaned to speak in Rodney's ear. "The Curate of Highburn does not normally attend Council meetings. Pekka refused the Curate's blessing when crowned. Why Falco wants him present is the question?"

Curate Bennet began to speak. "In place of a Prime Minister, I have the honor to preside over this Council. Today, we gather to begin the proceedings of crowning Orrin's new king. Although we mourn the death of our late King Pekka, the line of succession must continue. To that end, I bid Devon Falco to join me on the platform."

Bennet's first sentence answered Simon's question of *why* and alerted him to his opponent when issuing the challenge. Legal versus religious.

At the end of the Great Hall, Falco appeared dressed in regal clothes of white, silver, and gold. His head was bare in anticipation of receiving the crown. Sergeant Cadel escorted Falco with a squad of royal guards walking behind them. Falco mounted the steps to take a seat on the throne.

Simon stepped forward. "By law, the Council is permitted to make inquiry before swearing fidelity to the king."

Curet Bennet nodded agreeably to Simon. "I was about to say the same, Lord Chancellor." He turned to the eldest noblemen. "Lord Lionel."

Leaning on a cane, Lionel stepped forward. His shoulders bent and wrinkled face showed a man very advanced in years. "Devon Falco, by what right do you claim the throne?"

Falco flashed a tolerant grin. "My lord Lionel. It is an honor that our eldest stateman graces this Council and asks the validating question posed to each sovereign. I do so by right of succession granted by our late King, Pekka."

"When did this happen?" continued Lionel.

"Shortly before his death, King Pekka signed an order of succession that named me as his heir."

"Where is this document?"

Falco snapped his fingers. Cadel stepped forward to hand him the sealed document. Cadel bowed and returned to his position at the foot of the platform. "Here." Falco held it up. "The Curate will read it." He held it out to Bennet.

Bennet broke the seal and read. *"'I, Pekka, King of Orrin, being childless and devoid of bodily heir, do name Lord Devon Falco as my heir apparent.'* The King signed the document. Although the hand is shaky." Bennet's brow knitted in viewing the signature.

Simon again stepped forward. "Why is the King's signature shaky?"

"Lord Chancellor." Falco sneered at Simon's second interruption yet quickly recovered to reply. "An unsteady hand is a result of old age."

"Really?" Simon spoke in an unconvinced tone. He turned to Lionel. "Tell me, my lord, since you are much older than our late King, how is your writing? Does it suffer from *old age* by way of a shaky hand?"

Lionel held out his hand. "My shoulders may stoop, and my feet shuffle, but my hand is steady as a rock." He lowered his hand; his gaze fixed on Simon. "And my mind is still sharp, which makes me wonder why you ask such questions, my Lord Chancellor?"

Rather than answer Lionel directly, Simon addressed the Council. "King Pekka's health was in serious decline. Perhaps only hours of life left. Thus, he sent for me. As Lord Chancellor, all legal documents are my responsibility. I hurried to the king's chamber, where I learned Lord Falco had just left His Majesty with that document. One which I have not seen until now, nor has it been entered into the official records."

Falco fumed at Simon. "I have witnesses!"

Simon maintained calm in his counter. "Then why was I not informed before this assembly? To verify the document and receive sworn testimony from those witnesses?"

The Council and nobles murmured among themselves. Even Lionel and Curate Bennet became concerned.

"You did not inform me about witnesses, nor of the Lord Chancellor's ignorance in this matter. You assured me all was in order," Bennet said to Falco.

Uncomfortable, Falco shifted in his seat. "I shall summon them immediately! Sergeant Cadel—"

"There is no need!" Simon loudly spoke over Falco and the increased murmurs. "As Lord Chancellor, they are at my summons." He waved to Kincaid.

The lieutenant escorted the three physicians from the alcove to stand beside Simon.

Falco's eyes blazed at the physicians. "What trickery is this?"

Simon ignored Falco's outburst to take a satchel from Rodney and withdraw three sheets of paper. "I assume you recognize your witnesses. Doctors Herbert, Mason, and Brad."

"What lies have you told?" Falco demanded of the men.

"Say nothing," Simon advised the physicians. "I shall speak for you." He turned to address the Council. "For the good of Orrin and with clear conscience, Doctors Herbert, Mason, and Brad have given sworn testimony to exactly what happened at the supposed signing of the Order of Succession. They are here to confirm what I shall now read *and* has been entered into the official record of Court."

"Upon entry, Lord Falco proceeded to urge His Majesty, King Pekka, to sign the Order of Succession. He did so continuously and without mercy to the King's declining health. I, Doctor Herbet, as head physician, warned Lord Falco concerning His Majesty, King Pekka's, fragility, only to be ignored. Lord Falco ordered Sergeant Cadel to provide a small writing desk upon which King Pekka could sign the order. It was then that Lord Falco took King Pekka's hand, holding the pen, dipped the quill in the ink well, and forcefully guided the King's hand to sign the document. Lord Falco melted wax and used the King's hand upon which he wore the royal signet to press into the wax."

Grumbling from those assembled turned into outrage as Simon read.

Furious, Falco bolted to his feet. "Lies! All lies."

"No! We have not lied!" Herbert bravely spoke.

Curate Bennet moved to confront Herbert and his companions. "By all that is holy, do you swear what the Lord Chancellor just read is the truth? Be careful how you answer, for the Almighty is not deceived." He held the gilded staff in front of the physicians.

Herbert met Bennet's probing gaze. "It is the truth! My conscience is clear before the Almighty."

Mason and Brad also confirmed the truthfulness when confronted by Bennet.

Their answers infuriated Falco. "Then who shall rule Orrin since Pekka lacked an heir? A foolish queen?"

Simon hid a smile at Falco's inciting question.

"There is an heir!" a loud voice yelled.

Curious, everyone looked to identify who spoke. Five figures moved from the alcove. Two were shorter than their companions, and all wore cloaks with deep hoods.

Falco's eyes narrowed in rage as he watched them move to stand before the platform. "Who dares to make such a claim?"

Jayson and Rafe tossed back their hoods, which caused a stir among the Council.

"You?" Falco scoffed with laughter at Jayson. "Did Simon put you up to this charade?"

"No. *You* sent me to Thorndel, where I learned the truth about your scheme to gain possession of the royal jewel to become king. You made the mistake of including Captain Tolbert. His actions resulted in the death of himself and Balor."

Falco flinched in surprise at the news. Seeing all eyes on him, he again tried to laugh off the accusation. "I suppose next you will tell me you recovered the lost jewel."

Jayson flashed a wry grin. "As well as discovering the identity of the true heir."

Falco forced mirth faded into wrath. "A scholar's deception. You don't have the jewel!"

"What makes you so certain since we have the heir?" said Rafe.

"And what would a ranger know of this?"

"Before I became the Ranger of Morgrath, I was known here as Lieutenant Rafferty Clarke, junior aide to General Briggs."

Falco snorted. "The Lord Chancellor's little brother. How quaint. A family conspiracy."

Rafe ignored the insult to inform the Council. "I was dispatched by Prince Ennis to safeguard the royal jewel from

Lord Falco's ambition. Circumstances led me to discover the Piskie Tribe of Morgrath, those appointed by the Almighty to guard the royal jewel."

"The jewel came to men hundreds of years ago after we defeated the Piskies. Since then, the jewel has been lost!" Falco spoke in a dismissive manner.

"No! Scrutern is once more in our possession." Finn and Burdock revealed themselves.

Thunderstruck, Falco gaped in wide-eyed surprise. "The kingmaker!"

Finn slyly grinned. "You do recognize me."

"Who let them in?" Falco cried out in fear.

Cadel reached for his sword when Kincaid seized him. "Stand down!"

Simon raised his hands and called for calm. "Let them speak!"

Bennet and the herald also called for order.

The commotion made Winnie grip Jayson's arm.

"Courage. Wait until the moment is right," he told her.

Falco took the time to regain his composure. He spoke again once the hall grew quiet. "Maybe you are the *kingmaker*, but there is no heir. The queen failed."

"I did not fail!" Rona's voice came from the back of the hall. She shed her cloak to reveal her white and gold coronation gown, complete with her royal crown. In regal dignity, she approached the platform. A cloaked and hooded man escorted her.

Falco sneered. "You have no business here. Pekka forbade your regency."

"I am not here to claim the throne for myself, but rather the legitimate heir of Pekka and me."

"There is no such person. I would have known."

The cloaked man stepped forward to confront Falco. "You must have suspected a birth, why else order attempts on the Queen's life? Attempts that ended in the murder of Arabella Briggs and Lady Eleanor Bailey."

Falco gripped the chair so hard his knuckles turned white. "Who dares accuse me?"

Conor threw off his cloak to reveal his uniform, complete with crest, insignia, and sash.

Shocked, Falco uttered, "Briggs!"

Curate Bennet approached Conor. "General, you were reported dead."

"A false exaggeration by those complicit in the death of my wife and Lady Eleanor." He turned around while speaking to the Council. "As all can see, I'm very much alive."

"That is a serious charge. Have you proof?" demanded Bennet.

"I do!" Simon said. He again took the satchel from Rodney to produce the document. "Evidence of poisoned food and drink. Alas, the maid involved was found dead last week."

"Who gave her the order?" asked Lionel.

"Captain Tolbert. Lord Falco's deputy," replied Simon.

"Tolbert threatened me by mentioning Arabella's death when you and Pekka tried to convince me to go to Thorndel in search of the jewel," Conor boldly confronted Falco.

"Tolbert wasn't here when Lady Eleanor—!" Falco abruptly stopped.

"Indeed. *You*, however, have been here the entire time." Simon held up the paper to address the Council. "The maid's testimony suggests a connection to Lord Falco's involvement."

Rafe's anger exploded. "Only a coward poisons women!"

Winnie took hold of Rafe's arm to calm him. He clenched his jowls to contain his temper.

Seeing Rafe subdued, Conor again confronted Falco. "Being complicit shows that you suspected a surviving heir."

Falco avoided Conor's intense gaze.

Rona moved to stand beside Winnie. "You convinced Pekka to deny my regency and then forced him to name you heir before the truth could be revealed. The truth you feared!"

"No such person exists!" Falco again disputed. Only this time, less forceful.

"She does. And has lived and worked right under your nose." Rona gently removed Winnie's cloak. "Behold, the daughter of myself and King Pekka. Princess Winifred."

Winnie stood proud and straight under Falco's contemptuous glare. She wore a stunning forest green and gold gown. Upon her head, a diamond and emerald coronet. "No doubt you and everyone here see the striking resemblance between us."

"There can be no misgivings about paternity. Pekka once had blonde hair," added Rona.

Falco squirmed. "Bennet!" He waved the Curate toward Winnie and Rona.

"This is a stunning revelation," said Bennet to Rona.

Rona boldly regarded Bennet. "*You* have known the truth for years, my lord. As does Doctor Mason, who attended me the night of Winifred's birth."

"You showed Pekka a dead newborn!" Falco objected.

"She showed my daughter, who was stillborn!" said Conor, woeful. He then gave an explanation to the Council. "We feared for the Queen's safety should the King learn a girl survived birth and not a son."

Moved with compassion, Rona laid a hand on Conor's shoulder. "General and Mistress Briggs made the switch of newborns at my request. Not for my benefit, rather to save Winifred from Pekka's wrath. All here experienced his frightful, violent temper, and his relentless desire for a male heir. He scorned those stillborn girls I lost before Winifred. No mourning. No hint of compassion. Tossed onto a heap like dead fish!" Rona's voice broke due to passion. Winnie gripped her mother's hand in a show of support. At this gesture, Rona swallowed back emotion to proceed. "What would he have done if presented with a living daughter?" Her sharp gaze scanned the crowded hall. "I did what any mother would to protect her child."

No one dared to answer. Even Falco remained silent during Rona's impassioned speech. However, his face told his true feelings on the matter. "This fiasco has gone on long enough! Pekka never acknowledged this mistress of the wardrobe. And this raving woman knows it."

Winnie's temper gave way. "How dare you scorn the Queen!"

"I am king!" Falco angrily thumped his chest.

"No! You are an ambitious pretender who seeks to usurp the crown by any means, including murder and forgery!" Winnie shook off Jayson's warning touch on her shoulder. "For too long, I have watched you belittle and humiliate my mother. Well, no more! Your treachery has been revealed for the Council to see and hear! As the rightful heir, I will see justice done for my mother, Mistress Arabella, Lady Eleanor, and all those you have harmed."

Falco's eyes narrowed and fixed on Winnie. "There is no proof of your birth past a grieving woman and traitorous general."

"Wrong!" Simon pulled out another sealed document from his satchel. "Prince Ennis' sworn testimony as he was also present at Princess Winifred's birth."

Bennet stepped to stand beside Simon. "Doctor Mason and I can attest to the princess' birth."

Winnie smiled smug and triumphant. "Will you accuse the Curate of Highburn of lying? Mock a representative of the Almighty in front of all gathered here?"

"And I, Kingmaker of the Piskies, appointed keeper of Scrutern by the Almighty, declare Princess Winifred rightful heir to the throne," said Finn.

"Scrutern has vanished—" Falco stopped speaking when Winnie revealed the glowing necklace from under her collar.

Finn withdrew the large piece of Scrutern, it, too, glowed. He stood before Winnie. When the larger piece came close to the necklace, an explosion of bright red light blinded everyone. When it faded, the pieces had fused together and hung as a whole jewel around her neck.

Burdock raised his hands. The excitement on his face was visible as he looked up. "By Scrutern, the Almighty has made his choice known. A new sovereign to unite men and Piskies once more." He cried out when Cadel attacked him.

Conor intercepted Cadel before he could strike Burdock again. Swords clashed.

"Guards!" Falco yelled.

The great hall erupted in mayhem. Soldiers loyal to Falco rushed in. Nobles and Council members tried to avoid confrontation.

Conor shoved Cadel aside. "Kincaid!"

Lieutenant Kincaid raised his sword. "To the Queen and Princess!" he shouted.

At the battle cry, some nobles aided Rafe, Kincaid, and Conor in the struggle. The general once more engaged Cadel steel to steel.

Jayson and Simon ushered Rona, Winnie, Finn, and Burdock toward the alcove for safety.

Falco quickly descended the platform and seized the staff from Bennet. He raised it to strike Conor from behind.

Zane suddenly appeared between Falco and the unsuspecting Conor. He tried to dodge Falco's swing. Unfortunately, the hard blow struck him behind the shoulders and sent him sliding headfirst into the base of the platform.

"Zane!" Winnie screamed. She broke free from Jayson. She fell to her knees. "No." She gathered Zane in her arms and wept. "Lord, why?"

Conor just wounded Cadel when he heard Winnie. He saw her cradling Zane. "Oh, no!" He then noticed Falco attempting to leave. "Kincaid!" He waved for the lieutenant to aid him in pursuit. They intercepted Falco near the door.

Cornered against the wall with swords leveled at his face, Falco offered little physical resistance. His lips snarled. "You have no authority here," he chided Conor.

"I am still General of the Royal Army." Conor roughly grabbed Falco to drag him back toward the platform. Kincaid followed with a sword, poking Falco in the back to keep him moving.

Rona, Zoe, Finn, and Burdock surrounded Winnie, who held Zane. Zoe wept in her father's arms. Rafe breathed hard in grief, while Jayson lowered his head and bit his lip.

Burdock tried to comfort Finn and Zoe. He noticed a faint red glow. For a moment, he watched. Winnie held Zane against her chest, weeping. The glow came from … "Scrutern!" he muttered in awe. He shook Finn's shoulder. "Look!"

Winnie continued to weep and rock Zane. She paused at hearing a faint moan. The glow from Scrutern intensified. "Zane?" His eyelids fluttered. "Zane. Can you hear me?" A loud inhale, and Zane opened his eyes. An exclamation of glee escaped her lips.

Zoe knelt beside Winnie, while Finn held her shoulder.

Zane glanced around in confusion. "What happened?"

"You saved Conor," Winnie said. Her eyes misty.

"You saved my son. Thank you." Finn touched Winnie's hair.

"Not me. The jewel," she spoke in wonderous regard of the necklace. "I have no power over life and death. But somehow Scrutern does."

"It is a divine jewel. Its powers are beyond what we know," said Burdock.

Winnie stood when she noticed Conor arrive with Falco.

"I have placed Lord Falco under arrest," Conor told her.

Falco tried to jerk free of Conor. "You may be the general, but without royal orders, you cannot arrest me."

Winnie glared at Falco as she spoke. "General, place Lord Falco in the dungeon until the Council determines his fate."

"Aye, *Your* Highness."

Chapter 37

UNDER CONOR'S COMMAND, IT TOOK TWO HOURS TO round up the turncoat soldiers, tend the wounded, and convince the Council members and nobles to remain at Highburn. In the Great Hall, servants scrubbed away signs of a brief battle, repaired damaged garlands, and replaced broken flower vessels.

While all this happened, Winnie, Rona, the Piskies, and Jayson retired to the Queen's chamber. Burdock lay on the sofa sipping an herbal remedy to help his aching body from Cadel's assault. Zane showed no signs of injury or being near death.

Rona paced. "Though I am glad Conor persuaded the Council to remain, will they accept Winnie as heir?" she asked Jayson.

"I'm certain my father and Conor are providing a full explanation along with all the evidence. If they can get Lionel and Curate Bennet to vote in favor of the princess, the rest of the Council will agree."

"After witnessing Scrutern's affirmation and miracle, they would be foolish to refuse," argued Finn.

"Men are stubborn," droned Rona.

"Chosen by the Almighty, she can rule without the Council," huffed Burdock.

"That could cause rebellion among the populace," warned Jayson. "And certainly not a way to reestablish friendly relations between Piskies and men."

The discussion upset Winnie. "I don't want my claim to cause further division. If needed, I will step aside in favor of my mother. Let her regency serve as a bridge to mine."

Rona softly smiled at the offer. "By right of birth, the throne is yours."

"Reinforced by Scrutern," Finn added.

After a brief knock on the door, Conor entered, joined by Simon, Curate Bennet, and Lord Lionel.

"Your Majesty." The men bowed to Rona.

Their respectful action prompted Rona to ask, "Has a decision been reached?"

Simon flashed a friendly smile. "It has."

Lionel leaned heavily on his cane as he approached Winnie. "Your Royal Highness." He bowed at the waist.

Winnie blinked back a sudden wave of emotion. "My lord," she managed to speak.

Lionel rose to stand as straight as his condition allowed. "Since the Council has assembled for a coronation, we see no reason not to proceed as planned. To crown a queen rather than a king."

Overcome, Winnie shivered slightly. The moment had come. Rona immediately placed an arm around Winnie's waist in support. The action made Winnie brace herself and gather her composure. "So be it, my lord."

Lionel and Bennet bowed. "We go to prepare the ceremony. We shall be ready within the hour," said Bennet.

When the door shut on their departure, Winnie felt her knees go weak and forced to sit.

Rona knelt beside the sofa. Smiling through tears, she held Winnie's hand. "All the sacrifices, risks, and dangers are finally over. You will take your rightful place as Queen of Orrin."

"It's overwhelming," said Winnie.

Conor's lips curved into a rakish smile. "You'll have me and your mother to help you."

Winnie rose and embraced Conor. "I could not have done any of this without you."

"Well, there were others involved." He nodded to them. "And remember, in public, I am *General Briggs.* You cannot be so affectionate as to show favoritism."

"Everyone is aware of our relationship, but" she added when he frowned, "I will refrain from showing you favor in public." She then asked Burdock, "Are you recovered enough to aid Finn in whatever is involved for the Piskie blessing?"

"Try and stop me!" Burdock pushed himself off the sofa. He wobbled, unsteady, so Zoe and Zane helped him sit back down. He shook them off. "I'll be ready!"

"You're still cranky," teased Winnie.

The Great Hall buzzed at the dramatic turn of events. Even the servants were caught up in the whirlwind. A thwarted coronation, the imprisonment of Lord Falco, the revelation of Piskies, a miracle healing by a jewel, and finally, a ceremony to crown a queen. The most striking was learning the identity of the heir, which they considered among their peers. A fellow servant yet born royal! By order of Winnie, the servants were permitted to gather in the hallway near open doors to the Great Hall.

Now adorned in a white, gold, and silver gown, Winnie sat on the throne. She bore the pomp of tradition and long speeches by individual noblemen and Council members with a nervous smile. She had yet to be crowned. During the proceedings, she cast side glances to Rona and Conor. Rona stood to the right of the platform while Conor on the left. Finn and Burdock flanked Rona. Burdock held a wooden case. Jayson, Simon, Rafe, and the twins assembled behind Conor.

Like earlier, Curate Bennet conducted the ceremony. "With the fidelity of the Council concluded, it is now time to welcome our honored guests. His Highness, Finn of the kingly Piskie tribe and Burdock, High Priest of the Piskies."

Finn and Burdock stepped into the center of the hall. "My lords and ladies," began Finn. "After what happened this morning, there should be no doubt that the ancient jewel, Scrutern, confirmed the next sovereign. A courageous young woman to unite Piskies and men. To heal the wounds inflicted so long ago. Wounds that divided our races can now be healed. Just like you saw the joining of the broken pieces and the restoration of life by Scrutern. The Almighty has spoken." Finn turned from addressing the crowd to face Winnie. "Since Orrin's founding, though interrupted by two centuries, Piskies have validated the new Monarch. Today, the privilege is restored." He motioned to Burdock.

Burdock lifted the case for all to see. "This contains the ancient crown once worn by human Monarchs, yet hidden after the Great Struggle. Today, it will once again grace the head of a uniting sovereign."

Burdock held out the box to Finn, who opened the lid. Finn removed a beautifully crafted, gold and silver crown filled with stunning diamonds. Finn mounted the steps of the platform and spoke to the crowd.

"It is my honor and duty, as the Almighty's appointed kingmaker, to crown Princess Winifred as the new Queen of Orrin." When he stepped in front of Winnie, the jewel erupted from the necklace she wore. In a flash of light, the jewel fitted snuggly into the center of the crown.

Burdock enthusiastically spoke, "Another sign!"

Startled, Finn paused in placing the crown on Winnie's head. Finn pushed aside his brief fright to continue. "You are now Winifred, Queen of Orrin, ruler of Piskies and humans alike." He placed the crown on Winnie's head.

"Long live Queen Winifred!" Conor shouted. Echoed by Rafe, Jayson, and Simon.

Those in the hall and servants at the doorways loudly repeated Conor's declaration.

Winnie's cheeks hurt from holding a nervous smile so long. She saw her mother gently wipe the tears from her face. Pride made Conor stand ramrod straight. Rafe's grin showed approval while Jayson's smile quivered slightly. He bowed to her.

Conor presented himself to the newly crowned queen. "What are your first commands, Majesty?" When she hesitated, he spoke specifically. "About Lord Falco."

"Oh," she sighed, uncertain. She caught Rona's glance as her mother shifted her eyes toward Lord Lionel. Winnie understood. "I leave his fate to the Council."

Lionel made a head nod. "We shall take up the matter before leaving Highburn, Majesty."

"Is there anyone else I should consider, General?" she asked.

"Far be it from me to influence your generosity to those who helped you." Conor motioned to Rafe and Jayson.

Winnie smiled at Rafe. "What can a sovereign give a ranger? A title? Land?"

Rafe stepped forward and bowed. "I crave none of those, Majesty."

"What do you crave, sir?"

"If it pleases Your Majesty, I will remain Ranger of Morgrath to act as intermediary between the Piskies and humans."

She smiled, grateful. "That would very much please me. Only don't stay away from court so long this time."

Rafe chuckled. "As you wish." He bowed and returned to his position.

Winnie fought a teasing smile at Jayson. "Master Scholar." She beckoned him.

Jayson stopped before the platform and bowed. "Your Majesty."

"What advice would you give a new sovereign in need of a Prime Minister?"

Jayson thought for a moment. "To immediately begin the search for one in which Her Majesty could confide and trust."

Her smile turned affectionate. "I already have such a man." She nodded to Zane.

The Piskie came forward. He carried something wrapped in a velvet cloth. He held it out to Jayson. Puzzled, Jayson looked from it to Winnie.

"Unwrap it," she said.

Beneath the velvet lay the great necklace of state. Stunned, Jayson said, "I'm merely a scholar. Not a statesman."

"I don't need a statesman. The Council deals with politics. What I need is a man of reason and logic. One who knows mythology and history enough to advise me on the two races I am to rule. You showed those qualities during our journey to Thorndel." Her smile grew. "Take it."

Jayson picked up the necklace and put it on. He made a reverent bow. "Your Majesty."

Rona gently guided Jayson to stand beside her in a place of honor.

Winnie sent a questioning glance to Conor, he simply nodded. She took it to mean all was complete. She addressed the crowd. "I am not one for long speeches. I leave that to the Council." She paused as the statement drew chuckles from the crowd. "These are tokens of gratitude I feel toward the individuals who helped me. My deepest appreciation is towards my mother and General Briggs. Just as this is a new day and experience for me, may it be the same for Orrin. A new day of hope for the future for both our races. With the Almighty's blessing, Orrin will return to the days of peace and prosperity between our peoples."

About the Author

Shawn Lamb is a multi-award-winning author of Christian fiction ranging from age 8 to adult. She is also an event speaker. Since 2010, Shawn has participated in homeschool conventions, book fairs, comic cons, and festivals throughout the Southeast, Midwest, and Mid-Atlantic regions.

As a former screenwriter for children's television, and author of numerous books, she brings over 30 years' experience dealing with publishing and Hollywood to her speaking engagements.

For more information about Shawn's books and possible speaking engagements, visit www.allonbooks.com.